JANE AND THE BOY WONDER

JANE AND THE BOY WONDER

a novel by AARON DONLEY

LANGAN MAE

For Mom

Happiness is like a butterfly: the more you chase it, the more it will elude you, but if you turn your attention to other things, it will come and sit softly on your shoulder.

—Often attributed to Nathaniel Hawthorne or Henry David Thoreau, this quote is by neither.

TABLE OF CONTENTS

PART I

CHAPTER 1

Each night, I sat alone on my small porch with a book. Occasionally, people would pass, and I'd say hello. Rarely did they stop for an extended conversation, and never once was one of any substance. I'd have some luck reeling them in with gossip, but in this small town, even the scandal should be ashamed of itself. At 8:30 p.m., I'd go to bed with my book—the consummation of reading lust.

I am the primary school teacher for rural Stramwell, Oregon. The town proper has a larger school, but I instruct in a two-room schoolhouse outside City limits.

It used to be a traditional one-room schoolhouse, but a politician some years back ran on education reform for the poor and fulfilled his promise by building a second room. The new room now houses old brooms.

A broom salesman came to Stramwell shortly after the politician built the second schoolroom. The salesman told his would-be clients that purchasing his broom would allow them to do a good deed, as they could donate their old broom to the rural school. The salesman did not inform customers that the rural school doesn't need fifty used brooms. I bought two brooms from him myself. If anyone should be donating an extra broom, it should be me.

I received my first broom donation from Margery Plimpton, an agreeable gal with a crooked chin and significant hips.

"The broom man said to give you my old broom," Marge said, poking her head into my classroom just before school started. "All the Civic Club ladies are buying them too. I bought one because of this new broom technology the salesman talked about. He's very becoming. He'll be coming down your side of Elm tomorrow."

"How becoming." I rolled my eyes. "*New broom technology.*"

Marge cautiously leaned her worn broom inside the doorway.

That was the same day I met Tobias Randall. It was October 30th and an unusual time of year to receive a new student. Tobias had shown up with no paperwork other than a note from his father:

This is Tobias Randall. He is fifteen. It is his final year of school.

—*Mr. Roy Randall 32 Rochester Lane, Stramwell, Oregon*

"That's the old Ellis farm," I said. "You must have just moved in. Where did you move from? Is your father

3

a farmer? Can you read acceptably for the ninth grade?"

"Idaho, yes, and yes," he said, looking past me at the other children.

"Where is your mother? Why didn't she write this note?"

The boy's overalls were worn but not too dirty. His blonde hair looked freshly cut by an inexperienced hand. He was tall and slender, and I assumed his father to be the same. I instructed him to sit down.

Tobias said nothing for the rest of the day. When school let out, he tried to leave without the schoolbooks I had provided.

"You'll need your books to study over the weekend," I said, catching him at the door. "Plenty of catching up to do. The others have been in attendance for well over a month now."

"No," he said and ran off in a sprint.

The following day was a Saturday and unseasonably warm. In the morning, I was gardening in the front yard. I find gardening more accessible in a short skirt. The broom salesman appeared as I bent over the dahlias.

"Excuse me, Miss?" he said, removing his hat.

I turned to greet the unexpected visitor. Due to the heat, a freshly curled lock of hair cascaded across my partially un-buttoned shirt.

"What's this I hear about new broom technology?" I said.

"Oh yes, this is the modern age of brooming," he said.

"Why, a girl just can't keep up!" I laughed heartily.

I invited the salesman inside where he could lay his display box on the table. He swung a broom like a samurai sword down with a smack.

"I didn't mean to startle you, ma'am," he said. "Only to prove the indestructibility of the new Oliver IV model. Made in the largest factory in the world, designed by Mr. Oliver himself in Hartford, Connecticut."

"Why!" I said, "You could knock out a nutria with that swing!"

"I'm sorry, ma'am?"

"A nutria. Surely, you've...? It's a large rodent with a hairless tail?"

I imitated buck teeth and clawed at his arm.

"Feisty as the dickens too." I clawed once more.

"No, sorry, ma'am, I'm unfamiliar with that type of rodent. So, the broom is quite strong."

I grasped his bicep. "Speaking of strong. Wowee zowee!"

He pulled his arm away.

"Yes, ma'am. Much like the Mark IV. Let me explain its patented new sweeping technology."

I put my hand on his forearm. "Perhaps you could explain it to me on the couch? I'm dying to put my feet up."

"Ma'am, I think I should be going. I just remembered I have another appointment. But I'd be happy to stop back by another time. Perhaps I could do a group presentation if you have any friends?"

He made it to the porch, where I pulled a trick I'd seen in a film and pinched his backside. He halted and dropped his head.

"Two brooms," he said.

"I beg your pardon?"

"Two brooms. And I'll sit on the couch."

I squinted. "How dare you presuppose a lady would—"

"Two brooms, ma'am," he turned. "I've got a busy schedule."

"*One* broom," I said.

"Two."

I slapped him then and there.

***

At noon, I visited Mother at the Blue Valley Nursing Home.

"You married?" Mother said.

She was sitting in the corner of her tiny upstairs room.

"No, Mother."

I straightened her bed sheets and dusted pictures of Dad along with her collection of glass chicken candy bowls.

"Careful of those chickens now. The last maid broke one."

"I've never broken a chicken."

"Well, chickens don't just break."

"It must have been one of your other maids."

She rolled her eyes. "I can't imagine why you're not married."

On my way out, I attempted to sneak past the reception desk, but the new girl had instructions to inform Administrator Roberts when I visited.

"Honey, we can't keep her for free," Mrs. Roberts said for all to hear. (Truthfully, she'd been patient with me in several discreet meetings over the past year.)

"Dear, you're six months behind," she said. "You'll have to take her home if we don't get payment."

"I know," I said, digging in my purse. "I've got thirty-five dollars."

Administrator Roberts put her hand on my shoulder.

"Lots of ladies take care of their mothers. You could get help from friends or the church?"

I took her hand from my shoulder and stuffed the cash into it.

"This is all I have," I said. "She goes to the restroom by herself and takes no medications. I'll do her laundry, and if she complains about the food, turn up her radio."

I stopped by Great Harvest General Store on my walk home to buy a pickle as a treat. Upon entering, I encountered the board of the Stramwell Civic Improvement Club (SCIC), led by chair president Mary Thompson Smith (MTS).

"Hi Jane," MTS said. "Out for a walk?"

"Just a stroll," I said, nodding to the ladies.

MTS knew quite well I went to see my mother every Saturday.

"Well, don't wear yourself out, darling," MTS said. "You're planning on attending Gay 90's tonight?"

"I have a scheduling conflict and will have to decline."

"Oh, that's a shame," Mary said. "Not family trouble, I hope?"

"Heavens no. I'm referring to a social engagement."

"Oh, well, enjoy your evening then."

"Please do have a gay time without me."

I smiled at the group and approached the counter.

"One wrapped dill, please," I told the store owner's daughter, Charlotte Cadwallader.

"It's self-serve," she said, nodding to the enormous jar of brine to my left.

The lid was tight, but I did not grimace or grunt. Still, my hand slipped, and the jar came down, spilling a hundred pickles and three-and-a-half gallons of vinegar.

"*Murder!!*" MTS screamed.

Charlotte leaned over the counter. "Lady, you're gonna have to pay for that. It's ten dollars' worth of pickles you just ruined."

"Ten dollars!" I said louder than I meant. (I honestly had given my last thirty-five to Administrator Roberts.)

"Well, I can't sell 'em now," Charlotte said. "Look,

there one clear over under Ruth Nelson."

Ruth, one of the SCIC members, shivered behind MTS as if witnessing a kingsnake.

She kicked at the dill three times, each attempt more pathetic than the last.

"Well, I beg to differ," I said, standing ankle-deep in brine.

I lifted a pickle and cut my palm on a shard of glass embedded therein. I picked off the chunk, placed it in my pocket, and raised the dill again for Charlotte's examination.

"That pickle's got blood on it," she said.

I ignored her nonsense and went about collecting the others.

A number required me to get on my hands and knees. Helen Brown, also of the SCIC, nearly toppled when I came near. She flung her arms wildly, crumpling the newly installed *Twinkies* display.

When I snatched the final king-sized dill between Ruth Nelson's legs, Charlotte slapped it out of my hand.

"I'm not spending ten bucks on pickles!" I yelled.

"I'll call the law!" Charlotte said.

"Ladies, please," MTS said, reaching into her pocketbook. "It's only money, for heaven's sake."

Charlotte took her cash and told me to get out.

"I shall repay you immediately," I said to MTS. "I just don't have the funds on my person. I was out on a stroll, as I previously stated."

I left with my head held high, nearly breaking my

hip on a stray pickle near the door, as Ruth let out a final scream.

***

That night, I attended a rival event of 'Gay '90s,' called the 'Single's Mingle,' held at the United Methodist gymnasium. I required Marge to go with me, and we walked the two miles in heels. She wore a flower print dress and a sizeable, white-brimmed hat. I donned a tightly fitting black skirt with pearls.

Other attendees to the mingle included church secretary Anne Huff and her disabled brother, with whom Marge and I had already been on uneventful dates. Also present was Sadie Becker, a widow with three young children in tow. I nodded at Sadie respectfully, and she moved in on Anne's brother.

Decorations included two paper streamers, a punch bowl, assorted cookies left over from the Sunday morning fellowship, and flyers inviting us to Pastor Reynold's latest sermon series, '*The Way of All Flesh*.'

After five minutes, I stood swinging my pearls in a variety of circular motions while Marge studied her hat.

"This is a bust," I said.

"Maybe it's all there is," Marge said, pulling a dead fly off the brim.

I swung the pearls in full force.

Two unknown men walked in. Marge moved on the tall one before I could.

The short one was named Hank. He and his cousin stayed at their great uncle's farm, two miles outside town. Hank owned a car and worked as a day laborer.

His hair was oily but full.

"Were you in the war?" I asked.

"Nancy, France," he said. "We were the first."

"Must have been awful."

"It was war."

"Do you know what a nutria is?" I asked.

"Yep."

Marge and the tall man approached.

"Well!" the tall man clapped his hands. "This has turned out to be a nice evening. Hank here said it was going to be a waste. Say, we got a car for the night. You ladies wanna go for a spin?"

Hank and I sat in the front while the tall man, Billy, sidled intimately to Marge in the rear. We parked outside Great Harvest and ate ice cream.

"Word has it there's youth going to houses demanding candy," Billy said. "And if they don't get it, they throw mud."

"Oh, that's awful!" Marge said. "I don't think any of our young people would do that, do you Jane?"

"Probably," I said, my attention captured by a couple dressed in full 1890s attire. I knew both by sight but couldn't place their first names. The woman forced a laugh and patted the man's chest, then nestled her arm into his crook—a well-orchestrated move.

Billy patted Hank's shoulder.

"Hey, turn on the radio. Remember?" Billy turned to Marge. "They're doing the seance for Houdini in Hollywood. Supposed to be on the radio tonight."

11

"But Houdini's dead," Marge said.

"That's why they're doing a seance!" Billy said. "Try and raise him. Supposed to be on the radio." Billy patted Hank again.

Hank turned on the radio and swiveled the dial until we heard speaking, but it was just the weather.

"They tryin' to raise him like Jesus?" Marge said.

"Yeah, like Jesus! Him and his wife had a deal: if he ever died doing a trick, ten years later, she'd do a seance. And Houdini promised to let her know if there was an afterlife."

"But Houdini ain't in heaven," Marge said. "He's a magician. They don't got radios in the hot place"

"How did he die?" I asked.

"A fan punched him in the gut on a dare," Billy said, fake punching Marge in the stomach. "He got a ruptured appendix. On Halloween."

"Ten years ago," Hank said.

Billy said 'Halloween' in a spooky tone and attempted to tickle Marge.

"You don't get appendicitis from someone punching you," I said.

"How do you know?" Hank said.

"Because it's a bacterial infection."

"It's been ten years since he passed?" Marge said. "That don't seem possible."

Hank kept turning the dial but was unable to find the broadcast.

"Ah," Billy waved his hand. "Podunk town like Stramwell. They could prove the afterlife and we wouldn't hear about it till we're dead."

"Are children throwing mud?" Marge said. "What if you're not home?"

"And besides," I said. "Houdini didn't believe in the afterlife."

"That don't mean there isn't one," Billy said.

I turned to face the backseat, noticing Billy's hand resting on Marge's thigh. "Church in the morning for you, Marge?"

"Oh, yes, that's right," she said, straightening.

"Well, we'll give you a lift home then," Billy said.

"That won't be necessary," I said. "We live close, and you've done quite enough."

Billy asked Marge if he could see her again, and she beamed like a lighthouse.

I was about to shake Hank's hand when I remembered something. I grabbed his lapel and leaned in.

"You can take me out on the last Saturday night this month," I whispered. "But I need ten dollars cash right now. And I won't be able to pay you back, ever."

"Ten dollars?" Hank said.

"Cash. And I can't pay you back. Then you can take me out in three weeks."

"Uh—"

"I need it tonight, right now. If you're willing."

"Ok, well, I guess," he said.

Hank took out his wallet and handed me the money, which I tucked away.

"Don't tell your cousin or anyone else," I whispered again, "and I'll see you in three weeks. And don't wear that cologne. Just bathe regularly."

"Thanks?"

Marge walked light as air on our journey home, twirling like a ballerina. I laughed out loud.

"What's Hank like?" she asked.

"He thinks war is hard and knows what a nutria is."

"Well, that's a start," she said.

I almost mentioned I was going out with him again but didn't, as my three-week delay was nothing more than a stall in hopes Hank would forget or move on. The truth is I felt slightly sour as he didn't deserve it.

"Oh! I forgot to ask you," Marge said. "What did you think of the broom salesman?"

***

After separating from Marge, I rerouted my journey to MTS's house, where I wedged the $10 bill in her door jamb with a note:

For MTS.

From JWA.

For PP.

(Pickle payment.)

It was nearly ten o'clock by the time I was home and settled. Just barely in time to catch my second favorite program, *Live from the Stork Club* in New York City. (My favorite is the Sunday night *Winchell Jergens Celebrity Gossip Program*, also broadcast from table 50 at the Stork.)

After the show, I had just bundled down with a blanket and book on the porch when I noticed a dark figure standing next to Mrs. Higdon's arborvitaes. I couldn't tell if it was holding a mud clot.

When I entered the yard, the body turned slowly and walked away.

Before going to sleep that night, for the first time, and for reasons I still do not understand, I shut my curtains.

CHAPTER 2

Acorn

Rigby, Idaho, 1926

The boy danced for his mother, who was lying in bed at 2 p.m. It was his birthday.

She instructed him to repeat certain motions. The boy's father entered, dirty from a day's work. The boy stopped.

"Don't stop," the mother said.

The man sat on the bed and grunted, taking off a boot.

"Aren't you going to tell him happy birthday?" the mother said.

"Happy birthday, kiddo."

"Thanks, Dad."

The boy did a little more of the dance.

"That's all you've got?" the mother said.

"Give me a break."

"No, I won't give you a break. You know why? Because I talked to Nancy today, and she said Bill told her you two were going fishing this weekend. Well, you're not. We're going to my mother's."

"We just saw her Sunday."

"Sunday is the day when people see their mothers. This Saturday is special. She wants to see Tobias for his birthday."

The man pulled off his other boot.

"Nancy said you and Bill spent ten dollars on new lures at the bait shop. Ten dollars?! All for some dirty old fish?"

"We still talking about your mother?"

The man walked past the boy.

"What's that supposed to mean?" the mother said. "What's that mean, Toby?"

"It's a euphemism," Toby said.

"A what?"

"Dad's comparing grandma to a fish, using your words."

The man reappeared.

"What are you saying to your mother?" he said.

"I was just explaining your joke."

"Take her side. You always do."

"Toby, leave. I need to talk to Dad," the mother

said.

Toby sat in the bathroom against the radiator, rocking. His parents yelled, the bed shook, and his dad left.

The boy removed the contents of his pockets, including a metal slug, an agate with a blue vein, and an acorn.

"Boyhood collectible trash," he said, examining the acorn. "The acorn falls like a bomb to the soil," the boy mumbled. "It is eaten and deposited far from the tree."

His mother called, and the boy joined her in bed. Once she was asleep, he crawled onto the floor.

The boy placed the acorn on the floor, rested his head on it, and whispered:

A squirrel

Is hit

with a falling nut

Confirming life

is a joke.

In his den,

He ices his head,

Plotting against

45ZED.

The license plate

From the car

That killed his Miss

With a passing squish.

CHAPTER 3

The following Monday, I was in front of the class, teaching addition by carrying multiple numbers.

"For example," I said. "Let's say you wanted to add all the numbers from one to ten."

I stacked the numbers on top of each other. One, two, three, and so on.

"Fifty-five," a small voice from the third row said.

Tobias had his head down. His desk neighbor, Timmy Porter, nodded in his direction.

"Yes, that's correct," I said. "But we all need to learn the carrying addition method for much larger problems we can't do in our head. For example, adding all the numbers from one to forty-seven."

"One thousand one hundred twenty-eight," Tobias mumbled between his arms.

"Tobias Randall, raise your head, young man. If you're going to address an adult, you look them in the eye."

I noted 1128 on my pad and dismissed the class for a brief recess.

I had been a Stramwell public school teacher for fifteen years. In all those years, I had asked each class this same question: What is the sum of all the numbers between one and a hundred?

The famed 19th-century German mathematician Friedrich Gauss's work was beyond me, save for the anecdote of his early primary teacher giving him a similar question. (As the story goes, the teacher asked young Gauss to add up all the numbers from one to one hundred, and within seconds, Gauss stated the correct answer of 5050.)

He accomplished the feat by adding the numbers in pairs: $1 + 100 = 101$, $2 + 99 = 101$, etc. In doing so, Gauss realized all of the pairs totaled 101. Then, he simply needed to determine the number of pairs (50) and multiply that number by the sum of each pair (101) to get to 5050.

I was busily trying to remember Gauss's process to fact-check Tobias's 1128 sum when I noticed the boy still standing at the door.

"Prodigy," he said. "In Idaho, I heard a doctor say it."

"Were you at my house on Saturday night?" I said.

"Yes, I often sneak out of the house."

"You shouldn't do that," I said. "Your father will be worried."

"Can you take me to the library?" Tobias asked. "I need an adult to get a rental card. You could let me keep the books here, and I could read them during recess."

"Why? Just ask your father, I'm sure—"

"No, that's not possible."

"Why not?"

"Because some things aren't."

We examined each other.

"Let me present to you a scenario," I said. "A young relative is starving and will die if they don't eat some bread. But you don't have money for bread, and the baker won't even give you old bread he is discarding anyway. So, would it be *wrong* for you to steal bread from this baker to give to the needy child?"

(When you ask young children this question, they will almost always say 'yes,' that stealing is wrong. By the time they reach Tobias's age, they can embrace advanced thinking and often reason it is better to steal the bread.)

"It is not wrong to steal the bread," Tobias said.

"I see," I said.

"It is also not wrong to let the child die."

"But... what would you do, personally?"

"Steal the bread and tell everyone the baker saved the child. This will increase his business, and I will insist he hires me to help with the added work. I need a guardian if purchasing bread to save a young relative is my responsibility. I have many other plans for the bakery, and the baker, for that matter, but the details are not important for your exercise, and you only called a ten-minute recess."

"I can get you a library card this Saturday," I said.

Tobias was silent the rest of the week but at least didn't have his head on his desk. Instead, he watched me, which isn't unusual for a student, but most don't scan my person so intensely.

***

"You married?"

Mother was still in the corner of her tiny room, watching me once again dusting chickens. I considered breaking one for a change in conversation.

"Your father died of the flu," Mother said.

I paused mid-chicken.

"Everybody got it," she continued, looking at the floor. "But he was the only one who died."

My father was indeed the only documented Spanish Flu death in Stramwell during the two years it came through.

"That's called bad luck," Mother said.

***

"Ok Tobias," I said. "What have you read in the past?"

"Well, there was a school in Idaho that had an encyclopedia set."

"I see. So, you read sections as part of your previous schooling?"

"Not exactly," Tobias said. "On my first day I noticed the encyclopedias in the back of the classroom, but the teacher wouldn't let me read them. So that night I stole them."

"You stole, an encyclopedia set?"

"Yes. There were thirteen 1933 World Book volumes. I read through the set twice before my father discovered where I'd buried them by the river."

"Buried them?"

"It was my best option. I subsequently learned the mayor of the town had purchased the set at the Chicago World's Fair and loaned it to my teacher. The volumes got a bit soiled in the burial process, so they wouldn't let me return to the school."

I checked out several books for Tobias, starting with classics I also owned so I could reread them simultaneously for discussion. We read Homer, Shakespeare, Eliot, Hugo, and Dostoevsky, then moved to Wharton, Woolf, and Huxley.

While I fancy myself a bibliophile, I could not hope to keep up with the boy's voraciousness. I was already far behind by the time he finished Shakespeare's *First Folio*, and by *Les Misérables* I had resorted to *Shaum's Outlines*.

The Stramwell Public Library librarian is an old friend of mine, Rebecca Miller. (Late twenties, mousy brown hair, mousy face, mousy everything.)

"Have you considered asking him what he would like to read?" Rebecca said.

It was my tenth appearance at the library in two weeks.

"I am first prescribing him the classics," I said. "Once digested he will be on healthy footing for diversions."

"Sounds like you're feeding him medicine."

"I'm amazed a librarian would say such a thing."

"Sorry dear. But perhaps you should test his overall aptitude, rather than just reading comprehension? There are several high school level tests in the reference section."

"Hmm," I thought. "Got anything stronger?"

***

I met the boy's father, Mr. Roy Randall, only once. It was after I'd provided Tobias with graduate-level aptitude tests in mathematics and science, for which after two weeks of prep time he scored perfectly. I felt it at that point my duty to follow the young man home to discuss advanced teaching plans with his guardian. (This was not my usual practice, but invitations for Mr. Roy Randall to meet at the school were not returned.)

After some prodding at the screen door, I achieved said meeting with Mr. Roy Randall on his porch. Tobias remained in the house.

Mr. Roy Randall was a calm man and a natural listener. He was indeed tall but also possessed lean muscular girth. It occurred to me that Tobias's frame was likely the same except artificially slender due to malnourishment.

After hearing my laudatory comments on Tobias's mental abilities, Mr. Roy Randall nodded and said, "*Yeah.*"

When I proposed an individualized course of study for Tobias under my care, Mr. Roy Randall released a resounding sigh. He removed his cap, wiped his head, replaced it, and summarily re-entered the house.

"Yeah?" I said to myself, then waited in stunned reaction for several moments until Tobias emerged and notified me his father had decided against any accelerated training.

I placed my hands on my hips.

"And what do you want, Tobias?"

"I think the question is, what do you want, Jane?"

"How do you mean?"

"Does helping me make you feel like a good teacher?"

"I would say yes. It does."

Tobias nodded. "Ok, let's do it then."

***

We met for an hour after school each day at the public library, where we studied the major disciplines, including science, math, English, and history.

On Saturday mornings, Tobias was allowed to research whatever topic he wanted. During these times, he received my and Rebecca Miller's full attention and assistance.

"What would you like to learn about?" I asked on

our first Saturday.

"People like me," Tobias said.

"Prodigies," Rebecca said. "Well, there's Mozart and Pascal, of course." She paused and bit a pencil tip. "And I recall a particular young man receiving a fair bit of attention in the early teens."

Rebecca raised herself from the table and left us without saying a word.

"Mozart and Pascal?" Tobias said, wandering off to the biography section.

Rebecca returned and placed an enormous bound book of newspaper pages on the table. I waived Tobias back over.

"Here," Rebecca said.

The New York Times headline read: *Boy of 10 Addresses Harvard Professors on Imaginary 4th Dimension.*

The article claimed the boy, named William James Sidis, could read *The Times* at 18 months and spoke seven languages by age six. He passed the Harvard and MIT entrance exams at ten.

The paper was from January 1910. In that same month, follow-up articles appeared saying Sidis had fallen gravely ill from 'mental exhaustion' and was under the care of his parents, both of whom were doctors.

By April 1910 a new article proclaimed the boy recovered fully, adding that 'theosophists claimed him to be the math genius Euclid reincarnated.'

A flurry of news followed, portraying Sidis as a national sensation, even calling him 'the most famous young person in the country.'

Tobias devoured them all. He then requested any works by Sidis's father, Boris, a famous psychologist considered in his time to be in league with Sigmund Freud.

Boris Sidis wrote on various subjects, including abnormal psychology, sleep, and hypnosis. He studied under the preeminent American psychologist William James, after which he named his son.

The final article we uncovered, written in 1914, claimed the boy Sidis had just become the youngest Harvard graduate in history.

"I want to meet him," Tobias said, running his fingers over the newsprint as if trying to feel the letters. "Also, please see if any of the libraries on your regional share program have *Philistine and Genius*. It's a book Boris Sidis wrote about child-rearing. As for today, Jane will check out both volumes of Otto Jahn's *Life of Mozart*."

***

"What do you want to do beyond teaching?" Tobias asked on our walk home, attempting to balance one of the *Life of Mozart* books on his head.

"Isn't teaching enough?" I said.

"Not for you."

"Well, I enjoy reading on the porch at night. But you already know that," I said. "So, I guess, like anyone, I've thought about writing a novel someday."

"What kind of novel pleasures you?"

I thought for a second. Having spent many hours with my nose in a book, I never took a step back to analyze my reading patterns.

"Stories about women."

"Like yourself?"

"Yes."

"Have you written anything?" Tobias asked.

"Heavens no. I wouldn't know where to begin." (This was a lie, as I'd tried to write a novel several times, only to end knee-deep in crumpled wads of paper and wasted ribbon.)

Tobias stopped abruptly.

"Thank you for taking me to the library," he said. "I want you to know I've considered giving you a hug at some point."

"Well," I said. "At some point, I would like that."

Tobias nodded, tossed me the Mozart book, and ran off like a bolt.

***

Upon returning home, I immediately placed my typewriter on the kitchen table.

It was decided: I would write a bestselling novel clearly explaining the human condition. Then I would shun interviews, save perhaps for the local Stramwell Chronicle, staying true to my roots. My statesman husband and I would move into a grand house in the country, where the waiting list for our dinner parties would be long and selective.

An hour and a half later, I was knee-deep in crumples. Writing a bestseller seemed like alchemy. I didn't even know where to begin.

I picked up several books to see how they started.

28

Elmer Gantry – Elmer is drunk and in search of a fight.

Crime and Punishment – An impoverished young man plans the robbery and murder of an older woman with an axe.

The Private Life of Helen of Troy – Menelaus goes looking for Helen *"with a sword in his hand. He was undecided whether to thrust the blade through her alluring bosom or to cut her swan-like throat."*

Then I remembered an ad I'd seen in a *Family Circle* two years ago. (The last time I'd sat down to write the great American novel.) At the time, I mocked the ad, but now I was on my hands and knees in the closet, searching back issues of my collection.

The closet was a bust, so I went to the fireplace stack, cursing my hubris and hoping it wasn't too late. I found the magazine near the bottom and crawling with bugs.

I remembered the particular issue because a chimpanzee named Jinxy was on the cover, one of eight chimps saved from a Brooklyn fire through artificial resuscitation. (I'd been inspired by Jinxy to include a series of chimps in my previous attempt at a novel. In fact, I sent an outline and sample chapters to no less than thirty literary agencies, receiving only one reply: a form rejection letter with the handwritten note, *"The monkeys are unrealistically tidy."*)

The desired page was second to last—an advertisement for 'The Plotter,' a step-by-step tool for aspiring writers to craft a masterpiece.

Of course, I didn't have 'The Plotter,' and, according to the fine print, an order would take 6-8 weeks.

I studied the ad, seeking anything to glean from this magical wheel.

There was an image of a woman seated at a book signing with a long line for autographs. Another woman getting her copy signed is saying, "*I always wanted to write a novel but didn't know where to begin!*" A man in a suit is next in line. He turns to an elderly woman behind him and says, "*Shakespeare never looked this good!*" ('The Plotter' conspicuously peers out from the author's purse under the table.)

"Oh *dear*," I said, imitating the woman author. "I'm just a simple girl, but people seem to like my stories!"

What *do* people like? I said aloud to myself.

I decided my story should happen somewhere glamorous, like the South of France. But I knew nothing about the South of France. So, I got an encyclopedia and came across the French city of Marseille. But then I read that Marseille contained nearly a million people, and I wanted a smaller town feel where a girl could make a difference. So I made up a town and called it 'Montelle.'

The story opens with the nation of France on the precipice of a civil war. (I wasn't sure if this was true for that time but was sure I could find some war to reference.)

A 16-year-old daughter of a wealthy farmer falls in love with a neighbor man, who is engaged to her cousin. At their engagement party, a different, more mysterious man flirts with the girl.

The girl ignores the mystery man and declares her love to the neighbor man, who rejects her. The girl is embarrassed and begins flirting with every man at the party, eventually accepting an invitation to marriage from the neighbor man's fiancé's brother. After a quick wedding, the girl becomes pregnant right away. Within two weeks, her new husband dies in the war. She dresses in black.

I looked up from my fury of typing, realizing I had just rewritten *Gone with the Wind*, set in a historically inaccurate France.

There was a knock at the door.

I flung open the door, bearing wild hair and eyes. The short man jumped back, nearly dropping a small bouquet.

"What?" I said.

I had forgotten about my date with Hank.

"Oh, yes. Hank."

"Um, yeah," he said, not moving. "It's me."

I hurriedly started picking up my mess but decided there was no point.

"I'm gonna be honest," I said, dropping an armful of papers and magazines onto a chair. "I forgot about our date. The truth is I'm not that interested. I'm sorry if I lead you on. And I'm sorry about the ten dollars. I can pay you back, just not today."

"That's ok," he said, tossing the flowers onto my stack of papers. "I'm not interested either."

I offered Hank coffee and a bit of leftover cake. We ate on the porch in remarkably comfortable silence.

Hank thanked me politely, then said he had to get

up early to take his aunt to Church. It was a lie.

I picked up a novel I was midway through, *Miss-Bee-Havin's Weekend*. Miss Bee was on one of her many exotic holidays in Istanbul. A handsome young bellhop had just delivered her bags, and she had explained to him she had no tip money, but other accommodations could be made.

I slumped in my chair, glaring at my dahlias, now finishing their perennial bloom.

"I wrote something," a quiet voice said.

I blinked a few times, unsure if I had heard it.

"I thought we could submit it to *Story's* short story contest: *One thousand words for one hundred dollars.*"

It was Tobias, peering through my porch railing, not three feet away. He reached forward and handed me two sheets of handwritten paper, covered front and back.

I took the papers without saying a word and read the story he had written. It was titled, *More*.

The piece was in the format of a suicide note penned by a small-town teacher who kept a bottle of Elixir Sulfanilamide by her bedside. On her 40th birthday, unbeknownst to anyone, she traveled to get a tattoo in a place only a lover or husband would ever see. Having completed menopause on her 48th, (and after an incident with a pickle jar shattering she couldn't pay for), she wrote the note and taped it to her vanity mirror. The final line references the story's title, using a quote from Epictetus: "*Happiness has all that it wants.*"

"I've written the instructions on where to send the submission," Tobias climbed over the railing and pointed to the bottom of the page.

I hugged him to my bosom like a mother hen.

"Good boy."

That night, I typed the piece exactly as written, placed it in an envelope, and walked a mile to the post office. On my journey home, I twirled.

***

We continued our tutoring routine, but truth be told, young Tobias was already advanced beyond what I could teach him. I requested science, math, and English textbooks of the highest collegiate level possible from the shared library system to keep him busy. Finally, I introduced foreign language guides.

I had no knowledge of languages, so I took us to the back kitchen of The Tijuana Restaurant on Oregon Ave., where my old pal Fernando De Leon put Tobias to work washing dishes. The fellas back there were always chatting away, so I figured it wouldn't take long for the boy to pick up what he couldn't glean from a book. (I had previously given English lessons to Fernando's wife, Armida, also a long talker, and now in two languages. I do not believe Fernando has forgiven me.)

From there, we went to Becker's Sausage and Meats. Ingrid Becker nodded at me, then leaned over the counter and handed the boy a fly swatter.

"Die Fliegenklatsche," she said, motioning him to start swatting. "Muggebadsch!"

(I knew Ingrid to be a natural teacher, having invited her and Otto on several occasions to teach German heritage to my students. They provided samples of frikadelle for the children to take home with a

Becker's coupon for 5% off a quart of sülze.)

The only other foreign speaker I knew was Moses Hamburger, former owner of Hamburger's Department Store. His kids ran the place now, but I knew him well because Mother worked the counter at Hamburger's for years.

I dropped Tobias off for a single afternoon of Scrabble with the old man, and when I returned, Moses practically ran to greet me.

"This one is destined to be a great rabbi!" he said.

"Thank you, Mr. Hamburger," Tobias said. "But as I told you previously, I am an atheist."

"Able to argue with God Himself!" Moses kissed the boy on the cheek.

Later, I asked Tobias if his father worried about him being gone so much.

"He was upset at first," he said. "Now he's resigned to the convenience of you raising me."

I never did ask Tobias about his mother.

***

The boy continued to develop a growing obsession with all things Sidis. He was able to get ahold of more of Boris's work and eventually a copy of William James Sidis's book, *The Animate and the Inanimate*, which he dog-eared to the point it resembled origami.

Other articles we discovered filled out a picture of the prodigy. After graduating from Harvard, he taught math at Rice University before attending Harvard Law School. Sidis then dropped out of his law studies just before graduating, claiming the topic didn't suit his fancy.

In 1919 Sidis was arrested under clouded circumstances for participating in a socialist parade. At that point, the news grew quiet about the young man, save for an article in 1926 mentioning Sidis's presentation to a group of hobbyists interested in the bizarre practice of collecting used street cart transfers.

I also read Boris Sidis's work on child-rearing, *Philistine and Genius.* While I appreciated his insights, I remain doubtful they are applicable beyond one of every ten-billion children born with pure genius. I tried to read William James Sidis's work as well, but found it too dense a tangle of scientific theories.

One day in mid-December, the letter arrived. *More* had won *Story's* short story contest and prize money of $100. The piece was scheduled for publication in their January edition, and they cordially invited me for an interview by phone.

I tried to give Tobias the $100, but he didn't want it.

"At least take fifty," I said.

"The spoils of early success can only taint me," he said, swatting a fly onto Becker's meat counter.

Ingrid smiled. "The German way," she said, chopping schnitzel. "Durchkauen."

"To chew thoroughly," Tobias said, swatting again.

Across the street, Jesse Achey's son Leroy was hanging a new movie poster at The Starlight Theater. I had tried to take Tobias to a movie a couple of weeks prior, but it was a low-budget western, and he grew bored after predicting the ending early on. This new poster was radically different, portraying a striking image of a rather passionate-looking female humanoid. The title was *Metropolis*.

"Let's at least ask what it's about," I said, stuffing $50 into Tobias's shirt pocket. "Your treat. And I'd like a large popcorn."

To my surprise, the boy dropped the swatter and followed.

Ingrid shook her head and ordered her husband Otto to pick up die fliegenklatsche.

I endured through the film's first hour before falling asleep to dreams so disorientating I could not put them into words. Suffice it to say, the plot of *Metropolis* was not easy to follow.

From what I could gather, there were two classes of people, the wealthy leisure class, who lived above ground, and the poor working class, who lived below ground, slaving to make the above ground city (Metropolis) operate. Neither class were aware the other existed.

As the story goes, a wealthy young man from the leisure class and a fairy-like woman from the working class met and attempted to introduce the two classes. Also, a mad scientist who lost his wife created a robot to replace her. Somehow this robot was used in an attempt to take down the whole system. In the end, the young man united the two worlds, and I can't remember what happened to the robot.

***

I wore a green satin evening dress and a beret for my interview with *Story*, but the man who called only wanted my name and a list of hobbies.

"I got dressed up for this?" I said.

"Dressed up?" he said.

Tobias insisted on rewatching *Metropolis*, but I told him I couldn't bear it. Afterward, I started finding drawings of the female robot in the margins of books.

I received a letter from an agent out of Portland shortly after the *Story* January edition was released. Theodore Compton was the agent's name, representing the agency of Compton and Birdwhistle. He said he enjoyed the piece and inquired if I'd written anything in long form.

The only thing I'd worked on at any length was the *Gone With The Wind* rip-off, now titled *Les Fleurs De Son Sein*. (*The Flowers of Her Bosom*.) After collecting the wadded papers from the trash bin, I kept secretly working on it, convinced I could twist the plot enough to not be direct plagiarism.

I gave the work, which consisted of thirty-seven pages, one more read-through, changed a few names to add additional French flair, and sent a fresh copy to Mr. Compton, informing him there was more where that came from.

I counted the days until Mr. Compton could reasonably be thought to receive my work. Getting no response, I justified a bit more time as he was a distinguished literary giant with a large volume of material begging his attention. When still no call came, I wondered if the package had gotten lost in the mail.

I envisioned *Les Fleurs De Son Sein* falling out of a postal carrier's cart on some deserted country road, where two flower bushes would grow around the manuscript in the shape of mammaries.

As more time lapsed, I settled into melancholy.

Tobias had his own requited writing enterprise, sending frequent letters to William James Sidis's mother, Sarah Sidis, in his attempt to locate the reclusive genius.

William James Sidis's mother and younger sister, Helena, maintained the Portsmouth, Rhode Island sanitorium building and grounds Boris left them upon his passing in 1923. Sarah had since turned the property into a bed-and-breakfast resort and, as it turned out, was working on an autobiography of the Sidis family.

On one occasion, while Tobias was bathing, I entered his room and viewed a penned letter to Sarah Sidis.

I snapped a picture of the document with my Kodak Retina 1 and have reproduced the letter in its original form here:

Dearest Dr. Sarah,

I do thank you for your kind reply to my previous letter. My original intention was, again, none other than to share with you a few tales of Billy (William) and myself at Harvard in our early years so long ago.

I wanted to share a few bits of those intimate late-night conversations young pals often have when away from home and missing their mothers. (Alas, we each hoped to find a girl just like ours someday.) As you can well imagine, Billy was no different than other boys in this respect, made even more endearing by his talk of your good character and brilliance of mind, which I could tell he respected above all things.

But I digress.

Dear Sarah, as fortune would have it, my firm has been looking to establish an East Coast branch in Boston. (My partner is from Boston, another Harvard fellow who attended a decade prior. You might know him; Mr. James Theodore Williamson, Esquire?)

In any regard, I will be on business travel next month and was wondering if it was possible to connect with Billy. The only trouble is I can't find his address in the local listings. If you could provide this, I would be most grateful, and I will be sure to write back a complete summary of our time.

I will now admit some purely selfish reasoning as well. I am curious about Billy's employment availability. We are a successful, albeit small, firm and could use a man like Billy in any capacity he would see fit. I'm sure your boy is undoubtedly entrenched in some form of high finance, scientific research, or legal practice, and I would only be kidding myself with an offer of employment. Even so, I would greatly appreciate the opportunity to at least catch up over lunch and talk about our formative days when we were young and missed our mothers.

Respectfully yours in admiration,

Thomas Kingsford Howell

"I'll be hopping rail cars. I've planned a route," Tobias said during our library tutoring session one Saturday in late June. He was holding the newest letter from Sarah Sidis, containing William James's apartment address.

"Shh," I said, as he spoke in plain volume. "You can't do that, Tobias. I'm sorry. It's simply not reasonable."

Tobias furrowed his brow.

"Jane, it is unreasonable to *not* meet Sidis."

"What exactly do you expect from this man once you meet him? Are you going to ask him to take you in? To raise you?"

"Of course not. The experience of meeting him is the entire plan. Do you not understand me at all?"

"Shh," I said again. "Yes, I understand you, but hopping trains is dangerous. You'll be hurt or worse."

"Worse is having not met Sidis, but if you're so concerned, you could take me."

"How in the world would I do that?"

"I give you my remaining $45, and you use your $50 share from the *Story* contest. You tell the school district you have a female cousin in Portland who had a difficult emergency birth, and the baby needs your attention while she recovers. Your employment file says you have backlogged over a week's days off. It will cost $35 for gas and $60 for food and lodging. I've written it all out here."

He took out a detailed itinerary, starting with the very hour we were sitting there in the library.

"It would be safer and less conspicuous if we had a man. Do you know anyone that could drive us," he asked, "for a small non-monetary fee?"

I gazed at him, at once scandalized and tantalized. My work file was in a locked cabinet in the Superintendent's office twenty-five miles away.

And so, in early February of 1937, at the age of 37, I left the State of Oregon for the first time in the company of Mr. Hank Sebastian and young Tobias Randall.

While the boy was gone from his house for long periods during the day, a week-and-a-half absence would be a bit much for even the laxest guardian. So, I made up a fictitious camp for which I would claim Tobias received a full scholarship, including rail fare. The non-existent camp was located outside Beaverton and, according to a freshly printed flyer, taught boys farming and tractor repair.

On our way out of town, we stopped at The Fill n' Time near the highway. (Stramwell locals typically used the Jiffy n' Fill on Main St.)

Unfortunately, it so happened that Lillian Martin, a lackey of Mary Thompson Smith (MTS), was there with her husband. She noticed our luggage in the back seat.

"Going somewhere, Jane?" Lillian said, looking at her watch. "Isn't this a school day, or am I mistaken?"

She shielded her eyes from glare and, looking intently into our car window, jumped back when noticing Tobias's face pressed against the glass. Then she craned her unusually long neck over the car to get a good look at Hank pumping the gas.

"One of my prize students has a mathematics contest in Beaverton today. Mr. Sebastian is a mathematics professor at the University. He's a calculus expert who has made significant advancements in the field of derivatives. Consequently, he is also a contest judge, and was kind enough to offer us a ride. I notified the school district well beforehand and have their full support, with a suitable substitute managing my teaching duties."

Hank, still pumping, raised his brow with a dumber-than-dumb expression.

"The boy is going to be a state champion someday. I have no doubt," I concluded. "We'll be returning tonight. Say hello to your mother for me."

"Will do, I'm sure," Lilian said, walking back to her car.

As we pulled away, I heard her giving orders to her poor husband to abandon their plans and take her to immediately to MTS's.

"Cal-cul-uss?" Hank said.

Tobias and I exchanged smiles in the rearview mirror.

The boy's routing had us traveling through Las Vegas, where Hank wasted forty dollars on craps.

"A bunch of crooks," he said, sulking over his ham sandwich.

"A casino is honest by nature," Tobias said. "It's based on the objective reality of mathematical probability. Much like Einstein's perception of God."

Hank paused mid-bite.

We continued west.

At each motel, Hank and Tobias slept in the front and back seats of the car while I took the room.

As travel is of interest to many, I will add one side piece of information I learned while sojourning across our great nation: We like large balls.

The substance (stamps, twine, chicken wire, cheese) of said balls is of no consequence. Choose the matter, and someone will make a ball of it. As a prime example, we witnessed a hairball taken from a cow's stomach in Garden City, Kansas, that weighed 55 pounds. (It was naturally wet when first removed and lighter now from dehydration by 10 pounds, but still in ranks with other hairballs in Webster and East Lansing.)

Americans also play fast and loose with claims of the 'World's Largest.' (Bull, thimble, fishing fly, Blessed Virgin Mary, fork). After seeing no less than five frying pans claiming the title, I finally cried foul in Brandon, Iowa.

"Well, it's the largest pan West of the Mississippi," the old man sitting beside it said. He bore no teeth and folded his arms in consternation after I'd disputed his claim of their pan's size. It took ten more seconds of my non-plussed gaze to bring him to say: "Shoot, biggest pan in the Midwest for sure."

I placed my hands on my hips.

"Biggest in Iowa," he said.

I folded my arms, pivoted, and raised my brow.

"It's the largest pan in Eastern Iowa," the man muttered. "And I'll take that to the grave, lady."

We arrived in Boston late Friday night and found a cheap hotel on Shailer St. in the city's south end. As sleeping in a car parked on the street was unsafe, Hank and Tobias got a room next to mine.

When I knocked on their door in the morning, Hank appeared worse for the wear.

"Tobias was already gone when I woke," he said, scratching his backside.

I naturally started to worry, but Hank waived me

off.

"Aw, that kid can take care of himself."

"He's still a child. And it's cold weather. He's not used to it." I cursed myself for not providing Tobias with a heavier coat. It rarely snowed in Stramwell, but in Boston, there were several inches of hard-packed ice over the city.

"He slept on the floor in his underpants," Hank said. "I think he'll be fine."

Hank insisted we see some sights and attempted to cheer me up by paying for a ride on the famed swan boats at the Public Gardens, which I found banal.

I did marvel at the Custom House Tower. It stands 496 feet tall and has an observation deck on the 26th floor, which I stepped onto for a full minute. We ate clam chowder and then returned to the hotel, where we watched businessmen and secretaries scurrying by on the street below.

"I don't get the point of all this," Hank said. "Are we just here for the kid to get an autograph?"

"All we had to do was drive across the country," I said, fixated on a very rotund secretary walking more briskly than anyone I'd ever seen, big or small. She wasn't quite running but could have won a sprint, nonetheless.

"How is she doin' that?" Hank said.

After she passed, Hank walked about the room earnestly trying to imitate her.

"No, you've got it all wrong," I said, demonstrating. "You're penguining it because you've got no hips.

That's where the power comes from."

Tobias finally appeared, walking beside a stocky, unassuming man with his head down. The man had thick brown hair and wore a shabby wool suit. They talked for a moment, then Tobias hugged him. The man patted Tobias on the shoulder and walked away.

"That was him?" I said as Tobias passed our doorway on his way to the communal bathroom.

"That was him," he paused.

"What now?"

"We can go home now."

"You don't want to see him again?"

"Why would I?"

***

Hank and I got into an interesting discussion as we left Boston. He believed our treatment of the American Indians made us no better than the tyrants we'd left in England. I told him Indians would still be living in teepees if we hadn't done something, and at least now they had proper medicine and education. Then Tobias pointed out many of them still were living in teepees. Not knowing how to respond, I claimed that was *precisely* my point, causing Hank and Tobias to scratch their heads.

We pulled into a little motel in Ohio around midnight. Hank said he didn't care about decency and was going to sleep in a bed, and if I wanted to sleep on the floor, that was up to me.

Two men approached when Tobias and I were outside unloading our bags from the car and Hank was indisposed in the restroom.

"Give us your money and jewelry," The fat one of the two said.

"I'll do nothing of the sort," I said. "Besides, I only have twelve dollars, and my jewelry is costume."

It was a lie, as I'd had another twenty dollars stashed away for safekeeping, along with my mother's pearls, which never left my neck. (They were given to her by my father on their fifteenth wedding anniversary.)

"Then give us your wedding ring," the fat man said.

"She's not married," Tobias said. "She can't find a man."

The statement silenced all.

"What about the guy driving the car?" the fat man said, looking over us at the motel room door.

"He's my retarded brother," I said.

"He's retarded and can drive a car?" the fat man said.

"It's hard to find someone, ma'am," the thinner of the two men said. "Lord knows."

The fat man gave him a snarl, then looked me up and down.

"Well, I guess you're still a woman," he said.

He reached forward and squeezed my right breast like it was nothing at all.

Hank came from the darkness and punched the fat man square in the throat. The man fell to his knees, gurgling blood, near taking my breast with him. Hank reared towards the skinny man, who cursed the mentally unfit and ran into the night.

"Boy," Hank said to Tobias, "go tell the office to call an ambulance. Here," he handed Tobias a gold object. "Hide that in your bag."

Tobias studied the item.

"Go!" Hank yelled.

Tobias ran towards the office.

Hank started pressing the fat man's chest.

"Lift his legs," Hank said. "We need to keep him breathing."

With stamina I had never witnessed, Hank pumped continually until the ambulance arrived. The police came as well and took our statements.

After the police left, Hank insisted we return to the road immediately.

"Don't you want to rest?" I said.

Hank reloaded the car and slammed the trunk shut. "I'll be resting in prison if he dies."

"But it was self-defense," I said.

"Excessive force," Tobias said. "But the police have your name and plates. Won't they find you?"

"Yeah, well, let's not make it easy for 'em. Give cops enough distance, and they stop caring."

"This isn't your first time," Tobias said.

"Shh now, Tobias," I said, sliding into the front seat close to Hank.

Instead of sitting in the back seat, Tobias sat on the other side of me in the front.

Two hours down the road, well into the darkness of the country, Hank told us a story about the brass knuckles.

"I got them from my dad when he died," he said. "He got 'em from an Indian when he was younger. Indian wore a bowler hat with a bunch of blue feathers pinned to it like a headdress. Dad did a job for the Indian, but the Indian couldn't pay him, so he offered Dad the knuckles and told him either he took 'em or the Indian'd kill him. Because he couldn't have people goin' around spreading a bad word 'bout Indians."

"Why'd the Indian choose blue feathers?" Tobias said.

Hank furrowed his brow.

"I don't know why people do what they do," he said.

After returning, I attempted to make up the heroics to Hank through a series of chocolate cakes and handholding on walks, but the chemistry still wasn't there, and we eventually drifted.

CHAPTER 4

A Personal Letter from a Stramwell Rock

February 1937
Stramwell, Oregon

I am not accustomed to writing letters or sharing my thoughts in general, as I am a rock, approximately the size of a deer's nose. (I know this because a deer once ate grass next to me.)

I exist on a gravel road on the outskirts of Stramwell, Oregon. (I know this because I have had many years to determine it, and even common gravel knows the sun is up and the earth is down.)

(The remaining items below I know because rocks gossip more than you can imagine.)

For 10,000 years, the Kalapuya Indians lived in

small villages around the area of Stramwell. They numbered 3,000 in the human year 1780 when the white explorers brought disease. In 1856 they built a school to teach Kalapuya children English. The last Kalapuya Indian died in 1937.

Ben Holladay was a businessman who built his stagecoach empire through lies, manipulation, and force. Seeing the railroad endangered his mail delivery business, he sold out to Wells Fargo for $1.5 million. He then bought the O&C Railroad out of Portland, Oregon, with plans to build the rail line south into California. When construction of the rail line got to the Stramwell area, Holladay set up a post office. He named the little town that sprung up after US Postmaster General Jon Stramwell to cater favor. Holladay funded the rail expansion by selling overstated bonds to German investors, and they came calling in the economic crash of 1873. The rail line stalled in Roseburg, OR. Holladay lost everything and never recovered.

In 1909 a man named J.T. Baumgartner from Minnesota began selling tracts of land near Stramwell. The price was $90 per acre, and he sold over 1400 acres to Midwest and East Coast investors. The investors were poor farmers who'd collected their life savings and the life savings of all their relatives to buy the land. Baumgartner bought train tickets for all the investors and their families to move to Oregon. In those days Stramwell grew exponentially.

On the morning of April 17, 1913, representatives of Baumgartner Inc. stated they were bankrupt, with its founder and supposed cash reserves of over $100,000 nowhere to be found.

J.T. Baumgartner achieved the grift by setting up

multiple corporations to sell land tracts and the associated debt at an inflated rate. Most of the farmers who lost their land moved into Stramwell proper and took jobs in lumber mills. As a result, by the end of the Great War, the town population had more than doubled. Additionally, all indicators of civilization, such as birth rate survival, high school graduation, food plenty, and lifespan, had increased.

The problem with humans is their concern over lifespans. Rocks accept we belong to the earth.

(I know this because it is true.)

Cordially, or not, (politeness is no concern of a rock),

Jasper Pyrite

CHAPTER 5

A nd now to the heart of the matter.

How it all came about was Tobias wrote me a letter and placed it on my chair. The letter stated his proposition as such:

Dear J,

I have appreciated your many efforts to stimulate my mind by serving up the brains of others on silver platters for me to devour. But I am tired of brain and would like to grow my own food. Put simply, dear bird, I plan to endeavor the creation of a novel unlike the world has ever seen. It will be full of profanity, guilty pleasure, murder, corruption, intrigue, and all other suitable primordial ooze the masses crave.

Our goal is to escape. I will soon be pulled out of school to till dirt, and your biological clock is ticking so loudly every single man in Stramwell smothers his head at night to escape its drone.

We will use each other then. I will write the shite, and you will be the name and face. With our earnings and fame, I will send myself to university, and you will land a man and his seed.

If you agree to my offer, place a blue feather in your cap tomorrow, and I will begin in earnest. You shall receive five pages daily in your schoolhouse cubby to type and bind for publisher submission once complete in two months.

Yours in exodus,

T. Randall

I put a feather in my best cap straight away.

***

The pages came in swimmingly, well exceeding the five-per-day quota. The writing was buoyed with such gusto and bold voice I often had to stop my chittering flurry of pounding keys to pat my breast with a mild case of the vapors.

10, then 20, even 30 pages were filling my cubby daily. I was getting very little sleep and loving it.

The story was titled, *The Senators*. I've included the premise below in seven parts:

1. Two years before the novel opening, an African nation was overtaken by a totalitarian European regime. The world sat on its collective alabaster hands and did nothing.
2. Back in the States, in the past six months, sixty black American prostitutes have been impregnated by the seed of American senators. The pregnant women are being kept hidden in a barn just outside Washington, DC. (If the women could not collect the seed directly, it was procured by payoffs to the Senator's mistresses,

53

and delivered post-haste to black women stationed in an adjoining room.)

3. The group funding the covert endeavor is the former royal family of the African nation. They hold the release of news of the pregnancies as blackmail against the senators. To keep the story shut up, the senators must vote to go to war against the European nation and restore the royal family to leadership in the African country.

4. The senators refuse to comply. They discover the barn's location (housing the pregnant prostitutes) through violent coercion and plan a bomb attack on the hidden compound. The attack fails due to incompetency.

5. Enraged, the African monarchy plans to release all the prostitutes and their stories to the press. On the eve of that release, word spreads that an immense reserve of oil has been discovered in the African nation. Congress unanimously votes to go to war to remove the European totalitarian regime and return the previous African government to power. (With strong US oversight on their oil production to prevent other attacks.)

6. The prostitutes are shipped to a Caribbean Island to raise the children. The island serves ostensibly as a prisoner-of-war base. A lavish resort is built there, where the prostitutes work and are imprisoned. Senators visit occasionally for highly confidential meetings and return rested and well-sunned.

7. A former prostitute and her young boy escape the island and wash up on shore atop a makeshift raft. They've landed in America.

A week into the process, we were up to 135 pages. (We had reached the part where the Senators were in the basement of the Capital Building, scheming to bomb the secluded barn but realizing none of them knew how to build a bomb.)

I noticed young Tobias was looking gaunt. His hair, face, and feet hadn't been washed, nor had his overalls rotated every few days as usual. I thought perhaps the writing process was draining him, and then considered for the first time he might be doing his work secretly in the night just as I was.

"Father left," he said, almost to himself, sliding the pages into my cubby. "In the night."

I didn't know what to say. It took me just a moment to re-examine him as a young adult rather than a colleague.

"Well," I said, "we will visit your house after school to gather your living items for temporary residence at my house."

I considered an embrace but instead turned and entered the second room full of used brooms.

***

If I were to make a single remark about the Randall estate, it would be the adjective 'bare.' Intentionally, aggressively, bare. There were no pictures or personal effects of the family anywhere, and of course, no female touches of delicacy to adorn the windows or tables. In the cupboard were exactly two place settings of wares and cutlery: two glasses, two plates, and two forks. I inquired Tobias if his father had made a commotion from packing all their wares the night he fled.

"He didn't take anything," he said.

When I attempted to visit Tobias's room to collect his things, he stated he did not have a room. He slept on his father's bedroom floor without a blanket or pillow. Aside from his two pairs of overalls and undershirts, the boy had no personal effects either.

I will state for the record I made every attempt to implore the boy to tell more about his family background but could not harvest any useful information.

Tobias did mention his father left the family car.

He led me around to the back of the house where, under a canvas tarp, sat a teal green 1930 Buick Series 40 Coupe 258 CI, 3-speed with grey interior.

"He also left cash under the kitchen floor."

As I stood in the kitchen, I noticed for the first time how grand the house really was, and far more suitable for a shared dwelling than my small cottage.

We drove the Buick 40 to my place, loaded my typewriter and various other meager personal effects and sundries, and returned to the former Randall residence, where I established temporary occupancy.

I notified the authorities of the parental abandonment immediately the next day, or rather earnestly intended to. But the next day was the sabbath, and, given the sparsity of the home, decided for the wellbeing of young Tobias that some shopping was in order.

We drove several towns away, where I purchased suitable items for the house, clothing for Tobias, and a hat, or two, for myself. On our journey home, I asked the young man why his father would leave the car during his flight. Tobias said his father liked walking, which made sense as I, too, enjoyed the simple things.

On stable ground now, the writing accelerated in earnest. We set up shop at the kitchen table where Tobias would write the story, and I would type from his pages.

On our first night of work, I observed young Tobias mouthing words to himself as he wrote in long hand, and inquired whether we should skip that step and go straight to dictation.

You wouldn't know it unless you had a narrative going in him, but that boy could talk. I am an adequate typist, but no Lucy Lindross (the fastest typist in my secretarial class at Weston Academy – you know it as Weston Normal School.) Lucy was ugly as a hot poker, but her fingers flew like Gabriel and Michael combined.

Three and a half hours later, I collapsed over the typewriter. I lay that night in bed, thinking of whatever became of Lucy Lindross. I then passed into a fitful dream where I ran wildly in a field while Zeus tore apart thunderclouds above me.

Ms. Lindross, I was to discover the following day on my call to her, had taken a private secretary job with a powerful young lawyer in Salem. The attorney was tall, handsome, and unflinchingly faithful to his blonde bombshell wife. Lucy stated she could be on the next train to Stramwell, tomorrow a.m.

In school that day, I sat at my desk while the children read in silence. Tobias had already read every book available and was skimming through old *National Geographics* containing breasts of women graffitied by other pubescent boys. Tobias studied the doodles with his pinky finger as an archeologist might handle an artifact from the sarcophagus of King Tutankhamun. I thought about all the other women I'd gone to Weston Academy with.

Even though it was long-distance, I used the official school phone to call Ms. Lindross at work.

"Lucy dear," I said. "I was thinking about your sister Heather. What is she up to these days?"

Lucy informed me her older, (and even homelier), sister Heather was available.

"She's not as quick on the keys as me, I'm afraid," Lucy said. "But she's an absolute virtuoso at shorthand."

While I was at Weston, classes were provided on Gregg's shorthand methodology. As my intention was education, I spent my efforts elsewhere, although the concept always intrigued me.

"Tobias," I said, holding my hand over the receiver, "could you come forward, please?"

Tobias shut his *Geographic* and approached.

"Perchance, young man," I whispered. "Have you any *more* story ideas?"

"I have a plethora of novels in various genres plotted completely in my mind."

I confirmed that both Lucy and Heather Lindross could arrive on the 11 a.m. train.

After school, Tobias and I took a leisurely walk back to the farmhouse. I did not prod him for conversation or rush our pace. I also let him wander without guidance.

We walked along Carson's Creek, just west of the house. The young man hefted the largest rocks he could raise from the earth and tossed them into the water. He chose the same spot each time to land the rocks and began to build a dam of sorts.

This he would do each day. When exhausted of energy, we would continue toward the house, where the Lindross sisters were waiting with dinner ready.

During dinner we would enjoy light conversation about the weather or news. After cleaning up, one hour of leisure time was allotted. We ladies would listen to the radio and read or knit. I never guided Tobias during this time, in which he would disappear into a room I had established as privately his. At exactly 6:30 p.m., writing would commence.

I stationed myself at a typewriter desk near the east dining room window. Lucy was at her typewriter in the northwest corner, and Heather was stationed on the south wall near the kitchen. Marge, who was not much of a typist and didn't know shorthand, was tasked with housework upkeep, making coffee, and keeping the paper and ribbon stocked.

Tobias would dictate the remaining bits of *The Senators* with me for fifteen minutes, upon which my egg timer in the shape of a chicken would rattle. He would then move to Lucy, where he began a new story. The chicken would ding-a-ling again, and Tobias would step to Heather to start another new novel.

Lucy could keep up with straight dictation via the typewriter. Heather would use shorthand and then type during her off-rotation times. I struggled along like a turtle with colon blockage, continually raising my finger to pause the young man.

"Lucy dear," I said, a bead of sweat cascading. "Do you keep in touch with any other girls from Weston?"

"Oh yes," she said. "Abigail and Judy are both married and have—"

"No, not them," I interrupted, looking over at the elder Heather, typing furiously. Strands of her hair floated out of a poorly constructed bun. One slightly askew eyeball peered over the frames of her thick glasses.

"What I mean is… ladies such as us."

Lucy followed my gaze to her sister, who sat in an unusual legs-akimbo fashion. One of her orthopedic shoes was untied and off-kilter. Her wool skirt stretched at the hips from unworldly pressure.

"Oh," Lucy said. "Yes…" She bit her thumbnail. "Mildred Wadell, perhaps?"

Mildred Wadell, I thought, picturing her. "Oh yes, kind Millie. Any others?"

By the week's end, we had wholly reorganized the structure of operations. There were five stations, each with a girl taking dictation on 15-minute time slots, then typing like a beast from Hades while off rotation. (All took dictation except for Lucy, of course, as her typing skills did not require shorthand.) Beyond Millie, the additional girls included Frances Malloy and Virginia Gleason.

I supervised and researched submission opportunities for publication. We continued each night until 10:30 p.m.

During the first month, we created the following:

The Senators

The aforementioned first novel.

Ms. McGillicutty's Menagerie of Wonders

(Children's books I through VII)

In years past, pretty young teacher Ms. M. went through a terrible ordeal with a fire at her schoolhouse: Her beloved golden labrador Maximus was trapped inside with no escape possible.

Committing herself to a life helping animals, she started a traveling rescue wagon outfit, taking in strays and a wild variety of other creatures for redistribution to loving homes across Oregon. Along the way, she collected orphans to help her in the work, who also got redistributed.

She passed away as an old lady in Book VII, ending with a grand funeral procession of all the families and pets she helped.

For Women Only

A female self-help book gathered from candid conversations Tobias collected, partially from eavesdropping on the ladies of the house. Tips included properly setting hair at night for morning readiness, utilizing small-town community social circles to your advantage, and a strategic regurgitation planner to maintain proper weight. There is also a tiny appendix, authored by a fictitious Dr. Henry J. Wiles, containing a step-by-step clinical guide, complete with sketches, on achieving self-induced satisfaction.

Our Sky Was Not Yours

A harrowing tale of a plantation owner's son who must rebuild his family's fortune after he returns from the Civil War.

Man About Town

and

Man Goes Downtown

Two mystery novels containing 16-year-old English boy genius sleuth Garland Fernsby. Garland solves crimes revealing the torrid underworld of his wealthy and politically connected upper Manhattan neighbors.

Garland was orphaned when his parents were involved in a mysterious carriage accident at Christmastime near the family estate in Birmingham, UK. He now resides in the spacious New York townhouse of his Great Aunt Tilda, an eccentric, wealthy widow with a few tricks up her sleeve.

Aunt Tilda's live-in caretaker is Jeanne Albert, a bookish, quiet girl who desires adventure. Along for the ride is Bubby, Tilda's grandson, a dim-witted, anxious, good-natured, obese boy of Garland's age who, whether due to his girth or otherwise, was always getting into tight predicaments.

Watching young Tobias bounce between stations was nothing short of a revelation. The chicken timer would release, and he'd stop mid-sentence on one story, pause for a slight beat, pivot directly to the following table, and continue where he previously broke away. I could have sold tickets.

***

We decided to break for a few days at the end of the third week. The girls were spent, and I had the tilt of a wilted daisy.

On that final night, I laid all the manuscripts on my bedroom floor. Two thousand one hundred eighty-one pages of fully realized coherent prose that was, in my humble opinion, superior to anything on the current literary market.

I called a group meeting for the morning.

"The word… is confidentiality," I said, looking gravely into each uncomely face. (There were seven of us now, plus young Tobias.) "I will be the author and face of the books."

"Wait," Lucy raised her hand. "Shouldn't Beth be the face? I mean, of the books? I mean…"

It was true. 18-year-old Beth Meyers, a last-minute fill-in for Frances Malloy, who left us in week two to return to a teaching position, was by far the prettiest of the bunch.

Young Beth was the image of a camas flower, with the blossom of her impossibly thick golden hair forever tied in a blue ribbon. Her beauty was an anomaly I had been too busy to examine the meaning of until that moment.

Beth had come to us as the recommendation of the exiting Frances and was a recent graduate of her class at Monmouth High School. Tragically, Beth was an aged-out ward of the foster care system and had no real family.

Our other new member was Dorothy (Dot) Cox, who joined our group as a fill-in for Virginia Gleason after she left abruptly during the first week of our venture. (Virginia's sister had passed suddenly of pneumonia, leaving two young children and a handsome widower behind. Dot was new in town and happened to be at the library one Saturday looking through want ads at a table next to Tobias and me.)

"No," I said. "Beth, as cute as she is, is of tender age. The public won't allow it given the subject matter."

"But Tobias is even younger than her," Lucy said.

"It simply won't work," I replied.

"You're right," Tobias said.

It was a rarity when he would comment at our group meetings.

"No one person could have written these titles," he continued. "Even if they could, it would take many months at best, and I will continue at this pace for at least six more weeks before mental burnout. By then, we will have over 40 books. That level of prolific output would be suspect, to say the least."

"He's right," Dot said.

"Yes," Lucy added, with the others joining the murmurs.

I cleared my throat. "What shall we do, then?

Abandon the proposition altogether? Each return to our empty domiciles of budget sundries and torn hosiery?"

The tussle-talk elevated to a small roar.

"What if," Tobias said, "we were to print under the auspices of a unified group? An all-female collective of writers who chose anonymity as an unspoken protest against prejudices in the literary world and beyond? We could call it the 'UVW.' The Unified Voices of Women, with Ms. Jane Alexander as our president and spokeswoman?"

***

That Friday, I reported ill to the school board, put a feather in my new best cap, and drove to Portland with the manuscripts in tow.

I wore a scarf and slunk into my seat to avoid suspicion. Unfortunately, I had previously let the car tank run dry. So, I took a calculated risk and stopped at Fill n' Time.

The proprietor, Al, was there this time. A burley ape of a man, he had a reputation for being a lonely widower and war hero.

He saw me fiddling with the pump and ran out to assist, wiping his oily hands on a greasy rag before jamming it in his pocket. (How vast the world of grime and bacteria in that pocket I cannot imagine.)

"I'll help ya miss," he said, taking the pump.

We watched the gas pump drain while an old dog slept a few feet away.

"Ya know," Al said, "dogs are both happy and miserable at the same time."

I was also looking at the mongrel, wondering how much lye and elbow grease it would take to scrub it clean.

"This one seems content enough," I said.

"Dogs are content as long as they're not mistreated."

Al removed a cigarette and struck a match on the rough side of the tank. Rather than putting the flame out, he tossed it into a bucket of fuel. When I flinched backward, he steadied me using his free meaty paw, then commenced smoking.

"Good nature is fertile soil for happiness," I said.

Al pulled the gas nozzle from the car and placed it back in its station.

The dog turned on his back, full in an oil patch, and gnawed at its hindquarters.

"But misery comes with the smallest flea," Al said, opening my door. "Enjoy your travels, Miss. Everyone deserves a day off, most of all teachers."

I nodded and put it in high gear for the city.

***

The offices of Compton and Birdwhistle (C&B) were small and cluttered, with oil paintings of the founders on the wall. I took in their substantial mustaches and wondered if an unspoken competition had been at play.

C&B was the only literary agency within three hundred miles. They mainly specialized in nature guides and large photography books on lighthouses. After repeated inquiries, I had landed an appointment, given their junior agent Theodore Compton's one-time interest in our short story *More.*

I was greeted coldly by a woman so old she was likely the first Birdwhistle's mistress. She neither provided me coffee nor a place to set the hundred pounds of manuscripts I had carried from Burnside St.

The young Mr. Compton exited his office, addressed me warmly, and hefted my papers.

I eyed the secretary as I walked past. Compton was tall and young, with broad shoulders that narrowed to a waistline that could never be cinched enough. I picked my eyeteeth to ensure they were free of debris, as I had arrived early and ordered a plate of assorted breadless sandwich rolls at Le Club.

I was surprised to find Theodore Compton's office clean and airy, with modern straight lines and stainless embellishments. I sat in a curved chair that appeared uncomfortable but felt quite plumb.

"These stories," Mr. Compton sighed, dropping the massive stack on his desk. "How again did you arrive by them?"

"I... *we* are the UVW. That's the United Voices of Women, a writer's collective from Stramwell way."

"I see."

"You will also see there are no individual author's names, save mention of the UVW itself and me, as its president and representative." (I had "*UVW President: Ms. Jane Alexander Esq.*" typed on each cover.)

"So, no one wants credit?"

"Quite the contrary. Everyone wants equal credit."

"So, you have an agenda?"

"As far as you're concerned, Mr. Compton, our only agenda is to sell books." I took off the top manuscript (*The Senators*) and dropped it flatly on his desk. "Boatloads."

The thin man sighed and fanned through the pages. "Ok, I'll take a peek when I have time, but I can't guarantee—"

"Page one, Theodore. Continue to page twenty, and I will leave of my own volition. Stop prematurely, and it will take the hounds of Hades to drag me from this overpriced chair."

I took out my hook and yarn. Compton stared at me while I focused on the thread without additional expression. He sighed again, picked up *The Senators,* and read the first ten pages.

A short time later, he called in his partner Vernon Caul, and they read forty more in my presence together.

Upon completing a sky-blue knit cap, I announced my need to return home at a reasonable hour. The men offered to put me up at The Benson, but I declined out of principle.

Contract for literary representation in hand, I sped South to Stramwell as happy as I'd ever been. The tank was nearly empty when I returned to town, so I refilled it.

***

"So," Al said, "how was your day?"

"Rapturous," I said, without pause.

"Well, that sounds pretty good."

We stood listening to the steady sound of the

68

flowing gas. The dog must have called it a day. Then, without notice to my brain, my mouth began spewing a detailed account of all the day's events. Afterward, Al once again opened and shut my door.

"Miss, I want to say thank you," Al said. "I'll go for weeks hearing about nothing but the weather. But you had a real tale."

His face was no less ape-like up close, but his forearms were muscular as a steed's breast, and his finger bore no ring. I nodded and pulled away, looking back only twice in the rearview.

***

On returning to the farmhouse, I called for a gathering of the group.

"It is with utmost pleasure," I began, with the agency contract laid before me, "that I announce the formal union of the UVW with the esteemed Compton and Birdwhistle Literary Agency."

I let them applaud for twenty seconds before calming.

"And I've been personally assured by junior agent Theodore Compton that he fully expects the sale of all our intellectual property to New York publishers in short time."

"Oh my!" Marge shouted.

"What does that mean?" Lucy said, "I mean, financially, for the group?"

"Well, of course, it no doubt means," I said, "where's young Beth?"

"It means where's young Beth?" Marge said plainly,

"No. Beth, where is she? Has anyone seen her?" I said.

Dot spoke. "All her things are there in the room. I was just there. Her dresses are still hanging on the line." She pointed out the window.

After comprehensively checking the grounds, Marge and I went to town. We searched Great Harvest, Darcy's Cafe, and Donna's Salon. No one had seen a trace of pretty Beth. In fact, no one had seen her since that morning before I left.

Hesitantly, as I didn't believe it was time for alarm, we visited Sheriff Tawlins.

"She got a boyfriend?" the sheriff asked, his dirty work boots propped on his desk.

"Never," Marge said.

Sheriff Tawlins dropped his feet and leaned over the dirty desk. "Could she have one, just not to your knowledge? She's pretty enough."

"No boyfriend," I said. "We've already inquired at Great Harvest, Darcy's, and Donna's. They haven't seen a trace."

"Hmm," the Sheriff said. "How about Buell's? Maybe she went shopping and lost track of time."

"For nine hours?"

"Maybe she's related to my ex."

Marge and I sat erect and cast him the sternest of looks.

In the next two hours, we canvassed every

establishment in Stramwell. Sheriff Tawlins also reached out to Lane County law enforcement, but none had witnessed a lone young lady. By nightfall, a search party of no less than thirty men had formed, commencing on our house property and expanding in concentric circles.

The men searched into the night. Our house served as a base, with coffee and light refreshments provided.

It wasn't until after three a.m. when it was determined that I, in fact, was the last person to see Beth.

"We crossed paths in the hallway before my exit this morning," I told the Sheriff and Al Clifton. (Al, the previously mentioned proprietor of the Fill n' Time, was a close friend of the Sheriff and the first person he called to assist with the search.)

"You saw her?" Sheriff Tawlins said.

"Early this morning in the hallway, we passed as young Beth was on her way to the necessary room."

"Her hair already in perfect curls," Lucy interjected.

"Her angelic face requiring no garnishment," Dot said.

"The day started so promising," Al said, giving me a small smile.

Sheriff Tawlins pushed his cowboy hat back on his head, looking confused.

"And where exactly were you headed?" he asked me.

"My cousin had a feminine doctor's appointment she had been waiting on for nigh two months. She is a caretaker for a wealthy blind and partially deaf older woman living in the Irvington neighborhood in

71

Portland. I agreed to take Sissy's place at the last minute when no substitute could be found, as the feminine doctor's appointment was most needed. It achieved her finally addressing a private issue by medicating the affected area directly with a green yeast paste similar in consistency to mushed peas."

Sheriff and Mr. Clifton jumped to refill their coffee and continued their search without further questions.

The search party began to dissipate around dawn. By lunchtime it was back down to the Sheriff and Al.

In the passing days and weeks, nary a trace of Beth was found, save one of her customary blue bows, which I discovered the following day in the internal cavity of my typewriter.

With the books submitted to publishing houses, I thought it a good idea for a longer respite. I sent all the ladies home, leaving only Tobias and myself in the house.

The night after the search, I witnessed the silhouette of the boy at my bedroom door. I remained silent as he lay quietly on the floor. Two hours before my customary early rising, I jumped up quickly and peered over the bed, but he was gone.

CHAPTER 6

The toy wishing well

February 1937
Randall Farm
Stramwell, Oregon

The most common adult brain tumor is glioblastoma, discovered in 1926 by Percival Bailey and Harvey Cushing.

Baily would later author *The Isocortex of Man*, a seminal work on the cellular composition of the cerebral cortex.

Cushing went on to provide the first diagnosis of Cushing's Disease, along with composing a Pulitzer Prize-winning biography on William Osler, the founder of modern medicine.

Mr. Roy Randall died on the toilet.

Tobias Randall performed the autopsy, discovering his brain aneurism was caused by a glioblastoma tumor ruptured from extreme exertion during a bowel movement after gorging on cream chipped beef.

There was no phone in the Randall house, and Tobias's mother could not drive. In theory, Tobias could have performed CPR or aroused his mother to do the same while he sought help. However, the time until the boy's return would be 45 minutes. His mother would not have maintained CPR for that long, and would have felt repressed guilt about it for the rest of her days.

Factoring this, Tobias heard his father fall off the toilet, waited 10 minutes for total death, and located the tumor using a rusty hacksaw. Tobias buried his father before notifying his mother, who did not take the news well.

***

When Tobias was a small child, the family lived in rural Idaho. In the side yard of their house was an ancient well that had been made obsolete with the advent of modern plumbing. The original cylindrical guard was no longer present, and the hole was left uncovered.

As a toddler, Tobias Randall would lie on his stomach, resting his chin on the hole's edge, watching small pebbles from his shifting position disrupt the black water below.

The boy would imagine his mother and father's faces surfacing from the water then disappearing back within.

When Tobias first met William James Sidis, he said, "I am but a young stranger, but I know who you are and want to learn from your life. What advice do you have for me?"

"Accept reality, good or bad," the genius said.

Sidis pivoted to leave the boy, but then returned.

"Live life on your terms," he added. "It guards the only thing you have."

"Time?" Tobias replied. "Energy?"

"Nothingness," the genius said.

***

Years later, Tobias would shut his eyes and return to the well's black water. Instead of his parents' faces, a different, perfectly crafted round face would emerge. The water would cascade as she rose until he reached out a hand and felt the perfect curvature of her cheek. She would descend again, and, just before the dark liquid hid her completely, the boy would force his eyes open.

CHAPTER 7

In two weeks, I received a call from Theodore Compton from the Compton and Birdwhistle Literary Agency. He was in New York City visiting the esteemed offices of The Walsingham Pater Publishing Company and was nearly out of breath after running to a payphone in Manhattan to make the call.

Mr. Compton provided word the publisher had purchased everything, with plans for expedient publication. Our take on the advance would be $11,250, just shy of ten years' teacher's salary. Finally, Compton said, Mr. Walsingham Pater himself asked to meet me personally.

I could have fainted for a month.

I mailed my resignation letter to the Lane County School Board offices that Saturday morning on my way to see Mother.

"Are you married?"

"Yes, to a handsome young doctor," I said. "We're pregnant with twins."

That shut her up.

***

The following Thursday, all the ladies of the UVW, plus Tobias, traveled together on a grand cross-country train ride. Dressed in high fashion, we ate the finest food and drank not a small amount of wine imported from the State of California.

A curious event happened over the Snake River Canyon that we would not thoroughly learn of until our return journey. I will go into greater detail after discussing our New York visit. For now, I will merely note that Marge scandalously removed two buttons from her day dress, attracting no less than three suitors before we crossed the Idaho border. We were near Payette when I finally demanded her repair it.

The New York visit was lackluster.

We visited the sights and made no little amount of stir, bustling in and out of hotel lobbies and restaurants. (Truthfully, New York City is ill-prepared to hold a gaggle of full-hearted prominent women in even larger hats once freed the bonds of economic patriarchy.)

I have provided one example below of our encounter at the Stork Club on the Sunday night of our visit. We had no choice but to leave young Tobias in the hotel room preoccupied with a large stack of science fiction magazines.

Regarding the Stork Club affair, we first waited in line for nearly forty-five minutes, (this was after a full hour and a half of prep time at the hotel.)

I had informed the ladies the Stork Club proprietor, Mr. Sherman Billingsley, provided a gardenia corsage to any lady wearing an evening gown with silk gloves up to her elbow. (Mr. Billingsley reportedly spent over $7,000 a year on flowers.) Although none of us had gowns, we wore all gloves to ensure we received our flowers.

Then there was an issue with the doorman, Mr. Lopez.

When the queue had not moved for some time, and after witnessing many others pulling directly up to the front door and being ushered in, I broke line and approached.

"We, sir," I said, "would like very much to enter and be seated at or near table 50. I have a number of high-class ladies with me unaccustomed to waiting."

Mr. Lopez glanced around me. About thirty feet back stood Mildred and Dot with deep frowns, their shoulders hunched, arms folded, legs firmly planted in wide stances. Marge clutched the tiniest of purses with both hands, flinching wildly at every passerby. Lucy had removed her gloves and was using them to fan her elder sister, Heather, who sat on the curb in the throes of an epic hot flash.

"Do you have a reservation?" Mr. Lopez asked.

"Yes," I said. "I've heard Mr. Winchell invite his audience to join him on more than one occasion, and we are his loyal American audience. I, for one, have been faithfully listening for over three and a half years."

"I am sorry, ma'am, no one is seated without a reservation."

A younger man with two young girls slapped Mr.

Lopez on the back, entering the Stork without pause.

"Joey! How ya doin', pal?!" the man said.

"And where is the golden rope?" I inquired. (I had seen a photograph of a solid gold rope used at the entry of the Stork, whereas, on that night, there was only Mr. Lopez.)

"I'm sorry, ma'am, you'll have to make a reservation," Mr. Lopez said, as he allowed another stylish couple through.

"Clearly," I said.

I motioned to several ladies at the front of the line with a '*Can you believe this?*' gesture, but they pretended to ignore me.

"Can't take the risk of fraternizing with me?" I said, but the women just inched closer to Mr. Lopez.

"Ok, that's it!" I yelled and waved my UVW crew over.

Heather groaned so loudly on getting up the entire crowd turned, expecting to see a mugging.

Once the group was assembled, I folded my arms and confronted Mr. Lopez directly.

"We will act like chickens," I said.

Mr. Lopez squinted.

"Chickens," I repeated. "We will parade in a circle, right here on the sidewalk, flapping our arms and squawking until you let us in."

"Listen, lady- "

"Be-gawk!!" I yelled.

79

A genuine panic entered Mr. Lopez's eyes.

"Ok," he raised his hands.

"Be-gawk!" Marge yelled. "Be-gawk!!"

Sweet Mildred stepped forward and, her hands folded inward and legs akimbo, marched in a circle.

"Boooog boog boog boog boog!!" she yelped.

"That's not a chicken sound," a man in line said.

"Quiet you!" I turned to Mr. Lopez. "Now, what'll be Mr. Lopez? Six chickens for the night or a table near table 50?"

Mr. Lopez scanned each of us and nodded for me to approach him more intimately. I called off Mildred and stepped over.

"No one gets in on Sunday nights," he said.

"How do you mean? I just saw—"

"I mean," he leaned in. "No one in this line is getting in tonight. We're too full of regulars. And if you keep making a scene, the boss'll call the cops. They'll arrest you. I'm serious. They won't even blink."

His eyes were genuinely apologetic.

"I'm sorry. I really am," he said.

I observed the long line of well-dressed onlookers, each one of them hoping.

"Do you know what Mr. Lopez just told me??" my voice cracked, the words spilling out in a crescendo from deep in my belly. "He said not one of you is getting in tonight. They have 'raised the draw bridge' so the peasants cannot enter the feast!"

I planted my feet firmly and raised both arms. "But we will not let them do this! For we are the people—"

"Shut up, you!" a woman in front shouted.

"Yeah! Shut yer trap!" another woman yelled. "You're gonna ruin it for the rest of us!"

"Get back to your coop, ya big hen!" a man called.

"Your eggs are getting cold!"

"She ain't got no eggs!"

A police siren broke the cacophony. A squad car pulled up and a fat policeman stepped out and shone his spotlight directly on us.

"Retreat!" I yelled.

The United Voices of Women ran down West 58th Street.

And that, is New York City.

The following day, after some unpleasant exchanges with a delicate-boned receptionist, I met with a junior representative at Walsingham Pater Publishing Company, who informed me William Pater was out of country and that I really should have scheduled an appointment.

"You people need an appointment to breathe," I said.

I phoned Mr. Compton to notify him of the discourtesy. He couldn't believe I had traveled to New York with the entire UVW, then apologized repeatedly after I clarified that we were women of action.

The rest of the trip was acceptably fine. Still, it reduced my estimation of the Big Apple to the point I haven't returned or felt the desire to do so.

The Snake River Canyon is in Idaho Falls, Idaho, just outside of town. A body of a man was discovered at the bottom of the ravine three days after we first passed on our journey east. The man was identified as a passenger who failed to arrive at the Omaha stop of our trip. His family insisted he had no reason to end things prematurely, and an accident or foul play must have been involved.

As it turns out, the night we traveled over the canyon on our journey to New York, this gentleman, Mr. Henry Hames as he was known, was entertaining our very own Ms. Margaret Plimpton (Marge) over several glasses of wine in the cocktail car.

No one remembered if they departed the car together, and I corrected anyone who assumed as much on the spot. (I also scolded Marge once more for unbuttoning her blouse in the first place, a detail I determined the police not hear as it was impertinent to their investigation.)

For the first time, I will now discuss my conversation with Marge and Tobias on our return journey. I had just passed Marge's sleeping quarters and witnessed young Tobias speaking with her.

"Alright, out with it then," I said, stepping inside her cabin and closing the door.

"Well," Marge said, "the questions that detective was asking got me thinking about that night, the night Mr. Hames—"

"Plummeted. Yes, go on."

"Well, the truth is I can't remember much. But I do

remember him and me talking about my blouse."

Marge fingered her top button, and I swiped her hand away.

"Nevermind that. Woman, what is your point?"

"Well, after you left, Mr. Hames said, and I can't remember exactly because I wasn't of the soundest mind, but I believe he said, *'That old Jane lady is just jealous of your developments.'*"

Marge darted a look at me and then down to her hands. "Then he suggested he was someone who could appreciate my," she swallowed hard, "*developments.*"

Marge fiddled with her buttons furiously.

"Stop that," I said, glancing at Tobias.

"Sorry, Tobias," Marge said.

"Never mind him. Get to the point. Why is Tobias in here in secret?"

"Well... after we talked for a while, Mr. Hames sort of steered me to the car exit. Then I remember waking up the next morning."

"So?"

"So that's it."

"What's it?"

"That's what Tobias wanted to talk about."

"Why would Tobias want to talk," I sighed, dropped my head, and stepped back for the door handle.

"Tobias, please follow me to my quarters," I said. "And Margaret Ivy Plimpton, if I see you playing with that button again, I'll throw you into the Snake River

83

myself. Your developments have got us nothing but trouble."

Upon returning to our sleeping quarters, I inquired Tobias regarding the full details.

"I pushed Mr. Hames into the Snake River Canyon," he began.

"Go on."

"Marge was seriously impaired," he continued. "I estimated her to be unconscious in seven minutes. So, I followed them from the cocktail car towards her sleeping quarters, where I observed a dramatic uptick in Mr. Hames's wandering hands. Despite her condition, Marge began pushing him away, to no avail."

The drink cart man rapped on our window. Tobias and I took tea with no milk and crumpets.

"Do you like crumpets?" I asked.

"What's not to like?" Tobias said.

"Furthermore," he continued, "Marge is a virgin, and the loss of this treasure psychologically would cause her remaining few years of fruitfulness to waste with guilt. In no uncertain terms, preventing what was about to occur was a matter of life and death. Since Mr. Hames was stronger than me, I took the opportunity and timing of the canyon's approach to attack with surprise. I pushed forward as the pair transferred between the final car leading to her sleeping quarters. Marge saw nothing and passed out into my arms barely moments after. Mr. Hames, in the few seconds he was falling, did not even know who pushed him. After some struggle with Marge, due in no small part to the massive weight of her *developments* both front and rear, I dragged her into the quarters, secured the door behind me, and returned to the cocktail car unseen. Christ may judge me, Miss Jane, but no court of law can, unless you or I speak of it further. Presently, I was inquiring of Marge what she told the police, of which naturally there was very little she could."

I sipped my tea.

"Are you surprised by your actions?" I said.

"Yes, I overestimated the time it would take for Marge to fall unconscious."

Tobias curved his mouth in a slight smile but concealed it quickly after I did not return the gesture.

Tobias took a sip of tea. "Be-*gawk*," he said quietly, resolving what he had done that Sunday night, with the complete freedom of New York at his reach, was spy on us ladies.

"Well, the man is dead," I said. "And since there's no resurrection until Christ returns, let's wait and see what He has to say about it."

Tobias nodded, and we finished the tea listening to the steady pattern of wheels against connecting joints. My mind drifted to Beth Meyers and her pretty face.

I kept my distance from Tobias and the rest of the group for the remainder of the journey. Consequently, I learned a new board game in the dining car from an elderly woman who was traveling to see her grandchildren. The game was called *Reversi*, and I have since become quite taken with it.

Upon returning home, I received a personalized letter from Mr. Pater of the publishing company stating his profuse apologies for my treatment at his offices and confirmation the junior executive I met was reprimanded. Pater also contacted Mr. Compton, offering a guarantee of publishing at least three more works from the UVW.

We commenced the writing shop once again, developing the following novels over the next three weeks:

The Vice Admiral

A summer romance blossoms between a 14-year-old daughter of a Navy Vice Admiral stationed in Hawaii and an 18-year-old Seaman.

The girl becomes pregnant, and the Seaman goes AWOL. They escape on a raft to the island of Niihau, inhabited only by 100 native Hawaiians. Under normal circumstances, the islanders would not allow any foreigners. However, the girl becomes gravely ill on their journey and must remain bedridden to protect the pregnancy. The Niihau ultimately embrace the young couple and host a beautiful marriage ceremony.

After the baby is born, word leaks of their presence on the island. The Vice Admiral plans a Navy Police raid to capture his daughter and granddaughter, then imprison the Seaman for desertion. Their plans face immediate opposition from the Native Hawaiian Cultural Commission (NHCC), who argue that such an invasion would violate the Newlands Resolution of 1898. The Commission determines as long as the couple does not leave the island, they will not be extradited.

Each year on the little girl's birthday, she waves to her grandfather on a boat 100 yards away.

One day the Vice Admiral retires from the Navy and his daughter convinces the NHCC to allow him to live on the small island with her family.

Gigi

A lighthearted comedy about a scientist who, mourning his wife's death, builds a robot named Gigi to replace her. Gigi must navigate not burning dinner while protecting her husband from foreign spies aiming to steal his inventions (the greatest of which being her.)

Man About the Army

(from *the Man About Town series*)

In book 3 of the series, Garland Fernsby, now 18, returns to England to join His Majesty's Armed Forces. Bubby, also 18 and grown out of his baby fat, joins the US Army. They are in parallel boot camps with equally difficult drill sergeants and gain a new chorus of friends. Garland remains in touch with Jeanne Albert, who is now pursuing a career in journalism as a junior reporter for *The New York Times*.

The trio reunite for Great Aunt Tilda's funeral. Visiting a coffee house afterward, the gang discusses their apprehension about the future of the world. In a moment alone with her, Garland finally confesses his affection for Jeanne, who reciprocates. —"Well, it's about bloody time!"

Bubby says, interrupting their first kiss by poking his face between them.

A fellow reporter of Jeanne's (a handsome young man) interrupts the group to give Jeanne news America has entered the war. Garland and Bubby scramble back to report for duty, and the group is broken up again.

CHAPTER 8

Big Al here, or Alfred Clifton, as I'm known to the bank and my mother.

Anyhoo, Miss Jane asked me to write a piece in her book, so you're stuck with me for a few lines. Just know I'm not a writer. I'm a gas man. I sell gas and often have it. So, like with my underpants, I'll keep it brief.

Miss Jane asked me to shine a dim light on some of my experiences with the boy.

Let's start with the night of the search party for Miss Beth Meyers.

I got word of her missing from Big Taw (Sheriff Tawlins), who called me around 7 pm after Miss Jane and Miss Marge forced him to do something. (Big Taw is lazy as a constipated moose and as good of a shot, but a true friend.)

We met at Miss Jane's house, which used to be the

Ellis Family Farm when Old Man Ellis was a young man and had a family and a farm.

It was a big search, with all the men in town joining in. But at first, it was just me, Big Taw, the ladies, and Tobias.

We spread out, and I happened to wander to the creek, where I noticed a small dam of sorts made from relocated stones that moved the stream a bit for no good reason. Tobias jumped from the tree I was standing under, and I let out a plume of gas still hovering over the Willamette Valley.

"Al Clifton is your name," he said.

"Jesus lover," I said, clutching my heart. "You almost had two dead bodies on your hands."

"You're implying Beth is dead and at my hands," he said. "That's currently unlikely."

"Oh no! Sorry about that," I stuck out my hand. He gazed at it like a curious dog, then shook it limply.

"So, I hear you're a genius," I said. "You must have some thoughts on where she is."

"Jane told you about our publishing plans. She wouldn't have revealed my genius to you if not. She was flirting, no doubt, but not fully, as you aren't exactly her target. Rather, I assume she was exalting in a brief moment of eclosion, and you were her available witness."

I stared.

"Eclosion is when a butterfly emerges from its chrysalis."

"Right. Well, I'm happy for you anyway."

We turned our attention to the makeshift dam.

"You know," the boy said, stepping into the stream, "some physicists believe we create reality by our presence. It means you, Mr. Al Clifton, wouldn't have existed had Jane not stopped for gas this morning and created you."

"Well, I'm just happy to be here," I said.

I looked around for turned-up dirt or any sign of recent disturbance. But nothing looked bothered, and not even Tobias could make weeds grow a foot high in a day.

Tobias laughed.

"What's funny?" I said.

"You asked me what I thought," he said, turning his back to me. "I think she's gone."

CHAPTER 9

Marge here.

Janey asked me to write a piece about Tobias and I obliged. The writing came out in a few parts, as things sometimes do.

***

I first met the boy before even I realized it, on the day a man came to town selling brooms. I was walking down Main and saw a tall man looking through the windows of Delores Elow's house. (It was vacant as she passed three months prior.) Believing this was the rumored broom salesman, I called out.

"Unless a ghost with a broken hip can sweep, you won't find a customer in there!"

"A ghost would never sweep," a young male voice spoke behind me.

I turned to find a woman standing next to a tall

blonde-haired boy. The lady's head was covered like a babushka, and she wore oversized sunglasses.

"Miss?" I said. But she didn't reply.

"She's a ghost, too," the boy whispered.

***

On the night of my arrival at the farmhouse, I carried my suitcase to my room, but left my typewriter on the main floor, as Janey said that's where we'd set up shop. She hadn't told me yet what the work was; only it was the opportunity of my lifetime. I told her that wouldn't take much to qualify.

I was hanging up my Sunday dress when Tobias appeared at the bedside with the typewriter.

"Oh," I said, shocked to see him enter the room.

"Thank you, young man, but you needn't the worry. Miss Jane meant I leave the typing machine in the living room."

"Lovely dress," he said.

"Oh, yes. My sister made it for me." (It was a lovely dress.) "I'll take the machine back down. You can leave it there."

"You think it's too good for you, but it's not," he said. "You're a flower, too. A female by all rights. Capable and fit for nature's work."

"Why—"

"I know she wanted the typing machine downstairs," he said. "I carried it up because we don't have to do what she says."

He winked and took the machine downstairs.

I didn't wear that dress a single day I lived in the house.

***

This one entails a hazy memory during our train ride to New York.

I remember us all gathered in the cocktail car on the first Tuesday night, carrying on gaily. Next, I'm lying in my sleeping quarters, and the boy was petting my hair. My first instinct was to ask him to leave, but I couldn't gather the strength to utter a word.

Then, this part I remember clearly, as absurd as it sounds: The boy was whispering scripture.

I can see his mouth moving even now. It was the only darn tootin' thing I could do. Just lie there and watch him recite Ecclesiasticus 19, the very same chapter my father used to read my sister and me before bed. Daddy made us memorize it too, as it's about wine, women, and keeping your mouth shut.

***

On our last morning at the house, on the day Al Clifton chased off young Tobias once and for all, I woke at 3 a.m. in need of a visit to the necessary room. Once seated I saw a shadow move behind the shower curtain.

"I'm staying behind the curtain, Miss Marge," Tobias said.

"Well," I said. "I'll appreciate your discretion in also plugging your ears and shutting your eyes."

There was silence.

"Have you done so?" I whispered, bracing to stand and make my break for it.

"It's my last day and I feel nothing," the boy whispered. "Only forward motion."

CHAPTER 10

Jane back with you now.

On the last day Tobias Randall was in my care, Marge woke me up early messing about the kitchen.

Al Clifton stopped by with bread and milk at 6:45 am, and we all had breakfast on the porch. Marge mentioned we were out of typing paper, so Al gulped his coffee and offered to fetch more reams at Great Harvest. I required him to take me along so I could pay.

When we pulled onto Elm Street, the sun was in a particular position to cause temporary blindness. I pulled down the visor, and a dirty, bloodstained camas hair bow fell out.

I didn't cause a commotion, as one might think. I didn't make a sound at all. Instead, I studied the bow, peculiar as it was, a delicate, stained item.

Al noticed I wasn't talking.

"What's that?"

"It's Beth Meyers' hair tie, covered in blood," I said. "Fallen from a hiding place under your visor."

In that moment, Al Clifton, a red-blooded American bear of a man, turned into a hairless kitten.

"In the visor?!"

"Oh, of course, you didn't have anything to do with it."

I leaned over, grabbed his bicep muscle firmly, then returned to my thoughts.

"But how did Tobias get in your truck?" I said to myself. "It was in full view of us the entire time. He must have snuck out last night and walked to your house."

"That's six miles away. And I keep my truck locked."

I smiled in pity.

"I'm sure Tobias can figure out how to break into an old truck."

"But why plant it on me?"

"It's obvious, isn't it? You're a disrupter."

"I've done nothing—"

"You're a man, courting me, his surrogate mother, and the leader of the writing enterprise. Your impending marriage proposal will cause my attentions to be diverted to a wedding and eventual pregnancies."

Al swallowed hard as news from the future bore down.

"Preg—"

I squeezed his arm again then rubbed the bow with my fingers.

"Nevermind all that now. We need to determine exactly what steps to take."

"About... preg—"

"No, Silly. What to do with the fact Tobias killed young Beth, of course."

My mind was racing the way it does when I've suddenly seen three moves ahead in *Reversi*, and a corner piece is in sight.

Al started to turn the truck back to the house, but I stopped him.

"No," I said. "We should get the paper just as we planned. Tobias would surmise the sunbeams coming in on Elm would cause the ribbon to be discovered, but not if we were to take a detour on Reed St. first to pick up a necklace from Monte's Jewelers you just couldn't wait until my birthday to give me."

"Monte's Jewelers?"

"Yes, he opens early on Tuesdays. There's a necklace I've had my eye on I was going to have you purchase for my birthday. You can get it this morning. It will justify our detour from the direct sunlight on Elm St. and satisfy me for a birthday present, which I know you've been anxious about."

Al wiped his brow, turned on Reed, and proceeded to Monte's.

The yellow gold necklace included a red heart pendant with two crystal birds touching beaks.

On the ride back, I talked out the rest of my plan,

starting with the ladies throwing their expected fuss over the necklace.

On our return, Tobias peered down from the banister, watching the ladies swoon over my gift. I sensed the young man suspicious of the ruse but not altogether unconvinced, potentially blinded by the threat of Al's now escalated intrusion.

The rest of the morning continued as usual. Al left for the filling station, and the writing team began our Saturday morning session. Tobias introduced a new story about a troubled young man traveling the country in search of a miracle.

I spent the day thinking but not coming up with any concrete plans. Still, I trusted I could figure it all out if given the time.

If I reported him to the police, they would no doubt place Tobias in a troubled boys' home. His path from there would surely lead to destruction for himself and others, not to mention a perverse waste of his gifts. — No. I simply had to figure out how we all could continue life as it was while at the same time ensuring Tobias learned killing was wrong. (Something I truly wasn't sure he knew.)

At 11:30 a.m., Al returned, and we had lunch. We discussed the news, as usual, when Tobias offered a rare interjection on international politics.

It should be stated at this point that Al Clifton is a committed pacifist. He is no fan of war, having been drafted and forced to take the lives of other boys who, according to Al, were only different in 'where they didn't choose to be born.'

"They say Hitler is becoming a real threat across the

pond," Tobias said.

"Yes," Dot chirped in. "Getting the Germans all riled up again. Giving them hope, as if Krauts would know what to do with it."

"Something should be done," Heather said, "or we'll get pulled into another war."

"Can't trust Germans," June interjected. "Foreign ones anyway. Too ashamed of defeat."

"Nothing to show from the last war means nothing to lose for the next one," Tobias said.

"There's plenty of good Germans," Al said, "just bad leadership."

"Even more the reason to intervene," Tobias said. "A pre-emptive military strike now could save untold numbers from future suffering."

"A preemptive strike," Al said, "is no road to peace."

"Better we wait until it's too late?"

"That's not what I said," Al said.

"An attack today would be limited to government officials and military only," Tobias continued. "Wait a year, and the Nazis will make innocents their cannon fodder, forcing our men to kill their women and children, as you well know."

"Let's change the subject," I interjected.

"Beth Meyers was German, wasn't she, Al?" Tobias said.

Everyone froze.

"An innocent German if there ever was one,"

Tobias continued.

"And that!" I said, standing, "is the commencement of lunch. Tobias, may I see you privately?"

"I have no idea if Beth was German," Al said.

The ladies turned from Tobias to Al, then to me.

"Meyers? With blonde hair? She was Hitler's dream," Tobias said. "It's a strange phenomenon. All that hate our soldiers must still bear towards a white race so seamlessly intertwined in our society. It becomes hard to tell who is and isn't the enemy... unless, of course, a pure example like Beth sprouts up. German beauty, promise, German sexuality. A thing taken from so many men in the last war." Tobias paused. "A man robbed of his own vitality by a foreign country sees their perfect flower of youth... And how exactly did your wife die, Mr. Clifton? A hunting injury in the woods, with no witnesses?"

"What is all this?" Marge stood. "You'll hold your tongue young man!"

"It's ok," Al motioned to Marge. "It's fine."

"Weren't you the first one here at the house," Tobias continued. "When the Sheriff showed up to search, weren't you with him? Stayed until the end, too. Did you know Miss Jane was leaving town that day? Can you account for your time the day Beth Meyers went missing?"

Tobias sat directly between Al and the front door. When Al stood to leave, Tobias continued backing up before the hulking man until the boy stumbled out the door then clear down the front steps and squarely into the dirt on his hind end.

Al stood at the top of the stairs with the ladies gathered behind him.

"Are you ok?" Al said, coming down the stairs. "Here, let me help ya."

Tobias scrambled to his feet, threw two handfuls of dust, and began spewing a tirade of fury to match Krakatoa. He detailed his theory of Al's involvement in the murder of Beth Meyers down to the letter, then cursed the ladies for using him as the only escape from their dull lives. He saved the worst vitriol for me, though Al interrupted him before he could get going.

"You will show respect to Ms. Alexander before you return to this house," Al said.

Tobias started in about how Al had no man parts to speak of.

"You," Al said, walking calmly to face down the boy, "will show respect to Ms. Alexander before you return to this house."

Tobias, attempting to capitalize on surprise, reared back and took a full swing. Al, unaware I had stuck so close behind him, dodged out of the way, allowing the young man's fist to connect directly with my face and crack my orbital socket.

Without hesitation Al swung and broke the young man's jaw.

Al drove us both to the hospital, then called the police to turn himself in.

Sherriff Tawlins, determining the harm was already done, decided it would do no good to arrest either Al or Tobias. However, Tobias would need to be turned over to child services immediately and removed from my care.

In the middle of the third night of my hospital stay, Tobias, with a wrapped jaw, crept in and stood over my bed. Al was snoring in the chair next to me.

The boy reached into his gown, placed an item on my stomach, then turned and left. It was the very feather I had put in my cap at the commencement of our writing partnership. Tied to the feather was a piece of card stock:

Dear J,

I killed Beth because no one else would. She would eventually bring in men who would use her, betray us, and bring down the entire endeavor. All the women would lose the achievements and return to barren lives of shame. I accept my banishment and hope Mr. Clifton feels well justified in his actions towards me. He is a good man by all standards, and you will find happiness together.

Yours,

T

After he left, I grazed my bandaged face softly back and forth with the feather.

He was always correct.

CHAPTER 11

Letter Opener

May 1ˢᵗ, 1937
Eugene, Oregon

Adam discovered himself to be naked in the garden after the fall. Joseph ran nude after being tempted by Potiphar's wife. The young man in the Garden of Gethsemane ran garmentless when Jesus was arrested. Tobias Randall fled Peaceful Valley Hospital in the pre-dawn hour, dropping his gown at the door.

He broke a back window of Armstrong's department store and lay for several hours on the cement floor, attempting to achieve a thoughtless state. Then he stole a coat, boots, two sets of clothes, a tent, canned food, a can opener, a canteen, and a backpack.

The young man's original destination was New York City, but as plans and mice go, intrigue derailed him. He traveled by rail to the Hoover Dam, desiring to witness the Coriolis effect by tossing stones off the sheer face.

While searching for a large spherical rock, Tobias met an American Indian boy of the same age. The Indian was hanging signs inviting tourists to an upcoming event called 'Helldorado' in nearby Las Vegas.

The once small town of Las Vegas had benefitted from the immense Hoover Dam construction labor pool. With the dam completed, the business community foresaw their impending bust, and 'Helldorado Days' was their response, with local leaders pitching Las Vegas as 'the last chance for Americans to see the authentic Old West.'

"Lots of work if you're interested," the Indian boy said. "Name's Tommy."

Tommy said 'Helldorado' was the brainchild of two men; legendary carnival barker Clyde Zerby and Las Vegas businessman Big Jim Cashman.

"Zerby'll hire you on my recommendation. Thinks I'm wise cuz I'm Indian."

"Are you wise?" Tobias asked.

"I'm average for an Indian."

The next day Tommy got Tobias a job building a walled canvas structure at 6th and Freemont Street.

"It's a fraud," Tommy told Tobias in their sleeping bags that night. "Helldorado Days. Ain't nothing real about it from history."

"A dream is as real as anything else," Tobias said.

"Maybe in your world."

They'd been discussing the history of Las Vegas, which truly had nothing to do with the Old West. The town was founded after a land auction in 1905, but before that, it was just a small re-supply stop for Mormons traveling to Los Angeles from Salt Lake, and before that, it was nothing.

"Does it upset you to see white men being deceptive?" Tobias asked.

"Not to other white men."

Clyde Zerby had connections in Hollywood and arranged for a shipment of Western costumes for all the townspeople to wear. Tommy and Tobias were tasked to unload the outfits, and they snagged a couple for themselves.

Tobias dressed like an Indian, and Tommy like a cowboy, and they walked that way in the Helldorado parade. Right after the band led with war vets and flags, the boys came through, chasing each other in and out of the crowd, pulling down the biggest laughs of the event.

That night Tobias got drunk for the first time in his life. He revealed to Tommy and his older cousin Timmy that he was a genius.

The Indian boys shrugged.

After tearing down Helldorado, Zerby tasked Timmy to drive the shipment of Western outfits back to Los Angeles. Zerby's only caveat was the requirement a white man go with him, so Timmy asked Tobias and he agreed.

Tommy said he was staying in Las Vegas, as he had plans to pursue a legal career.

"You can get a divorce here with six weeks' residency," he said. "I'm helping a lawyer bring in customers. He's got a firm above The Boulder."

"Six weeks is a nice vacation with a mistress," Tobias said.

"Maybe you are a genius," Tommy said.

Timmy and Tobias didn't speak on the four-hour trip to Los Angeles. After unloading the costumes, Timmy announced he was stealing the truck to start a garbage-hauling business. Tobias said he planned to stay in town and visit an old friend. The boys parted ways on Paramount Studios loading dock 15E.

***

Fritz Lang, director of *Metropolis*, had left Germany several years prior, after being propositioned by Joseph Goebbels to lead the entire German film industry. As the story went, Lang told Goebbels he would be honored, then escaped to Paris and ultimately the United States.

Lang's wife was Thea von Harbou, a well-known author in Germany. Throughout the 1920s, she collaborated closely with Lang on many film projects, including writing *Metropolis* in both the film and novel form. But Von Harbou had grown sympathetic towards the Nazi movement and stayed in Germany when Lang fled.

Fritz Lang's first American film was *Fury*. It portrayed a man (played by Spencer Tracey) wrongly accused by a vengeful mob. Tobias saw the picture in Las Vegas and stayed through the end credits to learn the location of Lang's office.

"I've been hired by Louis B. Mayer to personally deliver a message to Fritz Lang," Tobias told the young receptionist in Lang's building.

"He's never here, sorry," she said. "You know Louis B. Mayer?"

"Of course. L.B. Mayer is my great uncle. Harold Mayer. Pleased to meet you."

"Wow, Louis Mayer's nephew is a messenger boy?"

Tobias leaned on the counter. "Only for the most important messages. He's slated me as an associate producer in his next film. It starts filming in Nepal in a couple. A sequel to King Kong. Have you ever considered acting?"

"Yes!"

"You give me Fritz Lang's home address, and I think I could tell Uncle Louis about a nice girl I met today."

Tobias took the address and sat outside Lang's office, drinking a Coca-Cola and watching the would-be actors and actresses come and go. It was the most densely populated group of attractive people he'd ever seen.

Lang's house was formidable but not outlandish. A blonde woman answered the door, and Tobias gave her the same line about the message.

"Louis," the woman rolled her eyes. "Always after something." She led the young man to a den where the director was sleeping in a reclining chair with his back facing them.

"Honey," the woman patted his shoulder and winked at Tobias. "There's a boy here with a message from Louis Mayer."

She motioned to a chair in front of Lang.

"Just wait a few minutes. He'll wake up and start talking. Then God help you. Hey, can I get you a soda or something?"

"I'll take a Coca-Cola with crushed ice in a thick glass."

"Now you sound like Louis." The woman laughed and left the room.

Tobias moved to the front of Lang and tapped him on the nose. The old director sneezed and adjusted his monocle.

"It's a good lad to be direct with women," he said. "What's this from Mayer?"

"I am not from Louis B. Mayer. I lied so I could ask you two questions."

The director furrowed his brow and sat up, looking over his shoulder.

"First, I saw *Fury*. You must have tried giving the role to a black man but were told the film would not be made?"

The director's brow softened.

"And what is your first question then?" he said.

"How do you keep track of your lies about the Goebbels story?"

Lang's face changed to confusion. Tobias leaned forward and pushed a letter opener against the flesh of

109

the old man's stomach.

"The second question," the young man said, "the Maschinenmensch, who inspired her?"

He pushed the letter opener further. Lang gasped.

The woman reappeared with the Coca-Cola. Tobias drank it down entirely and handed her back the glass.

"Thank you, that will be all," he said.

She paused for a moment and broke into a deep laugh. "Fritzy, keep your eye on this one," she said, leaving the room.

Tobias leaned in more and whispered into Lang's ear.

"Your inspiration for the robot?"

"The girl, of course," Lang gasped. "It has always been the girl."

PART II

CHAPTER 12

Al and I got married after the swelling in my face receded.

Who knew the level of machinery behind the simple promoting and selling of a novel, let alone seven? Interview requests came like a flood, which I was careful to allow only in writing and then with concise answers so I could keep track of my story. Theodore Compton initially frowned on the idea, but I convinced him the mystique only added to our allure.

The women's guide was our first and biggest bestseller. It still ranks in the all-time top twenty for nonfiction book sales. (I retain a first-edition dog-eared copy myself.)

The next book to jump out was *Our Sky Was Not Yours*. It garnered such attention the publisher demanded a follow-up immediately.

At first, I was doggedly determined to create a

sequel out of sheer force of will. But nothing healthy grows that way, and I was once again surrounded by crumples.

I then tried to achieve genius by committee, pulling in all the ladies to work on storyboarding. Even Al got involved (by making coffee and occasional jokes.)

We had a finished 150-page book at the conclusion of one month's work. Unable to sit in Theodore Compton's office with the same confidence while he read the pages, I mailed the manuscript with a note: "*Clear Skies a Plenty*, the requested sequel. Sincerely, JWA, President, UVW."

In three days, I received the call from Compton all writers dread. It starts with too long of a pause, continues with trepidatious pleasantries, and concludes with obfuscated disappointment. In short, he was saying it stunk.

"Stop," I interrupted him as he was politely inquiring if I'd had a recent illness. "It's a dud. I know it, you know it, your secretary listening in knows it. So then, what can be done?"

"Or a head injury perhaps, God forbid?" he continued.

It was decided Compton would bring in a ghostwriter he knew of the highest quality and discretion. (The man was a well-respected literary novelist before being arrested for consorting with men of the night. Unable to use his name and unsuitable for any other type of work, he was hired far and wide as a fixer by literary agents.)

Our hired gun salvaged the work into something that, if not of the same caliber as its predecessor, at least bore a passing resemblance to a novel.

While the publisher was naturally disappointed, the critics absolutely relished our fall from grace. Our kindest review announced: "The UVW gals have served us refried beans."

In retrospect, the experience allowed me to give up all pretenses of continuing the writing enterprise. Instead, I focused exclusively on promoting and licensing the already finished works for film and radio.

Our biggest hit over the wireless was the *Man About Town* series, as told via radio drama in weekly serial form. The program lasted four years until all the stories from the books were used up. NBC Radio wanted the rights to continue, with assurances their writers could maintain the same quality, but I firmly stated the UVW does not allow ghostwriting outside the group as a principle.

Two films were made, both forgettable. One was based on a short story Tobias wrote apart from the group called *We Should Struggle*. The film version was called *The Struggle of Bounty Hill*. The story was based on a trench battle in the Great War Tobias became particularly obsessed with. Critics of the film said it was 'too indulgent.'

I was surprised this story was chosen for a film, as the written version of the story centered around an opaque homosexual relationship between two men in the trenches. (The men speak about their fiancés back home as a veiled means of addressing each other. But in the movie version, the men truly do miss their fiancés.)

The other film was a financial failure but otherwise quite good. It, too, was based on work Tobias wrote alone. The piece was a novella I found among his things after his departure, and the storyline was loosely based on the life of William James Sidis. (The main character was a boy genius with overbearing parents whom he flees.) The young man travels the country by rail and writes a well-researched book on the life of hobos.

The film starred a very talented young actor who was a passionate fan of the novella, so much so that he vanished before wrapping up production to set out on his own journey of documenting hobos. His body was discovered outside Columbus, OH, after falling out of a moving train and freezing to death. As a result, the film's ending had to be dramatically altered.

The novella concludes with a large encampment of hobos in the center of an affluent suburb where several railroad executives lived. Now a man, the prodigy gives a compelling speech there on generosity, broadcast by radio nationwide. The speech becomes so popular it prompts widescale federal homeless housing and education policies.

The film, lacking the actor to deliver the final address, does not contain the large hobo gathering in the suburbs. Instead, the movie ends with a shot of a body double of the actor walking up the steps of the Lincoln Memorial. He places his handwritten book about hobos on the lap of Lincoln, then hops on a train while the national anthem plays through the credits.

The money from our projects allowed all but two girls (Marge and Dot) to snag husbands. Lucy and Mildred each gave birth nine months after their respective weddings and were with child again in two years.

Al and I bought the Randall property and a vast swath of surrounding land from the bank for a song. Al

115

hired a day-to-day manager and a couple of part-time high school boys to operate the Fill-N-Time. (Still, he found a reason to hang around the place a few hours a day.)

At approximately 9:30 am on April 14th, 1938, Mother died. The Stramwell Pioneer Cemetery had already sold the plots next to Dad, so she was buried several rows away.

***

It was becoming clear by late 1939 we were going to war.

Al had become obsessed with following the trajectory of Hitler and Mussolini, along with the growing Naval activity of Japan, and he was sure Roosevelt would not delay entry indefinitely.

"Well, I am for stopping Hitler," I said one morning over our coffee and first game of *Reversi*. "It can only be a good thing if he's gone."

Al was reading Harvey Hines' *News of the Globe* section from the Stramwell Chronicle. (I've admired Mr. Hines's character since he took my side on a Lane County School Board issue encouraging school uniforms. He even used my quote in his piece: "*Almighty God made the poor and rich look the same inside. We could do no better to follow suit on the outside.*")

Al glanced over his paper. "But how do we stop him?"

"Simple," I said. "Europe gets its act together and shares all its information on where Hitler sleeps each night. Then we bomb him."

"What about his replacement? They'll just make

116

Adolf a saint. Germans will fight even harder."

"So, we bomb the replacement. And the next one. Eventually, they'll put in a man too weak or corrupt, and the thing will topple."

"Don't you think the Brits would take Hitler if they could?" Al said. "They must not be able to get to him."

"It's likely a mismanagement of information," I said, taking a corner *Reversi* piece. "The Brits and Russkies need a woman in charge. Gather all the hearsay and scuttlebutt from cooks and maids onto a big map, then triangulate the gossip. We'd have Adolf roasting on a spit in a week."

"Dang!" Al noticed my corner move.

During our night *Reversi* match, Al broached the topic again.

"I've been thinking," he said, stacking my pieces and then his, "what if we look at war as a pure numbers game?"

"Go on," I said, laying my first piece.

"Let's say Hitler continues to seize land, and no one stops him. At some point, Germany will be stretched too thin. He'll have to compromise."

"Ok," I laid another piece.

"He's divisive by nature," Al continued, laying a piece. "And with such a big empire, it's gonna be a matter of time before it decays from the inside."

"True," I countered his move.

"In that time, lots of people are gonna die, that's sure. But there's a cap to it, see? Maybe, five or ten million tops?"

"This is a victory for pacifism?" I said.

"No." Al paused and fiddled with the black wooden piece in his meaty fingers. "It's terrible. But we could drop the number now by taking in the Jews and whoever else the Germans don't want. We've got the boats and could pay for it all. Us, England, and Russia. It'd be cheaper than going to war."

"Unrealistic, but ok. You're still at a few million dead."

"But another world war? You're talking fifty million. Maybe a hundred."

"We're already in a world war, dear. We just haven't printed the announcement."

"Yeah," Al said. "And they've already laid aside the printing blocks for the headline. '*Unavoidable*,' it'll say."

"Fine," I said, firmly placing down a Reversi piece. "Fine."

"Fine? What does that mean? What do you mean?"

"I mean as I say. Fine," I said. "You say we're going to war, and it's the wrong decision. So, I say fine then, Al Clifton. What are you going to do about it?"

"What *can* I do? Call Roosevelt?"

"Fine." I folded my arms.

"Wait, are you upset with me?"

"Fine."

Al pursed his lips. He knew he was in for something but was unsure what.

"What I mean," I said, "is you can do something. I don't know what that is, but I do know pacifism has at least one thing going for it: You. A fine man with a fine mind and fine ambitions. So again, I ask, what will you do with this fine opportunity?"

I took the final Reversi corner.

"Dang it!" he said, scanning the board for a strategic counter move, of which there were none.

The thing is, I disagreed with pacifism then, and I still do. But, for better or worse, I am Mrs. Jane Clifton. I married a sweet man on December 11th, 1937, and vowed to support his sweet path.

The next morning Al went to the library and stayed there all day. Had I known he would be gone all day, I would have packed him a bologna sandwich. As it was, I had to call librarian Rebecca and ask if Al had departed the building to get food anywhere. She informed me he had not, but she had a half plate of leftover spaghetti she could give him. I told her that wouldn't be necessary and made three well-supplied BLT sandwiches. (One was for Rebecca, as cold spaghetti is no excuse for a lunch.)

We three ate in the librarian's office. Al was positively bursting. He started the day reading commentary in the national papers about Roosevelt's recently implemented 'Cash and Carry Act.'

"It allows us to sell guns to the Allies if they pay in cash and use their boats to get them to Europe," he said. "Replaces the Neutrality Act. It was barely covered in the news."

Al took a giant bite and chewed. "I got to thinking today about this doughboy I fought with in Argonne, Corny Krahn."

"What?" I said.

"His name," Al said, "was Cornelius Krahn. A Mennonite. True pacifist."

"Hmm."

"See," Al raised a finger, "the draft board told him they'd hang him if he refused to serve."

"Hang him? Really?" Rebecca said, her mouth full.

Al nodded. "So now he's got a logic problem."

"Seems crystal clear to me," I said.

Al pointed with his sandwich. "By refusing the draft and getting himself hanged, he'd be *causing* someone else to do violence *on him*."

Rebecca nodded.

"So he gets drafted," Al took another big bite. "And Corny figures, well, maybe God's lining him up for some pacifist job, like a medic or a cook." Al burped and asked us to excuse him. "But that didn't happen of course. He got sent to the front line in France, just north of Verdun. Battles of the Meuse–Argonne. Highest body count in US history." Al covered his mouth with one hand until the next burp subsided, then took another huge bite. "So, Corny's sitting in a trench, supposed to be firing at German boys, but he can't do that. He also can't *not* fire because allowing Germans to live means you're letting them continue to kill *our* boys."

"Which makes our boys keep trying to kill them," Rebecca said.

"Yes."

"That's not a logic problem, it's a logic pretzel," I

120

said.

"That's war," Al said.

I put my hand on his forearm.

"Ok, well, so let's see," Al continued. "Yeah, so that's how I met Corny. I got stationed near no man's land, just a big empty field really. And somehow, one night, these five German boys made it across and slit our lookout's throat —oh, I'm sorry, maybe I shouldn't be— "

"Continue," both Rebecca and I said.

"Ok. Well, the Germans kill two more before our boys even wake up to fight. I woke up scared out of my life and started firing at anything moving. When the smoke cleared, I was alone; and they'd gotten nine of our boys. I was crawling over bodies when I found Corny. He was hiding *under* the bodies. I hugged him so tight. Man, was I happy to find someone alive."

"Well, that's just your holy nature," I said. "Any other man would've," I stopped myself, realizing I had veered towards insult.

"My brothers would've shoved that boy into no man's land for target practice," Rebecca said.

"Nah, you don't feel that way. Not when you're in it. So, anyway, I tried to convince Corny it was safe to come out. But he just started talking about his dilemma with the twisted logic and all. I told him to get out from under the bodies and we'd figure it out, but he still didn't move. So, I just sat there and listened."

"Sweet man."

"Anyway, after that, I made sure we were always on

watch together, which was easy because no one else wanted him. When the time came, I told Corny to at least fire a bullet now and then *above* the Germans. Not too far above, just barely above. Then I made sure to, well, shoot a lot more often. And I've always been a good shot. So that was that."

We all took a breath.

"So, what are you going to do now?" I asked.

Al took a look at his sandwich.

"Oh, I thought maybe I'd stay here and keep reading, unless you need me—"

"No, I mean regarding the war. What is a *fine man*, like you, going to do now?"

Al finished his last bite in thought, then said he had been studying the concept of something called 'conscientious objection,' or 'CO.'

After the Civil Service Act, a small faction of 'peace churches' (Mennonites, Quakers, and The Church of the Brethren) approached President Roosevelt with a plan for their boys to avoid fighting. They asked if their men could stay in the States and instead do work of 'national importance.' Ultimately Roosevelt agreed, and a system was established, mainly involving the men toiling in forest work camps or working at mental institutions.

Al thought we could start a publicity campaign to encourage local boys to sign up for the program.

"The key is to make them look brave for staying *out* of the war," he said. "There's already a CO camp near Waldport where they plant trees. And Oregon is gonna need those after the war to keep all the forestry jobs from going away."

Rebecca slouched, chewing on a pencil. She spoke quietly, almost in a mumble. "If we can convince the pretty girls in town to marry some pacifist boys, that would be ideal."

"Why pretty girls?" Al said.

"Sit up," I said, taking Rebecca's pencil. "Miss Miller, you are positively brilliant."

That day we began planning Al's second war. The first stage: *propaganda.*

CHAPTER 13

A Wooden Sculpture of Three Owls on a

Limb

June 1st, 1937

In early 1937, Tobias Randall selected the three greatest geniuses of his time and began a correspondence campaign with each of them, secret even to Miss Alexander.

William James Sidis was the first, introduced to Randall by Stramwell librarian Rebecca Miller. Through research and numerous letters, Randall discovered a man called Frank Folupa, who was, in truth, Mr. Sidis writing under a pseudonym. Randall communicated with Sidis (Folupa) by engaging in the hobby of streetcar transfer collecting, otherwise called 'peridromophilia.' Sidis coined the term and developed a small, devoted following through his newsletters and a densely written 300-page book he (Frank Folupa) published on the topic called *Notes on the Collection of Transfers*. (A work critics have called 'the most boring book ever written.')

Randall learned of Sidis' other interests, including that he taught occasional small group classes on Native American history. In turn, Randall wrote to Sidis about the Kalapuya tribe native to the Willamette Valley in Oregon and their fate of contracting diseases from the white man. (Sidis was also fascinated by the minutia of local American history.) The great genius wrote back, inviting Randall to join his small group on the first Thursday of each month should he ever visit Boston.

Randall discovered the genius Norbert Weiner as part of his research on Sidis. Weiner was also a prodigy and classmate at Harvard when Sidis was eleven and Weiner fifteen. Unlike Sidis, Weiner had led a very public life, publishing in scientific journals and frequently speaking while serving on the mathematics faculty at MIT. He eventually developed an entirely new realm of human endeavor involving the melding of man and machine, which Weiner coined 'cybernetics.'

Weiner led Randall to discover John von Neumann, another prodigy from the same generation as Sidis and Weiner. By age eight, von Neumann could divide two eight-digit numbers in his head. He had also absorbed Oncken's 46-volume *Allgemeine Geschichte in Einzeldarstellungen* (*General History in Monographs*), among other classic works, with the ability to recite them word for word, even decades later. Von Neumann could repeat exact telephone book information after glancing at a page for several seconds. (Randall attempted the same with only 18% accuracy.) Von Neumann published groundbreaking work in various fields, including mathematics, quantum mechanics, and economic game theory. He was the greatest genius of a group of geniuses out of Hungary about the same time, affectionately called 'the Martians.' Von Neumann's office at Princeton was next to Einstein's, whom von Neumann often annoyed by playing music at extremely high volumes. He once gave Albert a ride to the train station and intentionally placed him aboard a car going in the wrong direction.

Randall introduced himself as a similar prodigy to establish rapport with Weiner and von Neumann. By discussing the relationship between summability methods (for Weiner) and ergodic theory (for von Neumann), Randall only needed to pen a single letter to both men to garner their attention.

***

After fleeing from Stramwell to Las Vegas and then Los Angeles, Randall set his compass to Germany. His aim was to save Thea von Harbou, Director Fritz Lang's ex-wife (*The girl, of course. It had always been the girl*), from the Nazis. As this meant a trip to New England, Randall decided it was time to meet von Neumann and Weiner.

***

Randall's interest in computing led him to a knowledge of other players in the field. Most notable was research being done by International Business Machines (IBM).

As fate would have it, IBM's president, Thomas Watson, was headed to Berlin aboard a ship in late June. (The International Chamber of Commerce was to hold its annual global meeting there, and Watson was its president.)

***

As to the question of money and Tobias Randall: It is not difficult to steal and resell valuables in a manner without detection if one performs the acts in moderation, casting a wide net of targets over a large area where said person is unfamiliar to others. The process takes a willingness to travel and the discipline to hold steady to the parameters of a plan that only comes from having foundational confidence in self rather than the things or money accumulating. That year, Randall's voyage across the country provided ample opportunity for him to test this process in many large department stores.

***

The polymath John von Neuman was both extroverted and introverted and equally proficient in both. Tobias Randall met him at a loud party at the professor's sizeable new house at 26 Prescott Lane in Princeton.

When Randall entered the party, he first surveyed for children to engage with, and found von Neumann's daughter peeking around a hallway and hugging a dog named 'Inverse.' John von Neumann soon spotted the boy and, once identifying Randall as his young penpal, pulled him into a circle of laughing men.

"Gentlemen, I want you all to meet young Tobias here," von Neumann announced. "I receive letters from around the country penned by hopeful parents and teachers regarding their prodigious youngsters who are undoubtedly the next world-renowned genius." He

127

paused, "Which they never are."

The group laughed.

Von Neumann continued, "Tobias, however, wrote to me himself. Beyond whatever genius he may possess, that stood out to me. Determination, gentlemen."

The men raised their glasses.

Hear, Hear!

Von Neumann motioned to an older man possessing a full beard and pipe.

"Monsieur Rislan was about to challenge me with a riddle. I want the boy to be challenged with me and see if I've still got it or have already been replaced by the next wave of flesh."

Von Neumann motioned to Monsieur Rislan and then to Randall.

"Proceed, Monsieur."

Monsieur Rislan squinted his eyes and removed his pipe.

"Suppose two bicyclists start twenty miles apart," he stated gruffly, then cleared his throat. "They travel towards each other, each pedaling at precisely ten miles per hour. At that exact time, a fly traveling at fifteen miles per hour starts at the wheel of one bike in the direction of the second bicycle. Once it arrives, the fly instantly turns around and flies back, again and again, until it is crushed by the two front wheels meeting each other. My question is, what total distance did the fly cover?"

Randall and von Neuman both spoke at once: "Fifteen miles."

"Oh, you've both heard the trick before!" Rislan exclaimed.

"Nonsense," von Neumann said. "I merely—"

"Summed the infinite series," Randall interrupted. "I did the same. After I deduced the trick Monsieur is referencing, of course."

All froze, including von Neumann.

Randall continued, "It took the bicyclists an hour to meet as each traveled ten miles per hour, and the distance was twenty miles. If a fly travels fifteen miles per hour, it will go fifteen miles in that one hour."

The men laughed, appreciating the simple logic of the solution. Randall held up a finger and spoke over them.

"Then I thought, I bet von Neumann adds the infinite series. I wonder if I can beat him. Fortunately, there is an easy way to sum the series without all the steps: multiplying twelve by five-fourths."

"That's what I did," von Neumann said.

The men stopped laughing.

"Mr. von Neumann, can I speak with you privately?" Randall asked.

Randall walked away, with von Neumann following.

"Can I call you John?" Randall asked.

"Certainly."

"John, you're going to leave your wife. When you do, remain a good father. I spoke with your daughter in the hall about your marriage."

"My marriage?"

"The girl is astute, has tremendous potential, and loves you. Be a good father after you leave the house."

"What is this, a joke?" von Neumann looked back at the group of men. "Rislan gave you the answer ahead of time didn't he!"

"Good night, Mr. von Neumann," Randall turned.

"Wait," he grabbed Randall's sleeve. "Wait. You've spoken to me, and now I'll speak to you. By appearance, you're entering the peak years of your mental prowess. You'll then have seven or eight years before the gradual decline." He squeezed Randall's arm. "Harness the time," he said. "Use it."

***

Norbert Weiner had recently returned from China on a long trip teaching at the National Tsing Hua University in Peking.

Randall attended Weiner's lecture at M.I.T. on '*The ethics of advanced computing.*'

"Mankind thinks he will provide himself with infinite leisure by passing on work to machines," Weiner said. "But! We are creating a prison for ourselves. Our manual workload may decrease, true, but an entirely new order of exhaustion will set in, driven by fear. We will sense our replacement by the machines, then work ever harder to keep ahead of them. We will push ourselves to the breaking point and won't realize that's what we're doing until it's too late!"

Randall stayed after class until the sycophants with questions had gone, then approached as Weiner gathered his things.

"What is the defining element of the future?"

Randall asked.

Weiner paused and spoke as if they were old friends in the middle of a long conversation.

"The same defining element as the past, of course," he said. "Forward motion. As for the world, the near future is Europe. The far future is Asia. After that will come a blended form of humanity and computers, then just computers. But the Chinese are next, after the German issue, of course."

"Can we solve the German issue with computers?"

Weiner picked his nose, "We might. But, it'll largely come by flesh and blood, I'm afraid."

"What if Germany develops advanced computing?"

Weiner stopped.

"Well, of course then, —I'm sorry, you are?"

Weiner did not recall Randall's letters.

"I'm traveling to Germany," Randall told the professor.

"Why on Earth would you go there?"

"The International Chamber of Commerce annual meeting is in Berlin. I aim to learn about the mixture of science, business, and Nazism."

"You are a spy?"

"Of sorts. I am the only one aware of my plans besides you."

"So, you're a journalist? If so, you should have announced yourself to me immediately rather than conduct this charade."

"It's no charade. I'm a friend of William James Sidis."

"Sidis? What on earth are you talking about?"

"You and he were both prodigies as I am now. Sidis pursued seclusion. You chose fame. I'm choosing to rise to the occasion of my time. The president of the Chamber is the head of IBM. Our nation's largest technology company seeks a warm welcome from the Fuhrer, and I'm simply meant to find out why."

"You are proposing," Weiner said, resuming his picking, "not only that IBM is working with the Nazis at the highest level but also bringing in other players from the American economy."

"What I'm saying is three things," Randall said, "computing is the future, companies exist to make money, and IBM booked the ICC convention in Berlin."

"Why are you telling me this?"

Randall parted his thick blonde hair and spoke in a strong German accent, "Because, my fellow prodigy, I need a ticket on that boat."

Tobias secretly knew Weiner had been duped out of a lucrative patent invention with AT&T under opaque circumstances the professor was considering taking legal action on. Needless to say, Weiner had favors owed him in the corporate world. He was also troubled by a Nazi sympathizer of a wife and, like all geniuses, craved insider information.

Before leaving, Randall asked Weiner what his best-case vision for the future was.

"To have an economy based on human values rather than buying or selling," Weiner responded.

"Are we going to get there?"

"Only after flesh and blood."

***

Randall's next appointment was with Sidis, attending one of the genius's small group lectures at the house of Margaret McGill. Mrs. McGill was known to be a kind woman, and a secretary at Babson Statistical Office, a firm started by Roger Babson, who predicted the October 1929 stock market crash in September.

Randall arrived early and looked for children, of which there was one. A boy of three grasped a button in his tiny hand. Tobias performed a magic trick with it and the boy ran off crying.

The group of five men and three women, all in their twenties, sat in a room upstairs, where Mrs. McGill had laid out an array of snacks and pastries. Sidis stood at the front and, without notes or pause, lectured on the interconnectivity of obscure cultural minutia in Native American history.

After an hour, Mrs. McGill tempted Sidis with a bowl of chocolates. The genius wandered over without stopping his speech and plopped a handful into his mouth. Taking advantage of the momentary silence, McGill stood and thanked William for another brilliant lecture. The other men also chimed in, exhausted from the sheer act of listening.

Sidis seemed surprised and smiled as if coming out of a fog.

"Oh, well, yes. Till next time, then," he said, reaching for a bowl of shelled peanuts.

Randall approached Sidis as the group dispersed.

"Well, hello there, Mr. Randall," Sidis said. "Do you have a magic trick for me?"

The pair walked to Sidis's apartment. Tobias spoke of his visits with Weiner and von Neumann then outlined his plans to visit Germany. Sidis spoke of his goals for the street transfer collecting society.

"The most important thing to me is keeping the peridromophile community non-hierarchical," Sidis said. "Speaking of which, how are things in Kalapuya territory?"

Randall told him the story of leaving Jane Alexander.

Sidis sighed as the pair reached the steps of his building, his one sign of emotion apart from an ever-present smile.

"It seems Norbert was the product of a manipulative father, you a mother, and me of both," he said.

"And von Neumann," Randall said, "was made by the world."

Sidis's smile returned.

"Well, God help him then."

Without saying goodbye, the greatest of all the prodigies trudged the steps and vanished into his dirty apartment.

CHAPTER 14

We founded the SOB or the 'Save Our Boys' organization on September 18, 1940. It was directly after Roosevelt enacted the Selective Training and Service Act and fifteen months before we entered the war. (The SOB acronym would later prove a hurdle of our own creation, as critics liked the easy association with "sobbing" men. Additionally, many of our boys came from domineering mothers.)

SOB headquarters were initially established at the Fill n' Time. As the organization's vice president, I moved operations to our living room and brought Marge and Dot to work on the cause.

Our initial strategy was to hedge the rising tidal wave of patriotism overwhelming Stramwell from the impending war. More American flags appeared on houses and downtown shop windows by the day. If possible, our mission was to make SOB sound *even more* urgent and American than combat.

It was a numbers game from the start.

Using census data, we determined of the approximately 500 male souls in the Stramwell area, 135 were of draft age. We figured at least 15% of them would be drafted, and 5% of those would ultimately die in battle. This meant exactly one Stramwell boy was going to perish.

Al painted these numbers with his rough penmanship on the backs of soda refreshment signs and hung them on the highway side of the Fix n' Fill.

I promptly made Al remove the signs, instructing him our tactics were to be more subversive in nature, which he should leave to the girls and me to orchestrate. Sweet man.

"We need to create a local need more significant than the call to arms," librarian Rebecca said at our first meeting.

"A *perceived* local need," I said.

Ironically, this had already been created for us by the war itself. Many Oregonians could remember how The Great War and its demands for lumber to manufacture airplanes had decimated many forested areas of the state. Another war without replanting new trees, and our primary industry could move elsewhere or, God forbid, be outsourced to other nations.

Our soldiers would have no recognizable home to return to without the towering pines that inhabited nearly every memory of any true Oregonian. "An Oregon without trees? *Never!*" was our rallying cry. (That any tree planted would take many years to reach maturity for lumber harvesting was not worth mentioning.)

Rebecca dug up news stories on the impact of depleted forests on our local economy. Along the way, she discovered an equally grave threat in the potential for uncontrollable forest fires from uncleared dead trees. (Besides planting trees, the other primary work of the CO camp near Waldport was forest management.)

"The entire Willamette Valley could catch fire tomorrow," we proclaimed. "All our men will be in Europe, and Oregon will be left worse than a war zone."

The next step was identifying the boys and, more importantly, the girls, as it was their God-given talents we would need to utilize to overcome any objection to conscientious objection.

***

We held our first public meeting in the WOW Hall, recruiting famed naturalist Tom Sequoia for a presentation on the necessity of Oregon forests for the security of State, Country, and the world. Sequoia had explored the Amazon, witnessed firsthand the storied Arashiyama Bamboo Grove of Japan, and even spent a summer roaming the Monteverde Cloud Forest of Costa Rica. —But nowhere could replace the Oregon forests of his childhood. (I paid an extra $25 for Tom to replace his home state of Nevada with Oregon for the presentation.)

Afterward, we provided a large assortment of refreshments and a performance from the famous Burt Bingham Orchestra, direct from the Green Parrot on the University campus in Eugene. Nearly the whole town showed.

I assigned the ladies to run two free photo booths to take pictures of all the youngsters. An informational form was required to mail the photos once processed. Data gathered included the person's name, age, address, whether they were married or dating anyone currently, and if so, who. We also requested a list of their five closest friends and a simple questionnaire on primary interests and hobbies. After the grand event, we sent the photos in the mail, along with arborist literature and a flyer on the pacifism of Christ, complete with scriptural backing.

We kept duplicates of the pictures in our master file at the house. Each folder also contained the information sheets with additional notes from intel gathered at Darcy's Café and Donna's Salon.

We held three more events. The most notable was a picnic in the town park with a projected film about Teddy Roosevelt's mission to create our national parks system. We provided another free photo booth, with pictures only available to those who hadn't already taken one. We also gave a sizeable donation to the high school drama club, which agreed to put on a short play about the history of the Christmas Tree industry in Oregon, written by Tom Sequoia.

In a month, we had nearly every young person in town cataloged. Then came the organizing.

Over 300 quality black and white photos with comprehensive biographies filled a filing cabinet in the main sitting room. Persons were organized by a system of my own conjuring.

First, we selected from the boys those who didn't have girlfriends (as noted on their information sheets.) They and their families were organized by town area, general socio-economic background, and religion. After that, we started on the single girls.

Once the girls and boys were organized, it was a matter of lining them up. To start, we created common 'pools' of likely groupings based on the aforementioned categories while factoring in mutual friends.

After three nights of creating piles of photographs throughout the house, I sensed a rising tide of frustration among our group.

For example, I would place a photo of Mary Halligan into the 'East Side poor Irish Catholic' pool, but Dot would move her to the 'South Side upper middle class' pool because two of Mary's best friends lived there, and Dot believed the Halligans were only 'marginal' Catholics.

Jill Sterling's photo, once placed in the 'Northwest Hills' pool (the wealthiest area of town) by Al, was moved to the 'Southwest Valley' (the poorest) by Marge, who knew for a fact Ms. Sterling's father was not James Sterling, owner of Sterling's Fine Furniture, but rather Jimmie Sterling, rail yard worker.

Several arguments broke out over determining ethnicity by nose shape and whether a crucifix necklace was enough to categorize a girl as 'devoutly' religious, fashionable, or neither.

I trudged upstairs and peered over the banister at the chaos below. We would need Tobias himself to figure out the mathematical complexities. Fortunately, as I turned to go back down the stairs, I saw myself in the hall mirror.

"Pretty girls are to be eliminated altogether," I proclaimed to the exhausted ladies and Al. "We are only going to select from the less desirable ones. And I will be the sole arbiter of that determination."

I sat at the table. "You will each come to me with pictures of 20 girls," I said. "You will hold a photo before me, and I will decide on first instinct whether they are a flower or a weed. When the flowers have been picked from the garden, you will toss them in the trash bin. Then, you will group the weeds into eight quadrants based on their home address, with Main Street, First, Seventh, and Tenth Streets creating the dividing barriers. After this process is complete, we will take the boys, completing the same process of separating the wheat from the chaff. The chaff will be divided geographically by home address, and those eight pools will be our groupings and targets."

"The fact is," I said, "we will never save all the boys, and those devoted to nationalism are almost certainly the same ones who've lived a welcoming life in this town."

Librarian Rebecca stepped forward and interrupted me.

"Let the strong, popular boys get their bodies and souls ruined by the war," she said. "Let them write uninspired letters to their boring beauty queens back home. They are low-hanging fruit for war, not for pacifism. We shall save *our* kind."

My God, that got applause.

There wasn't a particular type I was looking for. Instead, I relied solely on feeling. Still, there were signs. A slight pig nose worked. Eyes a little too close together did just fine. A larger-than-average forehead was ideal. Thinning hair? You betcha.

After the pools were determined, it was a matter of targeting. How exactly did we get to know the girls, get them on board with the plan, and get them to work together? —We needed someone on the inside—a general to implement marching orders blindly, without hesitation or regard for casualties.

Charlotte Cadwallader.

CHAPTER 15

As careful readers will remember, Charlotte Cadwallader was the iron-fisted pickle-patrol checker at the Great Harvest General Store. Conveniently, her family, who owned the store, were Quakers.

The male child of a small-town general store is expected to learn the business from the ground up for eventual takeover from the father. There were no boys in the Cadwallader family, and the father was a drunk (a rarity for Quaker general store proprietors).

Charlotte's uncle, a tall, gaunt, permanent bachelor, was technically the store manager, but since she was sixteen, Charlotte was the boss. She dealt with the customers, placed orders, designed displays, and ran shoplifters off with a broom. (As a point of note Charlotte's father bought twenty-five Mark IVs from the broom salesman and graciously donated none to the school. Instead, they sat in the corner of the store with a 'make an offer' sign hanging for all eternity.)

Charlotte was nineteen now, having graduated the previous year with no boyfriend or prospects. The store was thriving under her leadership. They'd even put up a billboard on the way into town with the image of a giant rooster proclaiming: *You've got to get up early in the morning to beat a Great Harvest deal!*

I took note of Charlotte at the age of fourteen when her family moved to a farmhouse on Swale Valley Rd., and she joined my class.

In every teacher's career, they come across that one student they secretly fear could arrange a coup d'état. It's hard to define, but I immediately knew it with Charlotte.

Sometimes I would even excuse myself to the broom room and crack the door to watch in secret exactly how she would replace me.

"Ok, class," Charlotte would say, rising to her feet. "We are on page 81 of the literature manual. I want you four in the back to read that page, the next four here 82, and you four up front 83. You have one minute. Then, discuss a summary amongst yourselves of what was on the pages for 30 seconds. I will call on one of you to present a 30-second oral summary for the class to take notes." Charlotte would pause and look at the clock. "Miss Alexander usually goes to the necessary room for just over three minutes. When she returns, we will all be on page 84 and insist on it regardless of her protest. She might quiz us to prove it, so be sharp."

At this point, if any student asked 'why they were doing this,' Charlotte would overcome any grumbling by raising her hand, and dropping it. "Go!"

I would play along when I returned. I feared

Charlotte a bit, actually.

Of no little importance were her ample breasts. At the time, she hefted the largest in town on a girl her age, permitting her to command waifs with a single look and stop beauty queens in their tracks.

Presently, my plan was to approach Charlotte at the store and casually suggest we catch up over lunch. But on my way out of the house, I once again caught my reflection in a mirror.

"Oh, bloody hell," I said out loud.

I sat and drafted a straightforward proposition detailing our entire plan as if she were in the inner sanctum. Al slipped the envelope under the Great Harvest back door that night. The letter concluded with a request to put a blue feather in her hat during work the next day if she was 'in.'

A pounding woke us up early the following morning. I stood from the top of the stairs as Al opened the door to reveal Charlotte Cadwallader.

"I ain't putting a dang feather in my hat," she said, looking past Al up at me. "I don't wear hats normally, and it looked ridiculous. Don't tell Papa I said dang."

"Well, good morning, Char—" Al tried to say, but Charlotte walked around him and pointed up at me.

"I'm in."

***

Ms. Cadwallader possessed a near-encyclopedic knowledge of Stramwell's youth.

"Claudia Gordon, now there's a diamond in the rough," Charlotte said, smoking a cigarette while hovering over our dining room table full of photographs. A long ash fell onto the photo of Claudia, and she brushed it away, leaving a smear.

Charlotte tilted her head.

"Let's get a standardized makeup kit for all the girls."

We trained the selected girls to be more attractive by all means necessary. Hair, makeup, and clothing makeovers were conducted, along with training on submissive laughing, accidental well-timed cleavage, and flirty touches to the boy's arms.

It was a fantastic thing to see Charlotte reign over the selected girls. She told them what to wear, when to be seen, and what boys to talk to on what subjects. — Almost none of the young ladies even asked why she was doing it. They just obeyed.

Jenny Burton was the only one who mustered the fortitude to question Charlotte. I happened to be there as a witness.

"Um, Charlotte," Jenny Burton said, her head down, fingers trembling.

Jenny had seen us about to walk into Cassie's Emporium, where we would be choosing the contents of the standard makeup case.

"What?" Charlotte said, fumbling through her purse for cigarettes, then a lighter. She finally looked Jenny in the eyes, cigarette dangling. "Well, come on."

"Um," Jenny looked back at the Emporium from where she had just come. "See, Momma said you telling us girls what to do and all is, well... intrusive."

"Who?" Charlotte barked.

"Mama. I mean, my mother. It's just, sudden like, is all. You telling us what… to do. And all."

Charlotte bent to look around Jenny's shoulder into the Emporium Café window where Jenny's mother was sitting.

"Look at your ma," Charlotte said.

Jenny turned slightly and broke into a nervous laugh. "What, what about her?"

"Look," Charlotte demanded.

Jenny's mother stared back through the window at the three of us.

"You wanna be her?" Charlotte said. "You wanna wear old stockings and cheap, itchy skirts? Care for a fat man who couldn't give a dang about you? Cuz that's exactly where you're headed. —Stuck in a dead-end town with dead-end dreams."

Charlotte lit up without looking away, then placed both hands on Jenny's shoulders and turned her back to us.

"Live your own life. Right? Right?"

Jenny's lips started the tiniest quiver, then a full tremor.

"But dad's not fat. He's nice."

Charlotte tapped Jenny lightly on the cheek with the lighter.

"No one's gonna steer you out of this dead-end." She grabbed Jenny's chin with some force. "We gotta steer *ourselves* out. Right?"

146

Charlotte held the girl in silence.

"Right?"

Charlotte squeezed tighter.

"Ok. Right. Yeah, yes, you're right," Jenny said.

Charlotte's iron stare broke and she embraced Jenny, who began laughing to nearly full-on crying.

"Right," Jenny just kept saying. "Right. Right!"

When we turned to go into the Emporium, I held the door for Charlotte.

She paused before entering and spoke, (to either me or herself, I am still unsure).

"It don't make any sense, and it don't have to," she said.

Later that week, I came home from shopping, and there was Charlotte with five girls in our living room. She had them all reading from *The Journal of George Fox* and was standing before them holding a large world atlas.

"Who can tell me where Chechlov is?" she said.

The girls squinted earnestly at the map but ultimately gave up, looking ashamed.

"Are you telling me you can't even name the country Hitler invaded to start this whole mess?"

Michelle Sexton raised a shaky hand.

"Is it near Poland?"

"Near Poland?! You're joking, right? The whole world is sending their young men off to murder each other, and you think Chechlov is *near Poland*?"

Charlotte paced, incredulous.

"So, let me just get this straight, Michelle. You send your beloved brother off to get slaughtered in some muddy ditch, *then* get doused with so much poison gas so when he returns you don't recognize him… and when he gets home, you ask, 'Did you fight in Chechlov, dear brother? You know, it's that place near Poland?!'"

Charlotte wiped her forehead in wild fury.

"Michelle," she barked. "Read for us the second paragraph of page 164 in the Fox book. What does it say *exactly*?"

Michelle Sexton fumbled frantically to find the section. Two of the other girls reached over to help her.

"No! Don't help her. Unless you think she's too dumb to find both Chechlov and a paragraph in a book?"

"I've got it!" Michelle said. "Here it is, the second paragraph: '*From Newcastle, we traveled through the countries, having meetings and visiting friends as we went, in Northumberland and Bishoprick.*'"

"Exactly!" Charlotte proclaimed, "As clear as day."

Charlotte took the book from Michelle and slammed it shut.

"And we shall learn more in the next chapter."

Charlotte smacked the book repeatedly with her fist.

"We are always learning, always growing, and always changing," she said. "It is our duty to our fathers, brothers, future husbands, and sons that we do! And you are already doing just that."

Charlotte took Michelle's hand and the hand of another girl.

"All of you are together in this. We will not let our men run off ramble shot straight into harm's way without even knowing where Chechlov is, right?"

"Right. Oh, very right. Yes, right."

Charlotte shook her head with pity.

"But our boys, God bless 'em, don't know any better."

She placed her hand on her stomach.

"We are the guardians of life. Our bodies decide who comes into this world. It has always been God's plan. But men won't listen to God's plan when war is involved. Because war is man's plan. So, we need to use God's gifts He has given only us. Repeat that."

"God's gift, given, gifted—"

"Exactly!"

At this, Charlotte unbuttoned the top half of her blouse and bent seductively, revealing her full, canyon-like depths.

"To keep them out of the war," Charlotte giggled.

The five girls giggled, too, looking at each other, their eyes wide as saucers.

After the girls left, I asked Charlotte about the presentation.

"Choose pages at random," she said. "Especially when I need to make a point."

"So, and forgive me," I said, "but where, exactly, is Chechlov?"

149

"Who's that now?" she mumbled, searching again for her lighter. "Purses are designed by men, did you know that? It's ridiculous!"

It was time to bring on the boys.

***

We laid out the boy's pictures in our living room on tables. We then asked the thirty or so girls we'd selected to pick up the image of the boy they would find most suitable in a mate.

It appeared most of them had already spent considerable time on the subject beforehand, as nearly all went right to their selected boy with no other takers. Still, there were a handful of doubles and even a few girls who wandered for a bit looking for one of the football star types who'd been removed.

Charlotte stepped forward to intervene, but I stopped her.

"This piece," I said, "needs to happen as it happens."

Any girls who had doubled up on one boy decided on a compromise quickly, simply by choosing another close approximation. The girls looking for their football star also gave up without much resistance, realizing they needed to select *someone*.

In the end, there were a few unfortunate bottom-of-the-barrel photos of boys. The girls still waiting to make a selection got into such a scrum fighting over the remaining pictures that Charlotte and I had to pull them off each other and flip a coin.

Ultimately, all were content and excited when finally handed the image of a boy that was their very own.

Next, we scheduled a dance. Our challenge was we had to get each boy to ask out their assigned girl without knowing anything about our plan.

We accomplished our goal through unwavering organization. Once assigned a boy, the girls gelled together with a fever. Just like allowing the boy selections to happen naturally, this process took on a life of its own, becoming a strategic attack none of us could have organized.

"Who knows my guy, Jack Sutton?" little Maggie Abel yelled. "I've only seen him. Never talked to him. Someone know him?"

She held up a picture of a pimply-faced large-lipped boy with heavy eyebrows.

"He's my cousin!" a voice from the far corner of the room shouted. "Just moved here."

"Who's that?" Maggie called back.

"It's me, Ruth Ann Sutton."

Maggie made a b-line for heavy-eyebrowed Ruth Ann. Other girls got the same idea, raised their photos, and shouted boy's names.

"Tommy Lillard?"

"Dick Macklemore?"

"Harry Cock? Anybody know Harry Cock? Oh dear..."

"They got it wrong on the picture. It's spelled K-O-C-H. Like 'Coke.'"

"Benjamin Weisberg?" a girl with a large and beautifully distinguished nose yelled.

"They just moved to town, and his father's a doctor!"

"Whoo hoo!" the girls shouted in unison.

CHAPTER 16

We scheduled the dance for Saturday, August 9th, 1941, at the WOW Hall, with the theme, 'Peace in our Time.'

As I stated, our straightforward task in the weeks leading up to the dance was to align every chosen boy with his respective girl. Marge turned out to be Cupid's apprentice in this regard. She tracked all the alignments in a master ledger detailing each interaction and the progress we were aware of.

Margie used colored pencils for highlighting. Green meant the boy had asked his girl to the dance, and she'd accepted. Blue meant a courtship process was in full swing, but no dance request had yet been offered. Yellow indicated the boy was not picking up hints from the girl and would need a more focused approach. Red, of which there were only two, meant things were going *too* well. (With an enterprise like ours, it could quickly become scandalous should the town believe we were driving hormonal youngsters into each other's arms. Babies were strictly a last resort, and such preemptive behavior in that arena was cause for a painful dressing down by Charlotte.)

The young ladies created and mailed invitations to the dance. In addition, we sent letters to the parents detailing that the SOB committee had selected their particular child as an 'exclusive reward for citizen recognition.'

We encouraged the boys to buy lily corsages from the SOB stand we set up inside Great Harvest, with 100% of the proceeds going towards planting trees in Oregon. A complimentary copy of *Johnny Got His Gun* by Dalton Trumbo accompanied each purchase. (I did not enjoy the novel. However, Al ordered them by the caseload and spread them like gospel tracts.)

***

"*Having a Ball??*" Charlotte said.

She was holding the latest edition of the Chronicle. At the bottom of page two was an article about the upcoming dance, with the aforementioned headline.

"With two danged question marks?"

She read the article aloud:

> "*An estimated one hundred parents were surprised to receive letters stating their child was being honored with an invitation to the 'Peace Dance,' to be held at 7 pm on August 9th at the WOW hall in Stramwell. Each of their respective young adults also received separate formal invitations. A local anti-war group called SOB, an acronym for 'Surrender Our Boys,' appears to be spearheading the event.*

'They mean to indoctrinate our young people with pacifist propaganda,' states a source close to the group.

Girls are expected to wear peace lily corsages, which the group has provided for sale in the Great Harvest General Store for the past week.

While leaders of the SOB group could not be reached for comment, some community members are outraged.

'It's a disgrace,' said Mike Miller, local businessman, Great War veteran, and Secretary of the Stramwell Great War Veterans League (SGWVL).

'We raise our boys to love our country, and a group can come along and do something like this. They ought to be ashamed,' states Mary Thompson Smith, chair of the Stramwell Civic Improvement Club (SCIC).

Charlotte tore the paper and said a word not fit for a lady.

***

As the night of the dance approached, news of the global conflict grew increasingly worrisome. Hitler had invaded Russia, while England was still reeling from the air raids that killed over 40,000 Londoners. It was evident Churchill was in dire need of our entrance into the war, and rumors were cropping up he might allow nefarious activity to drag America in.

(Al had read a story about Churchill as a young lad that told me all I needed to know about the man. In a game of chase through the woods with his brother and cousin, the future prime minister found himself on a long bridge with his two pursuers having split up and trapped him, approaching from each side. Instead of conceding, Churchill jumped from the bridge onto a pine tree, thinking he could slide down as if it were a pole. Instead, young Winston fell 29 feet and ruptured a kidney. After six weeks of bed rest, he walked out of the house to go enlist in the Military Academy.)

The night of the dance there was a question if it would even happen. The board of the WOW Hall included three veterans of the Great War, one of them the brother of Mike Miller, (the man quoted in the Chronicle article.) A poster even appeared on the WOW Hall door, stating the dance was: CANCELLED BY THE BOARD.

Fortunately, my husband had a connection with law enforcement.

Sheriff Tawlins walked into the Crazy Horse and tossed the poster on the table where the WOW Hall board members sat.

"You boys are gonna allow this dance on Friday," he said. "I seen their contract with y'all, and they got a permit with the City a month ago."

"Under false pretenses," Jefferson Tawlins (Sheriff Tawlins' second cousin) said.

The sheriff bent to Jefferson's face.

"You mean like that moonshine still on the Hawthorne back forty your ma claims is for medicine?"

Jefferson snarled. "You leave her outta this!"

"I wish I could leave y'all outta everything," the Sherrif said. "Now, you can throw a fit on Friday if you'd like, but unless you want to face charges of disrupting the peace, then costly litigation for tortious interference, that's what there'll be: *Peace*. The dance stays as planned."

The old boys grumbled over their scotch but eventually relented. Except one of them called Big Taw a coward as he walked out. As the story goes, Taw pivoted on his boot heel, took his gun out of the holster, and slammed it on the table.

"Who's the coward here?" he said, "Cause by the way you figure things, a brave man would grab this gun and give me what for," he stared each one of them down. "And a coward, according to you at least, would know it's wrong to fight the law when the law is right." He paused and waited for a response, but none came. "Well then, we're all good, law-abiding cowards here. You and me both."

Sheriff Tawlins picked up his gun and walked out.

(Upon hearing the story I immediately considered which female in town would be best suited as a helpmate for the Sheriff. As it happened, there was a stately, mannish-looking blonde who'd moved into town to tend her aging parents. An anonymous call reporting chicken thievery was made regarding her property, but when the Sheriff arrived, the handsome woman was too forward in her pursuit, causing Taw to flee the premises.)

So the dance was on, at least from a legal perspective. But, given our recent negative press, there was still the matter of actual attendance. Word had it most men in town, of which a large number were veterans, forbade their sons and daughters to attend.

So, on the day of the dance, while Al and I were busy preparing the Wow Hall with decorations and making last-minute confirmations, Charlotte was ensuring no one backed out.

She made her way to no less than twenty

households. Some would later report she was gentle and sweet, encouraging families the dance was 'pro-war,' in a way, as it was to promote peace, and wasn't lasting peace the goal of any war?

At some houses, Charlotte instructed the girls to put on their dresses so their fathers could see how beautiful they looked, garnering soft-hearted approvals for their entry.

At most, however, Charlotte asked the mother and daughter to leave and had a frank discussion with the father about his uncomely daughter's bleak prospects should she turn down this golden opportunity.

All eventually gave their blessing, with more than one man thereafter heading straight to bed with a bottle of brandy.

Whatever the method, they started arriving at 6:30 p.m. on the night. All wore their best outfits, with nearly every girl donning a peace lily corsage.

I had assigned Dot to greet the couples at the door, checking their names against the guest list.

Al and I stood to the side, watching as the unattractive youths happily entered arm and arm.

"I'm gonna start calling you Noah," Al said.

I beamed.

"How dare you!" a boy said. He was standing with his date in front of Dot. "There's nothing wrong with her dress."

The boy's date was Mary Abernathy, part of what might have been the poorest family in the Willamette Valley. A dozen of them lived in a shack right in the middle of town.

"You can see all God gave her!" Dot said, squinting at Mary. "And *you know* what you're doing, too."

It was true, the dress was threadbare in all the wrong places.

"Ok, ok," I said, going over and ushering the couple through the doors. "Everything's fine. You children have a good time."

I nodded at Al vigorously for him to find Mary a suitable coat for covering, but he did not seem to decipher my message.

"We're trying to be *inviting* here," I whispered to Dot.

Dot scowled at me for so long I had to physically turn her back to the greeting table. She ripped the tickets from the next boy, who I believe needed a stop at the restroom after.

Inside were tables of light snacks and sandwiches, plenty of punch, fifteen round tables for socializing, and a medium-sized dance floor.

At 7:00 pm sharp, the band took their place on stage, all in singular uniform and polished to a shine. The lights dimmed, and Charlotte, the maître d', came to the spotlighted microphone with roaring applause.

There was shuffling of feet for a half-second, then a blast. Charlotte's face was blown to the left, splattering Burt Bingham and his famous Orchestra with flesh.

It was like a candle blowing out, her face escaping from her body, which then waivered for another half second while the gun blast echoes subsided, then fell in complete silence.

Among the six boys who ambushed from stage right were three sons of Wow Hall board members. The gang was led by Frankie Miller, the grandson of local businessman Mike Miller.

It would later come out that Brad Matthewson, the boy who shot Charlotte, didn't know the gun was loaded. (None of their other guns were, and Brad's gun only went off when his feet got tangled in a paper streamer.)

After seeking refuge at his grandfather's house that night and being turned away, Frankie Miller was ultimately discovered hiding in a truck stop restroom five miles south of Stramwell.

A short speech he planned to read at the dance, once commandeering the microphone, was found on his person:

> *We're here to remind you of the debt you owe to the veterans. You should be giving thanks for their sacrifice instead of dancing. Just because you're ungrateful cowards doesn't mean the rest of us are. God blessed the US of A in '76, and I'll fight to protect her in '41.*

The speech was, of course, never read, but it was also never publicized, as I took the only copy from Big Taw and secretly replaced it with one slightly truer to the boy's intentions.

I suspect Mike Miller or some other adult wrote Frankie Miller's original, but none owned up to it.

Here is the speech the Chronicle received and printed in their next edition:

> *My name is Frankie Miller, grandson of Mike Miller. These*

are my boys here. Y'all know who we are, and we know who y'all are too: A bunch of yellow-bellied scoundrels and ugly-faced sacks. Look at y'all putting lipstick on pigs—fatties, just like their mommas. Stramwell is full of 'em. Me and the boys here can't wait for war to start just to get away from this hog farm. Grandpa says the only thing a Stramwell girl is good for is getting exercise by running from her. So good riddance. Europe girls, here we come.

***

The Cadwalladers, as it turns out, consisted of a huge extended family stretching from Roseburg to Salem.

"We're the Cadwalladers," a sturdy woman said, standing at my door two mornings after the dance. She resembled almost exactly Charlotte, with forty years of fighting added on.

"And we're here for ya."

The huddled group behind her spilled out into the lawn, where a number of cars were already parked, with more pulling in.

Seeing the benefit of fully letting the Cadwalladers in on the details of our plan, I revealed everything to the woman (her name was Timey) in short order: file cabinets and all.

"Right," she said. "So we fight this one on both the land and air. Gather up every girl you've recruited. It's time for 'em to put the pressure on the boys." Timey pointed to me. "You and I are headed downtown. The Chronicle'll be needing a heroic story about Charlotte, and you're a writer, ain't ya?"

Within three days all our girls had clear marching orders to get as many of their boys registered for

161

conscientious objection (CO) right away.

(As Charlotte would say, 'the time to knock a trout in the head is before it knows it's out of the water.')

As for the Chronicle, I cast the tale of Ms. Charlotte Cadwallader as a quiet, serene local girl just trying to support her community. *Her dream,* I wrote, *was to mentor a generation of Stramwell women who would raise their children to be like Christ Himself.*

"Just like the good book says," Timey said. "It ain't a lie if nobody gets hurt."

Still, since the Selective Service had been activated, no less than twenty Stramwell boys had been drafted and scattered to boot camps. Another thirty enlisted voluntarily. Even with the girls pushing the boys to sign up for CO, stronger forces of history pushed them not to: Families in Stramwell had fought in American wars for generations, and many had lost men for lesser causes.

We were going to need to pour gas on the fire.

"Now," I said to a group of twenty girls making 'Charlotte Ribbons' at the house. "We're all adult women here. Let's not beat around the bush on what makes men tick."

Some girls giggled, while other's eyes widened in terror.

"The kettle of war is starting to shake," I continued. "It's time we dropped the heavy payload."

I fiddled with my top two buttons, stood square with the group and bent over.

"If we're going to win the game, it's time to advance the runners."

162

"My Frankie loves baseball!" Jackie Bentley spoke up from the back.

I ignored her.

"We've got no petitions for conscientious objection so far," I said. "I want to see ten by next week, by *any means necessary.*"

We got ten. Then fifteen in two weeks.

Then, our progress came to a halt.

It seemed the local draft board had sensed a rising trend of Stramwell CO applicants and started denying our boys outright on principle.

Fortunately, draft boards are comprised of local citizen volunteers, and the Cadwalladers just happened to have a large number of volunteers that were in for the cause.

The CO applicant flow resumed in a few weeks. And, needless to say, if a draftee said he was a Quaker in Stramwell, Oregon, the board believed him, whether or not he could recite the *Beatitudes*.

All of this was good and well, but not nearly enough when December 7th came.

As the news of the Hawaiian ambush rolled in like waves, our boys rode them straight to the enlistment office. They promised to write home to our girls and were grateful for the good times of late, but the lure of national vengeance rivals none.

***

Around this time, we started to hear more about the conscientious objector camp near Waldport on the Oregon coast called 'Camp Gabriel.' As a point of interest, we heard the men there worked all day in the forests, then spent their remaining energies writing and making art.

Librarian Rebecca Miller showed us one of their handmade poetry periodicals, which she said were gaining a reputation amongst the small, coastal-town librarians as being of the highest caliber.

Al and I even traveled to the Camp to watch a particularly hilarious retelling of *The Mikado*. That night, we met many of the men, who were enthralled to meet the leader of the famed UVW.

Two young leaders and a young lady who volunteered at the camp returned to our cabin, 'The Whale Inn,' just across the road. We stayed up talking until 2 a.m., with spirits running high and plenty.

The topic of discussion that night wasn't the European conflict, Hitler, or even how the young men were prisoners for simply not wanting to kill.

Tom Graves, a tall, skinny, wild-bearded man of twenty-four, raised his glass high in a toast to Al and me.

"As outsiders to Camp Gabriel," he said, "and proof there is an outside, which we were beginning to doubt, please do us the honor of being the impartial judge for a debate my colleague and I, the highly esteemed and smelliest coward in the woods, Jonathan Abernathy, have been having this past week."

"Go on," I said, primly crossing my legs and sitting erect.

"The question is this," Tom continued, "exactly what *is* a well-lived life?"

"Oh Lord," Mae Close, the young female of the

group, rolled her eyes and grabbed my shoulder. "When they're not fighting over a patch of mud, they're still killing themselves."

"No, no," I said, holding back laughter. "I shall hear both sides and judge accordingly. And don't pull the Solomon trick where one of you offers to cut the baby in half, because I'm liable to let you do it."

"Al, you got a wild one on your hands!" Mae said.

Al lifted his drink, grinned, and nodded vigorously through the laughter. (Sweet man.)

"Jonathan!" I said, "State your case, young man."

Jonathan was an even thinner young man but shorter and fairer. He claimed a somewhat distant Quaker heritage as his justification before the Selective Service board. (Still, he more likely was granted CO status by a kindhearted staffer who knew the intolerable ridicule he might face in boot camp.)

Jonathan jumped and took a dainty bow.

"I shall present my case with brevity because it needs no embellishment," he said. "My argument is a simple definition of the way of all life: A life well lived is simply one that grows under any circumstances."

Johnathan took another bow and sat down to Mae and Al's applause.

"A naturalistic approach. Very well," I said. "Tom, certainly you cannot disagree with the way of all nature?"

Tom took a princely bow, then stepped toward Mae and requested her hand. Mae played the part and stood like a debutante being presented at a ball.

"Take, if you will," Tom said, "pure beauty."

Mae snorted in laughter and doubled over, causing all to break.

"As I was saying before being rudely interrupted by a stray swine," Tom continued, lifting Mae's hand in the air once more.

"Beauty, not just in the female or male body, or even the heart, or soul, but beauty *itself*, the chasing after it even though we never fully obtain it, is a life well lived."

Tom placed Mae's arm down gently, then walked to the single potted plant in the room and felt a leaf.

"In the fullness of nature, is it not what every living thing is striving for? Why else does the mighty fir grow a hundred feet in the air if not to receive more light? If there is any purpose in life, it must be the appreciation of beauty, in whatever form the beholder determines it most pure."

"And what form," I said earnestly, "do you determine it?"

Tom stepped back, took Mae's hand again, and kissed it.

"That," he said, looking into her eyes, "I hope to one day know."

CHAPTER 17

For several years up to that point, Al's right-hand man at the Fill n' Time was Jake Fairfield. Al had taken him under his wing after observing his innate talent for machinery work. Such was the quiet young man's competency, that by early 41, Jake was running the place and only checking in with Al periodically. Jake's wife, Sally, ran all the Fill n' Time bookkeeping, with their two little ones toddling around the shop, (which I believe Al loved even more than the cars.)

In late-December of '41, Jake stopped by during breakfast.

"I've got Sally minding the station for just a few, Mr. Al," he said, standing in our doorway. "She knows more 'an I do about the place anyways. But, well, I'm just here letting you know my number's been called. I'm sorry sir."

"Oh Jake," Al said.

"I come to tell you first, even before my pa. It's the shame of his life I haven't enlisted yet. He'll probably hug me."

Jake let out a half-smirk that faded as soon as it came.

"Anyway," Jake said, raising a finger which, just like sweet Al's, contained deep crevices of grease. "Pa got me thinking, and I had an idea I thought I might share with you and the Mrs. if that's ok?"

Al invited Jake in for breakfast, but he politely declined.

"See, Mr. Al," Jake continued, "there's only one thing my old man likes more than patriotism. And that's capitalism."

"Is that so?" Al said.

"It was always his dream to own a business. He was gonna work on train boilers for hire. But he never got to it. And when you let me and Sally run the shop... well, he was proud. So it got me thinking about an idea."

Jake's basic concept was that Al and I would move to the cabins across from Camp Gabriel, where Al would set up a satellite auto repair station. The shop could serve as a training ground at night for men at the camp who wanted to learn the mechanic trade. Once the war was over, we could offer the most promising young men an opportunity, with our financial assistance, to set up their own Fill n' Time location. It would give the boys an actual career path and the girls' parents something redeemable in place of them marrying a pacifist.

"But what about you?" Al said to Jake, choked up.

"Oh, I'll be alright Mr. Al," he said. "Figure the army'll have me working on some machinery somewhere. But, I was hoping Sally and my children might have a place at the coast with you? To work, of course. Help you set things up? We'd have to shut down the station here, but I'll help you restart it when I'm back. You can count on it."

***

Al and I packed our necessary belongings and moved into cabin #5 of The Whale Inn on January 13, 1942, reserving cabin #6 for Sally and her boys.

We left Marge in charge of the CO recruitment operations back in Stramwell, along with Dot and a couple of the Cadwallader clan still hanging about. (After a long talk with Dot she still would not apologize to young Mary Abernathy. However, Dot did agree to get Mary a new dress, which I ended up picking out and paying for.)

Timey Cadwallader died of lung cancer a couple of weeks before we left, on Christmas Day. She had me pre-write an obituary and post in three papers around the area, promoting her and Charlotte as angels of peace, along with mentioning their association with the UVW and our plan for the mechanic's training program at Camp Gabriel.

As for the Fill n' Time 'satellite' shop, the obits garnered interest from no less than twenty boys from as far out as Corvallis.

Al got to work having the participating CO men build a garage on the property we'd purchased adjacent to The Whale Inn, conveniently located off the main highway and 20 miles from the nearest auto mechanic shop. Al wanted to call the new place 'A Real Peace of Work Auto Station,' but I decided that would be bad for business and encouraged him to keep the name Fill n' Time.

"Honey, I never disagree with your instincts on planning," Al said. "And I'm sure I'm wrong about this from a business standpoint. But this isn't about business."

So, 'A Real Peace of Work Auto Station' it became. Internally, we called it the 'Peace Station' for short.

***

Life at Camp Gabriel for the CO men lucky enough to be stationed there involved:

1. No pay.

2. Hard labor.

3. No veteran benefits for their families.

4. Life in an isolated camp.

5. An obligation to continue working at the camp until six months after the war ended, whenever that would be.

6. Being branded a coward.

A growing number of men reporting to Camp Gabriel had wives and children at home who were left to fend for themselves or take from charity. Not knowing what else to do, some women moved into The Whale Inn cabins just to be close.

Most of them worked at the Peace Station during the day while the men worked in the forests.

At night, the men would train with Al in the garage.

Naturally, everyone wanted to be together, so we often held buffet-style dinners. We kept expanding too, so purchasing The Whale Inn outright ultimately made sense.

While learning the mechanic's trade was an excellent opportunity for many, it wasn't for everyone. In fact, at the same time as we were busily growing the Peace Station, other projects were flourishing at Camp Gabriel.

Our early friends Tom Graves and Jonathan Abernathy had finally acquired a small, manually powered printing press and were now printing formal anthologies of their poetry and short stories for distribution to a broader audience.

I was never a fan of poetry myself. (Part of me thinks it's silly.) With that said, Mae Close had a piece in the first anthology I quite enjoyed that Al took note of and framed in our cabin.

Calling in the Wilderness

I am a person

even if

I don't do

many of the things

other persons

say I should.

After all,

other persons

aren't the ones

that make me

a person.

I sent Marge and Dot a copy of that first anthology with an update on our newest endeavor. I also sent a copy to Theodore Compton, notifying him we would be submitting no more work as the UVW, and if he was looking for the next big thing, here it was.

Mr. Compton wrote back warmly, saying even though the anthology wasn't a work of the UVW, it was still quite good.

"Unfortunately, prospects of selling anti-war poetry to a major publisher at the moment," he said, "are not optimal. But keep me posted and tell them to keep up the good fight. Also, I've received word from the production company in Los Angeles who expressed interest in adapting *The Senators* for film. Unfortunately, they are putting the project on indefinite hold. Something about a war going on and people wanting combat films. We will still hang tight on the novel's publication until there's a picture deal, as the global conflict will surely resolve itself shortly."

It was no matter to me financially *The Senators* was

on hold, as we had been printing money on the other works. (It had been the marketing plan of Mr. Compton to withhold publishing *The Senators* in novel form until it was released in movie form, wherein both would be released simultaneously in an avalanche of publicity, or what Mr. Compton called, 'synergy.') Still, it saddened me the work wouldn't be shared yet. It was the first novel Tobias crafted in our partnership, and secretly, I always believed the best.

I told Tom and Jon at Camp Gabriel the bad news about the anthology's formal publishing hopes, and it didn't seem to faze them one bit.

The lads were most excited about a new play they'd written, hoping to perform for a public audience at the camp. It was based on our conversation in the cabin that late night when we visited early on.

They even wanted Al and I to play minor but key parts.

"Oh, my heavens," I said. "No one wants to watch an old couple! Me with my wrinkles and Al with his hobble. I can see the reviews now. Well, I'll think about it. And just how do you plan to promote the play?"

Tom and Jon stared back, blank-faced.

"Don't worry," I said, "I'm sure the ladies and I can figure something out."

***

One of the interesting things about camp life was how little anyone talked or even seemed to think about the war. It was why we were all there, uprooted from our everyday lives like the rest of the world, yet it was almost like the conflict didn't exist. Rarely did anyone play the news on the radio or even read the paper. Apparently, life provided enough trouble working the hillsides, planting trees and making fire stops; hard work made more difficult by the six consecutive months of cold Oregon rain.

For eight and a half hours a day, six days a week, the men worked bent over, ankle-deep in the mud on steep slopes, soaked cold through. With frozen fingers and toes, they'd take three small steps, lift their shovels, dig a hole, and put in a seedling they didn't own and wouldn't see grow.

The group was also responsible for 'forest maintenance.'

I happened to be in the dining hall when the men were getting their training from the forestry service on removing snags while making fire stops.

"Snagging," a Ranger standing at a chalkboard said, "Is the most dangerous work in forestry. It takes having your head about you at all times. Being proactive. Remember that word, 'pro-active.' You don't re-act, you pro-act."

He drew a downed tree.

"Here is the dead tree. Fell, who knows how long ago. Vegetation grew all around it, other trees even. Absolutely ripe for a fire. And it's in the middle of the woods, a mile from the nearest road if you're lucky."

He drew more trees.

"You can't get a crane in that far. So, we use more rudimentary methods."

"I'm sorry, sir," Jon raised his hand. "We are unfamiliar with rudimentary methods at Camp Gabriel."

The defining quality of the camp was mud. Thick clay with chocolate slosh, omnipresent and impossible to clean. You can't wet it, and scraping only makes it multiply. The only rational thing to do was accept it.

I made Al pull up the little carpet we had in the living room the second week we were there. Each night I'd move my feet in the bed sheets and feel dirt.

("The real curse," my Mother used to say, "is putting women in charge of housework when the very thing we detest most is filth." She might have been right.)

Sugar and fruit were under rationing but made available in enough supply for baking when all of us combined our allotments. So, we sold pies and other bakery goods at the Peace Station. We were making quite a name for ourselves, too. Travelers regularly stopped for nothing else than a piece of pie at a premium price.

When completed, Tom and Jon formally presented us with copies of their play. Each night in bed, Al and me read our lines out loud in earnest, Al always had a copy rolled up in his back pocket in case there was a lull in the work at the Peace Station. I do believe his restroom trips were doubled in length because of intensive study.

Two weeks before the first show, some ladies and I drove into town to hang flyers. We visited all the major stores asking if we could leave copies on their counters, and inquired if the businesses were interested in sponsorship.

We received three takers on the marketing opportunity, all with in-kind trades, one of which was the movie theater, providing us with free tickets to shows.

I assured the theater manager, Mr. Kimball, we would highlight him as the 'Presenting Sponsor of the Arts Locally' (PSAL).

Mr. Kimball invited me to stay to view their current film, *High Sierra*. As he was speaking, several newsreels played about the war.

Having been insulated from the news, the images awakened me to the sheer grandness of the effort. One shot was a panoramic view of the ocean, with warships and planes dotting the horizon like a plague, while the narrator voiced impressive statistics I couldn't comprehend. (Partly because the manager was speaking so loudly. -He seemed nervous about the prospect of a theater at the camp, taking people's limited free time away from the movies.)

"I care deeply about the arts," he said, fiddling with the flyer I'd handed him. "So important for a community, now more than ever. How many plays do you think you'll be putting on?"

"Boo!!" the crowd groaned in unison at the image of German tanks. The manager paused and smiled. "Go to hell, krauts!" someone yelled.

"It happens every time," Mr. Kimball said. "There's nothing like seeing a moving picture in real life."

A scene of Hitler played on the screen, watching the endless, tightly organized ranks of men marching past, looking more like mass-produced machines than humans. Then, the monster shouted and screamed from a podium, making it hard to tell if his arm swings were sped up as a trick of the camera or if he genuinely moved so frenetically. Finally, a group of Nazi officials stood at a large banquet before an elaborate spread of food unimaginable to the locals there in Waldport.

"And this play," Mr. Kimball said, his hands still shaking the flyer, "you have full permission from the publisher to use in a production of this nature? Don't get me started on the troubles that result from not dotting every tittle."

"It was written in-house," I said, still watching the screen.

"Oh, I see."

And then I caught a glimpse. Only a glimpse, mind you. A single second, or less.

Tobias.

The young man stood on a stage with Nazi leaders, glaring directly into the camera with the slightest smile and a feather in his hat.

CHAPTER 18

INT. KITCHEN - DAY

ABEL, a mischievous young boy,
stands holding an empty glass. He
is wearing a white mustache from
having just drunk milk. He turns to
face CAIN, who is frozen in place
with a frying pan raised in the
air.

                    ABEL
              (looking amused)
              What are you doing
              brother?

Cain, usually quick with his words,
is at a loss.

                    ABEL
                 (teasingly)
              You're not attempting to
              murder me, are you?

Their mother, EVE, standing at the
kitchen door, interrupts with a
loud yell.

                     EVE
                (disapprovingly)
              Cain! Murder hasn't even
              been invented yet! Just
              imagine the legal bills!
              Put that pan down and
              help me with the
              groceries, the both of
              you.

Reluctantly, Cain lowers the frying
pan.
Abel smirks, enjoying his brother's
momentary defeat.

                    ABEL
                 (mocking)
              Can't even be first at
              that.

                    CAIN
                (defensively)
              You think you're better
              than me.

                    ABEL
                 (confidently)
              No brother, I am better
              than you.

                    CAIN
                 (suggestively)
              Well, little brother, how
              about we prove it through
              life rather than death?

Abel looks suspicious but
intrigued.

                    ABEL
                 (curiously)
              How so?

Cain leans in, making a secretive
proposition.

                    CAIN
              Make a vow to me. We will
              each devote our lives to
              pursuing life in the
              fullest. In forty years'
              time, we allow a third
              party to decide who lived
              best. The loser takes his
              own life.

                    ABEL
                 (smirks again)
              A third party?

Cain points upward, implying that YAHWEH himself will be the arbiter of their contest.

Both boys look up, acknowledging the ombudsman in the sky.

Eve enters again, struggling to carry two heavy grocery bags.

Their father, ADAM, seated in the living room, yells from behind his newspaper.

> ADAM
> (demanding)
> Boys! Stop inventing murder and help your mother.

Adam's attention returns to the paper.

> ADAM
> (to himself)
> Or I'll never hear the end of it.

The boys rush to help their mother as the curtain closes, signaling the end of Act 1. Before the curtain closes fully, Adam shuts the paper and looks at it.

ADAM
How is there this much
news already?

***

The crew shuffled around us in a frenzy, rearranging the set backstage for Act 2.

"That was great, you guys!" Tom whispered, hugging Al and me. (Dressed as Adam and Eve.)

Act 2 also starts five years later. Both boys have moved out of the house and are well on their way. The first scene utilized a split stage effect, with two telephones connecting the action, and the lights only focusing on the scene(s) with activity.

Backstage was a kind of heaven, peering from the side through a hole in the curtain, watching the faces in the audience from the darkness, knowing when the laughs or shocks are coming. It all builds a camaraderie among actors that is hard to explain. Al and I crouched against each other, holding hands and trying to hold our laughter.

***

INT. CAIN AND ABEL'S CHILDHOOD HOME

Cain and Abel are wearing sweaters,
Santa hats, drinking eggnog, and
standing in front of a Christmas
tree.

ABEL

So what have you been up
to, old boy, murdering
for hire?

                CAIN
        Quite the contrary,
        child. I've committed my
        life to pacifism.

                ABEL
        Bullsh—

A 'lightning strike' hits from the
corner off-stage. (The effect is
achieved by the flicker of two
lightbulbs, timed an instant apart,
with the corresponding sound effect
from hitting a round cookie sheet.)

                ABEL (cont'd)
        (cowering, looking up)
            'Bulls sure are strong,'
            I meant to say. 'Bulls
            are strong!' Great work
            on them Yahweh.

The rumbling sound calms.

                CAIN
        (regaining composure)
            Anyway, it's true. Right
            now, I'm headed to work
            in a pacifist camp near
            an ocean. I hear it never
            rains there, and the food

                    is gourmet. (beat) I'm
                    thinking of calling it
                    the 'Pacifist Ocean.'

                         ABEL
                    As big and deep as your
                    bullsh—

A lightning storm hits as the boys
take cover.

                         * * *

The rest of the act continues with Cain and Abel losing touch as they live their lives through the next thirty-five years.

Abel is industrious, working his way up the ranks of the large meat processor Armour and Company before leaving to start his own company. He is happily married (there are jokes about his wife closely resembling their sister), has many children, and contributes mightily to his town, providing jobs at his slaughterhouse.

After leaving the pacifist camp, Cain rides the railroads as a hobo, assisting various strangers in ways they weren't even aware of. At the end of his journey, Cain is a hermit living in the woods alone, eating roots and writing poetry.

Both men feel they have won the bet they made many years ago to live their best life. They call Yahweh (played by the head of the camp, Joe Simmons, dressed in a bedsheet) on the phone and ask him for a verdict.

                         ***

INT. HEAVEN - DAY

Yahweh answers the phone.

>   YAHWEH
>   Have it Yahweh Pancake
>   House, Yahweh speaking.

Yahweh listens to a question.

>   YAHWEH (cont'd)
>   A life well lived, eh?
>   Hmm... Well, having never
>   been a human myself,
>   well, not yet anyway —
>   what's that? Oh, never
>   mind, you'll read about
>   it in the sequel. Anyhoo,
>   I think you'll need a
>   human judge for this one.
>   How about your old man?

Cain and Abel are both leaning into
the phone to listen. Cain
scratches his head.

>   CAIN
>   (to Abel)
>   I haven't checked in on
>   Dad for a while.

                    ABEL
          Yeah, it's been a stretch
          for me, too. But we live
          900 years, so missing
          forty is like a lost
          weekend, right?

                    YAHWEH
          Tell that to Moses.

                    CAIN
          Who?

                    YAHWEH
                 (to himself)
          Oh, right. He doesn't
          show up for a while
          either. Things have to
          get pret-ty wet first.

Cain and Abel look at each other,
confused.

               YAHWEH (cont'd)
          Then of course come the
          space squid attacks.

Cain and Abel's eyes widen in
terror.

               YAHWEH (cont'd)
                 (to himself)
          I probably shouldn't joke
          like that. Someone may
          write it down.

                    186

Yahweh looks at the phone, frustrated. He throws it down, snaps his finger, and walks over to Cain and Abel, still holding the phone, shocked to see Yahweh in the flesh.

                    YAHWEH
              (raising hands to
              mouth to amplify)
              Adam??

Adam leaps in from the side of the stage and stands at attention.

                    ADAM
              Present drill sergeant!

                    YAHWEH
              Knock that off.

Adam stands 'at ease' with his hands formally behind his back.

                    ADAM
              Whatever you say, drill
              sergeant.

Yahweh points at the others on stage.

                    YAHWEH
              He's the only one who
              gets to do that.

Adam acts nonchalant when Yahweh's back is turned.

                    YAHWEH
          I can still see you,
          Adam.

Adam and the others straighten up. Yahweh rolls his eyes and tousles Adam's hair.

                    YAHWEH
          Oh, I can't stay mad.
          You'll always be my
          number one.
               (beat)

          YAHWEH (cont'd)
          Now, Adam, it's a simple
          question. Who lived the
          better life?

                    ADAM
          Yes sir.
          (looking around)
          Just making sure there's
          no women around to mess
          this one up.
               (beat)
          Okay then, let's start
          with Cain, my firstborn.
          He put down his murderous
          frying pan and committed
          himself to peace. Very

commendable. And seeing
him living a life of
solitude in the woods
reminds me of the times
we had in the garden
before things got, well,
complicated.

                    YAHWEH
          (looking around himself)
          I don't see Eve anywhere.
                    (beat)
          Yeah, complicated is a
          good word.

All the men on stage nod their
heads.

                    ADAM
          You know Pops, no one
          ever asks me about those
          times.

                    YAHWEH
          Between you and me, I
          think they're afraid we
          were fine without them.

Adam and Yahweh share a moment.
Yahweh motions him back to the
topic at hand.

                    ADAM
          Yes, and Abel, my good
          boy. Always doing the

right thing. First in his
class. Captain of the
goat-sacrificing team.
Would make any father
proud. Even you.

Yahweh shrugs and acknowledges.

                    YAHWEH
          So Abel, then?

                    ADAM
          I didn't say that. See, I
          keep returning to one
          thing both boys failed to
          do with their lives.
                    (beat)
          Dad, what was the most
          common thing you and I
          did in those early days?
          Before the garden, what
          did we love most?

Yahweh pauses and smile.

                    YAHWEH
               (to himself)
          We danced.

                    ADAM
          Oh c'mon Pops, say it
          loud for those in the
          back rows.

                    YAHWEH

                         (booming)
                    We danced!

                         ADAM
         (pacing, acting professorial)
                    Exactly! One might even
                    argue it was the primary
                    activity of humanity.

                         YAHWEH
                    Interesting take on
                    things.

                         ADAM
                    Many thanks. Coming from
                    you, that means a lot.

                         YAHWEH
                    So what will you decide
                    then? Shall no one win
                    the contest? Are you
                    saying neither son lived
                    a worthwhile life?

                         ADAM
                    Not exactly. My answer is
                    neither this one nor
                    that. Neither yes or no.
                    Instead, my answer is to
                    step around the question
                    and see the backside of
                    it.

All on stage lean in with
anticipation turning to interest.

                    ADAM (cont'd)
                The true answer... is to
                absolve the contest. Like
                it never happened. And,
                in its place, and you're
                gonna love this Daddy-o,
                I offer a sacrifice.

The two boys talk at once, arguing
and pointing fingers.

                    YAHWEH
            (with lightning and thunder)
                Enough! My chosen one has
                made his decision, and
                all will respect it.
                    (beat)
                Adam, what is your
                sacrifice?

                    ADAM
                A sacrifice of dance.

The boys yell again in chaos.

                    YAHWEH
                    (raising arms)
                Wait, wait... I've gotta
                agree, Adam. A dance is
                not much of a sacrifice.

                    ADAM
                But Father, it's the
                purest form of sacrifice.

                        192

When we dance, we give up
our most valuable
possession, our time, in
celebration of our most
valuable gift: our life.

Yahweh ponders for a moment. He
walks over to Cain and stares him
down, then Abel and stares him
down, then walks to Adam and raises
a fist. Instead of smiting Adam, he
hugs him and leans in.

                    YAHWEH
              (privately to Adam)
               But Sonny, isn't ending a
               play with a dance number
               a bit… cliché? I mean
               what is this, amateur
               hour?

                    ADAM
              (motioning to crowd)
               Technically yes, no one's
               getting paid here.

Yahweh turns to the audience.

                    YAHWEH
               Good point.
              (booming with lighting
                 and thunder)
               Hit it, boys!

Drums start beating from the back.
Seven angels dressed in white robes
march in. Adam and Yahweh break
into a synchronized dance number.
The others on stage join them.

Yahweh puts up his hands to stop
the music.

> YAHWEH
> Wait, wait... Adam,
> where's that girl of
> yours?

A seductive drumbeat starts up, and
Eve sticks her leg out from behind
the curtain into the spotlight. The
actors whistle and go wild. She
continues until fully revealed.
Yahweh and Adam nod in approval.
Adam and Eve meet in the middle of
the stage for a silent moment of
embrace before starting an
energetic Charleston. They dance
like teenagers.

Yahweh joins in, and eventually,
Cain, Abel, and their whole crew
join as well. All the actors walk
into the crowd, dancing and
swinging with the outstretched
hands of the audience. The dance
continues for several moments until
the final note, when all turn to

Yahweh, standing alone at center
stage.

                    YAHWEH
          I am well pleased.

Lights go out.

THE END.

CHAPTER 19

A toy donkey

In late July 1937, Tobias Randall boarded a ship headed for Berlin. Technically, his job was to perform as General Assistant to the Senior Vice President of Marketing for AT&T. Practically this meant Randall was to provide the VP and his mistress with items and food at their whim.

Tobias befriended some of the other assistants, making a name for himself by playing cards. As a cover story, he claimed to be the cousin of the former General Assistant who had taken ill just before the journey. (In truth, the original assistant had been left at home on purpose, reassigned by top AT&T brass due to threatening demands by a certain M.I.T. professor.)

Upon arrival in Germany, a welcome party greeted

the passengers with a grand ceremony. The large group stayed at the Hotel Kaiserhof, where Tobias shared a room with two assistants of senior VPs at IBM, Hal Quick and Sutcliffe Horner.

After the VPs and their respective mistresses retired, Hal proposed the assistants get a taste of real German nightlife.

"You'll never have the chance again," Hal said. "All the bars'll be bombed to rubble."

The trio climbed out of the fire escape and walked down the block to a crowded coffee shop playing live music. They found a table in a quieter rear room.

Many young people were there, including four girls at a table in the corner. One was very attractive, and the other three tried very hard. The boys moved a long table over so they could sit together. Tobias sat across from a plain-looking blonde-haired female.

Tobias leaned in and whispered in German. "We'd make some great Arian babies."

"I've heard that one before," she said, smiling and revealing a crooked front tooth.

Aware of its crookedness, she closed her lips.

"It's ok," Tobias said. "You have a nice smile."

She smiled again with her mouth closed.

"You from Berlin?" Tobias asked, and the blonde shook her head yes. "I'm American," Tobias said. The girl shook her head again.

"You like the flag?"

Tobias pointed to a Nazi flag on the wall opposite

the group.

The girl shrugged, nodded, and took a sip of her drink.

"You like Hitler?"

She nodded the same way.

"You like coffee?"

She grinned, once again showing her teeth.

Hal smacked Tobias's shoulder.

"Our boy here can speak German perfectly," Hal said. "How'd you say 'perfectly' in German?"

Tobias said 'perfectly' in Hebrew.

The boys smiled at the girls, not knowing the difference. The girls looked at each other, not understanding.

Tobias stood and shouted, "Heil Hitler!"

The crowd erupted with cheers.

"Glory to the Nazi party!" he said, in German.

Cheers.

"And may their reign last a thousand years!"

The crowd roared.

Next, Tobias yelled in Hebrew, "Adolph mates with a donkey daily!"

Cheers.

The blonde girl kissed Tobias on the cheek. The boys raised their glasses.

Her name was Holly. She was a nanny for a wealthy

couple and their three children. The father was an official in the SS, while the mother held fundraisers.

"Oh, they're wonderful!" Holly said. "There's Renate at twelve, Hans at eight, and baby Dieter at three."

"What is Ranete reading?" Tobias asked. "*Max and Moritz*?"

"Yes, of course!"

"Don't you find their punishment a bit over the top?"

"It's just a story. Besides, they had it coming!"

"They certainly did," Tobias said.

(*Max and Moritz* is a classic German children's book about two prankster boys who are ground up and fed to ducks in the end.)

They finished their drinks and left the café as a group.

Everyone begged Tobias to continue with them, but he was getting tired. Holly pleaded with him, whispering a proposition in his ear that bears not repeated.

Tobias walked towards the fire escape where they'd escaped the hotel and waited until the rest of the group was out of sight before going in the other direction.

At the first bridge Tobias approached, he expected several drunks to be camping underneath but found none. He walked to the next bridge, which was also empty, and then the next. He went into a nearby bar and noticed, for the first time since entering Germany not a single person looked poor or disheveled.

He jogged down back alleyways, ducked under more bridges, and entered every bar in the area. There were no vagrants anywhere.

Tobias finally sat on a bench. A man walking a dog passed, and Tobias asked him for a cigarette in German.

"Nice night," Tobias said.

"Hmm."

"Used to be you couldn't enjoy an evening alone without getting robbed. But no more."

"Heil Hitler," the man said, lighting a smoke.

"My mother was attacked by a tramp once."

"Work-shy trash," the man said.

"They certainly are."

***

The next day, a luncheon was held at the hotel, with an awards banquet planned for that night.

The AT&T vice president and his mistress went sightseeing during the luncheon, leaving Tobias to do their laundry.

Tobias learned from the other assistants that hotel staff performed the service. So he went to the basement laundry facilities and watched the workers load and unload the large machines.

That night's awards banquet was a massive affair. While all the VIPs waited their turn in the lobby to be transported by chauffeur, the AT&T VP and his mistress sat silently at the bar, trying to get drunk; by that point very well sick of each other.

Hal leaned over to Tobias. "A moment made

possible by Americans paying their phone bills."

"It certainly is."

When it was their time to go, Tobias climbed in front with the driver.

CHAPTER 20

A piece of sheet music

Tobias stood in the shadows along the wall with the other aides. He positioned himself next to the stage, watching the dignitaries of commerce shuffling to their seats inside the cavernous Berlin Opera House.

"This is the best we can do?" he said.

A Nazi guard grinned and replied with the only three English words he knew, "Yes! Very exciting!"

After a few speeches, the man of the hour was greeted with worshipful applause.

He displayed the rarest of poise: entirely uncomfortable while fully relishing the moment. A boy who became all-powerful without friends. It was as simple as that.

Hitler's speech was 357 words, of which 67 were lies. His foundational fabrication was a 'proposal for world peace through shared economic success.' -The same message IBM President Thomas Watson had pushed earlier.

Hitler finally sat in a folding chair on stage not twenty feet from Tobias, where he remained for the next hour.

Neither fat or slim, short or tall, handsome or ugly. The man smiled, nodded, coughed, and shifted his body position at appropriate times and in regular intervals. — The exact image a visitor to Earth, upon returning to their home planet, might portray while describing a human.

CHAPTER 21

A hole punch

That night, Hal and Sutcliffe insisted Tobias go out again, saying Holly had been asking about him.

"It's the perfect opportunity for hedonism without moral consequence," Randall said. "In a year, these girls'll be bombed to pieces along with the bars. Our activities will exist in memory alone and fully justified in our deepest psyches as an act of war."

Hal and Sutcliffe froze with their mouths open, then burst into laughter.

Hal brought hard alcohol and promised to show the group something they'd never seen before. After meeting the girls, he led their group on foot over two miles into an increasingly industrial area.

Hal studied a piece of paper and checked several back-alley doors until he found one open.

"If you're going to murder us, my compliments on your planning," Tobias said in German, but the girls didn't laugh.

Even before the door opened, they could hear the whirring. Down three flights of stairs, the cacophony morphed into crunching. When Hal opened the final door, the unbuffered sound waves blew the little group backward.

The low-ceilinged room was the size of a city block, full of running machinery.

They moved ahead, twisting their bodies nimbly through rows of spinning gears. Beige punch cards shot from here to there, pushing through the intricate mess with instantaneous speed.

A card fluttered off track and landed at Tobias's feet. It contained print on both sides and small punched holes throughout. He read aloud the name printed thereon: *August Seibert.*

Amidst the deafening noise, Hal pointed at his lips and mouthed with exaggeration three letters: "I-B-M."

CHAPTER 22

A porcelain angel

Tobias Randall was there, on Peacock Island, for the night of the grandest Nazi extravaganza ever held.

Hundreds of pre-teen girls dressed as angels greeted the 4,000 guests as they exited their ferry boats. The winged beings lined either side of a walking path leading to a grand castle intricately garnished with Arabian décor. The expansive courtyard bar boasted 80 bartenders, ready to unleash an ocean of stockpiled wine. A thousand waiters distributed storerooms of food sufficient to feed a small nation.

On the guest list was Thea von Harbou, former wife of Fritz Lang and screenwriter of *Metropolis*.

Tobias located and followed Ms. von Harbou until

she was alone.

"Fritz still thinks of you," Tobias said in German.

Von Harbou turned and, seeing a young man before her, smiled.

"And what are his thoughts?"

"That you are the maschinenmensch."

Von Harbou laughed.

"Did he tell you that?" she said.

"In a round-about way."

Von Harbou rolled her eyes.

"Is it so impossible you were his only love?" Tobias said, inching closer.

Von Harbou took a drag from her cigarette. "Oh, I'm sure of that, but I'm not the maschinenmensch."

"If not you, then who?"

"Boys and control," she said, stepping closer to pat his cheek and study his features. "Why are you so interested in the love life of an old woman?"

"Why are you not in America with him?"

She laughed and motioned around.

"Isn't it obvious?"

"Smoke and mirrors, my lady. You're better than this."

"Oh child," von Harbou said, "and Fritz is not in the land of smoke and mirrors?"

The legendary screenwriter sat and took a drink, deciding whether to continue with the young stranger.

Several German couples passed and greeted her.

"I am Fritz's second wife," she continued when they were alone. "He had a first."

"Lisa Rosenthal."

"Yes."

"Did he kill her?"

"Doesn't matter," she shrugged. "The maschinenmensch is dead."

She blew smoke at the young man.

"Come back with me," Tobias said, extending his hand. "Unite the head and hands with the heart."

Von Harbou laughed. She stood, patted Tobias again, and walked away.

There was a commotion in the crowd. Tobias looked up and saw Joseph Goebbels standing at a podium with Hjalmar Schacht, the Nazi Minister of Economics. They were motioning to Thomas Watson, seated in front with a large medal pinned to his suitcoat.

"The Order of the German Eagle," Schacht proclaimed, "was awarded to a foreign diplomat who has made himself worthy of the Reich."

Tobias grabbed a feather from a nearby girl's angel wings and stole a hat sitting on a table. He climbed onto the stage next to Schacht and looked straight into the camera.

Tobias abandoned the International Chamber of Commerce group that night, finding passage back to America on a different steam liner. He kept silent the entire trip, watching immigrants eat their few pieces of stale bread, never seeing people so grateful.

At Ellis Island, Tobias bought a train ticket west, finally getting off in Waterloo, Iowa, for no reason at all.

CHAPTER 23

Two weeks to the day, we held our second performance. Word had gotten around Waldport, and we had to stack the dining room tables and push the stage back thirty feet to make room for the crowd.

At the very moment Cain raised his frying pan to smite Abel, Horris Caldwell burst in through the back doors.

He shouted inaudibly and collapsed to his knees, covered in mud.

"Oh, my God!" a petite brunette named Carol Burton screamed. (An unfortunate term, as the audience thought it was part of the play. Rather, Carol knew Horris was her husband Peter's tree-snagging partner.)

"Trunk crushed him," Horris was panting. "Pete's still under it." He swallowed and pointed behind him, "Truck's stuck, ten miles up."

The CO men grabbed Horris by the arms and piled into the camp's other truck.

Al moved to go with them, but I grabbed his arm. Carol was trying to leave with the men, but I had her elbow with my other arm.

"You'll go with us in our car," I said.

All three of us sat in the front seat, silent except for the jostling of the car's suspension against the forest road. I was still holding Carol's arm. The road got rougher a few miles up, and we slowed to a crawl in the dark, our headlights bouncing through the coastal fog. Five, then eight miles passed. Finally, we saw the Camp Gabriel truck stuck on the side of the road, with the other eight men from the snagging outfit sitting in the bed. Tom Graves emerged from the forest. A newer man I didn't know spoke with him. Then Tom approached Al's window.

"It's about a mile-and-a-half northeast into the woods," Tom said.

Carol leaned over Al, "Is he ok?! He's ok? You're getting him?"

"We're heading in," Tom said. "But it's pitch dark out there, ma'am. All manner of tangled undergrowth. I barely trust myself—"

Carol wiggled over my lap and grabbed the door handle, spilling us both out.

"I'll stay with her," I said, regaining Carol's arm. "We'll be right close behind."

"It's too dark," Al said.

"We'll be right behind."

211

Tom was right. It was an ancient virgin forest, and the undergrowth was substantial. The night was starless, and with the tree cover, it was nearly a blackout. Even walking a few feet behind the men, it was impossible to move forward without looking down. As a result, Carol and I got separated from the group.

"We need to be still," I said, squeezing Carol's shoulders. "Stop now. Listen."

We stood in place, hearing no sound of the men.

"Pete?!" Carol yelled.

She moved us forward; her hands outstretched, tugging us this way and that.

I bore down with all my might and felt for her face.

"Stop this!" I yelled, patting her cheek with my hand.

Carol leaned her whole weight on me, releasing proper sobs.

"All alone!" she yelled, right next to my ear and loud as the confusion of hell.

When she quieted, I heard Al's call.

"Al?"

"Jane?"

"*Al?*"

"Jane!"

After a couple of false starts, we finally connected. (Al, who was always gentle with me, pulled the wind out of both us ladies with his embrace.)

The group was only a short distance ahead, stopped

in a clearing which allowed more light.

"Peter!" Carol screamed. She ran to some men standing by a giant fallen Douglas fir. Her husband was pinned underneath, still clinging to life by a ligament.

"He's alive?" I asked.

Tom nodded.

"The tree's too large to lift," Al said. "Even if we could… we're too remote. We're just too remote."

The felled tree had taken an odd turn when breaking due to extensive rot in the low trunk. (The reason why it was being cut.) Peter had wisely stood off to the left when it fell, but its upper branches snagged on neighboring trees, causing a twist. It first landed on another downed tree, creating a pivot fulcrum, then swung back and settled with its enormous base squarely on Peter's chest.

It had already been four hours since the accident when we arrived. (After the tree fell, Horris panicked and started running for help, but he got lost and couldn't remember where the tree was when he finally found someone.)

Carol cradled Peter's head until he passed and stayed with his body until sunrise. What they whispered to each other in that forest, I never asked and didn't want to know.

The next day, the entire camp of men abandoned their regular duties to lift the tree and recover the body. The U.S. government provided $100 for the funeral. It was the only support Carol would ever receive. The casket cost $125.

***

"How terrible that was," I said, handing Al a bowl to dry. "Dying so far from home."

"Indeed," Al said. But his voice cracked, finally sparking my memory of his own tragedy in the woods with his first wife.

I hugged him.

"Not Jane," he said, leaning into me.

He shook his head.

"Not Jane," he said.

"No, of course not," I said. "Not Jane." I patted the back of his neck. "Not Jane."

The sweet man stepped back, wiped his eyes, and kept drying the dishes.

"I've been thinking," he said. "Carol and the kids have nothing."

"I don't know what you're going to say, but I agree to it already."

Al's plan, as we would work out almost entirely by the time dishes were done, was to give 'Al's Fill n' Time' to Carol Burton and Sally Fairfield outright.

We returned to Stramwell to help the ladies start it back up and Al hired a couple of retired mechanics who owed him favors. The ladies and their kids would live behind the shop in Al's old house.

Once back at camp, Al and I approached four men from the camp who showed the most promise and began planning the opening of four different 'Peace Stations' in their respective towns after the war.

All four men selected were from the West Coast—

Sam from Salem, Tom from Tacoma, and Sal and Mick from Los Angeles.

Shop locations were quickly scouted by their respective family members back home. Two men, Sal and Mick, had wives who would return home to prepare the way so that they could launch directly into business when the men were released.

Word spread of our arrangements, and no less than ten other men approached us with interest. To not extend the endeavor too thin, we devised a system whereby these men would assist with the start-up of the initial four shops. The group would pool money and when they had saved enough for expansion, these men would start new shops.

At night in our cabin, listening to Al's snores in concert with the far-off ocean waves, I pictured the camp from above. All of us, asleep on cots or worn-out mattresses, tired from hard labor, taking hold of a plan.

CHAPTER 24

A tin can

Tobias Randall exited a train in Waterloo, Iowa, and entered a diner. He opened the local paper and put his finger on the first classified ad, finding a job and renting a room the same way.

Randall began work the following Monday at 4:00 a.m., standing in the darkness of a truck yard while a man named Aloysius instructed him to hoist a large metal can onto his head.

"Use your legs," Aloysius bounced. "Let it sit on your head. Other guys say shoulders is fine, but their backs are messed up and they wonder why. Use your head. They don't like the juice, see. But juice is a part of life. It'll run down your neck, but that's better'n a screwed-up back."

"Juice?"

"Garbage juice. You'll be takin' your clothes off outside 'fore you go in the house. You got a wife?

"No."

"Find one. You're gonna need her."

Three minutes into his first day, Tobias started developing a concept for a wheeled bin collection system using a truck mounted, hydraulic side-arm tipper. He was midway into mentally drafting the necessary additions to city code language when he realized what he was doing and stopped himself.

Tobias focused on breathing and the weight of his body against the earth with each step. He set his mind to notice the flaking paint on the houses, the cut grass blades on the lawns, the face of an elderly housewife through a window as she made her husband's coffee at a stove, how a child stared with curiosity when he entered a backyard.

This all gave him another idea.

CHAPTER 25

A Children's Book of ABC's

Tobias found a wife in 1940. Her name was Helen, and she was the waitress who served him when he first came into Waterloo off the train from New York.

Helen was quiet and polite. Tobias took her to see *Buck Rogers* on their first date.

"I'm going to be an airline hostess," she said. "I'll play with the children to keep them busy and point out places of interest down below for the adults."

Tobias Randall spent what von Neuman called 'the best years of the mind' collecting garbage. At night, he read.

On his arrival, the Waterloo library had 10,345

books, and Randall set a schedule to read them all.

The first book, organized by the Dewey Decimal System, was *Flatland* by Edwin Abbott. The book begins:

Of the Nature of Flatland:

I call our world Flatland, not because we call it so, but to make its nature more apparent to you, my happy readers, who are privileged to live in Space.

The story centers around a 2-dimensional 'flat' world that comes into contact with a 3-dimensional spherical character.

Out of curiosity, Tobias went to the last book in the library before starting his reading journey. It was *Through the First Antarctic Night 1898-1899*, by Frederick A. Cook, an American explorer.

The book concludes:

The favourable criticism of the geographers of all lands convince us of what we had hardly dared to hope, that the expedition was an entire success. I am sure that I voice the sentiment of every member of the expedition when I say that in receiving the substantial recognition of King Leopold, of the various scientific societies, and above all of our fellow-countrymen, we feel that we have been rewarded beyond our deserts. Such appreciation by knowing critics is indeed the highest honour which falls to man.

The author, explorer Frederick A. Cook, actually ended his life in public disgrace. He claimed to be the first to reach the summit of Denali in 1906 and the North Pole in 1907, and both were publicly proven wrong. In 1923 he was convicted of stock fraud and sentenced to 14 years in prison. Roosevelt pardoned him in 1940, shortly before Cook's death of a cerebral hemorrhage.

During the Antarctic voyage detailed in *Through the First Antarctic Night,* their ship, the *Belgica,* became irrevocably lodged in ice for months during the season when the sun did not rise above the horizon. The captain and many other men began losing control of their minds and bodies from scurvy and mental malaise.

Dr. Cook remembered his experiences with the native peoples of Greenland from years prior and, on a hunch, prescribed the men eat only a diet of fresh penguin and seal meat, which Cook hunted for them. Cook also required the men to stand naked before a fire each day for an extended period, a therapy he called 'baking treatment.'

The men ultimately recovered from their scurvy, and Cook had made a breakthrough in modern medicine. (The meat contained vitamin C.)

Famed explorer Roald Amundsen was the first mate on the Belgica. He credited Cook for saving his life and later visited the doctor in prison several times to show support. In 1911 Amundsen became the first human to reach the South Pole. In 1926 he was the first to the North Pole.

The only thing that slowed Tobias's reading quest was the physical turning of pages, so he built a small machine to do it for him at the twitch of a finger. To combat eye fatigue, Tobias invented a powered device set to a metronome at 57 beats per minute to move a book slightly from left to right so that his eyes might stay fixed in one position.

After acclimation and much practice, he sped up the device and improved his already expeditious reading speed by a factor of 2.12.

Averaging his usual 4.14 hours of sleep per night, Tobias calculated it would take 7.00 years to finish the library.

Work continued as usual, walking to the back of four hundred houses daily, lifting the garbage from the house can into the bin on his head, and depositing it in the truck when full.

Tobias and Helen honeymooned over a weekend at the Corn Palace in Mitchell, South Dakota, where they observed the newly installed Russian-style onion domes.

In a burst of passion, Tobias impregnated Helen in a small upstairs restroom, but the baby did not take.

CHAPTER 26

A baby doll

Helen eventually gave birth to their only child, William Norbert John Randall, at midnight on January 2nd, 1941. Holding him for the first time, Tobias wondered, also for the first time, if his gifts were genetic. After determining his capabilities were a fluke of chance and that the baby should be treated as commonly as possible, Tobias laughed uncontrollably for two minutes.

CHAPTER 27

A rock

Aloysius Matthews filled the waste bin and lifted it smoothly, carrying over a hundred lbs. on his head from house to house. He was a large man in his mid-50s, well-built and agile. Aloysius had worked for the sanitation department for thirty-five years, and, like all other sanitation workers except for Tobias, he was black. He made a barely survivable wage for his family, with no pension, health care, or savings. Tobias Randall worked under the man, hauling cans on the same route for seven years. They ate lunch together and took turns riding in the hopper when it rained.

Tobias visited Aloysius Matthews's house only once, when a call came over the radio that Mrs. Matthews was in labor. They broke route and drove the garbage truck over.

The Matthews house leaned six and a half degrees to the left and had one bedroom. It was still early morning when they arrived, and two children were sleeping with blankets on the living room floor. Aloysius's wife was in bed.

"Dr. Wilbury's comin'," she whispered.

When Dr. Wilbury arrived, Tobias took the small children to the porch, the distance barely muffling their mother's screams.

"She gonna die?" the boy said.

"Improbable," Tobias said.

The mother yelled again.

Tobias picked up a few rocks from the dirt in front of the steps, then drew a twelve-inch circle six feet in front of them, an eight-inch circle above it to the right, and a four-inch circle higher above to the left. He handed each of them a rock.

"It's one point if you get your rock into the big circle, three points for the smaller circle, and fifteen points for the tiny circle. You get ten throws each. What are your names?"

Tobias wrote all three of their names in the dirt. He tossed a rock and missed the smallest 4-inch circle. He wrote a zero under his name and motioned to the boy. The boy threw his rock and landed it inside the big circle. Tobias drew a one under his name. Tobias told the little girl to throw.

She turned the stone over in her hand. When Tobias tried to move her arm to display a throwing motion, she shook her head and held the rock to her heart.

Tobias and the boy smiled to each other and continued the game.

Tobias kept missing the four-inch circle. The boy threw his first four rocks into the big circle, noticed what Tobias was doing, then tossed at the eight-inch circle.

The boy scored nine points before their tenth and final throw, while Tobias's score remained zero. Tobias threw his last rock, again at the smallest circle, barely missing. He clapped his hands and laughed. The boy smiled and threw his rock at the smallest circle. The stone landed close but missed as well. He clapped his hands.

They looked at the little girl, who'd been imitating throwing. She noticed them watching and held the rock close again. When the girl finally did throw, they had to duck out of the way.

CHAPTER 28

A pill bottle

In July of 1944, Tobias Randall was twenty-three years old and had just finished the final book in the Waterloo Public Library. After returning the book, he pivoted from the circulation desk and picked up a *New York Times*.

The previous week, William James Sidis had died of a brain aneurysm. He was forty-six. The obituary labeled him a 'burned out' genius who lived in squalor collecting expired streetcar transfers from the ground. There was no mention of *The Animate and the Inanimate* or *The Tribes and the States*.

The article provided details that Sidis had sued, personally represented himself, and lost a libel case against *The New Yorker* magazine for a disparaging

'Where Are They Now' piece famed humorist James Thurber wrote under a pseudonym in 1937. Thurber claimed he gained access to Sidis's private life and impoverished living quarters via an anonymous source.

In the lawsuit, Sidis claimed he had no extraordinary gifts that would warrant public interest and that exposure from the piece had caused him irreparable harm. Sidis posited he was 'a private citizen with the right to remain so without a national publication exploiting the details of his life to sell magazines.'

The next day, Tobias Randall got his first headache. He immediately dropped his trash bin and walked to a train station storage locker where he'd kept new clothes, identification, and cash.

Tobias called the public works superintendent, a man he had made a private financial arrangement with, who informed Mrs. Helen Randall that her husband died that morning in the hopper of a garbage truck and was inadvertently crushed beyond recognition.

A box of ashes would be provided, along with a monthly check for her to accommodate Tobias's lost wages until she remarried. (Tobias arranged this funding separately with the superintendent as the trash company provided no death benefits. Randall also set aside a trust fund for their son, William, to provide for his education.)

Aloysius Matthews received a substantial check in the mail with no return address and only an account number listed as the payee. Mr. Matthews vigorously argued with the bank manager, saying the check didn't belong to him. But the manager, prepared for such a protest, held firm that it was authentic.

Aloysius tossed the check in the air and stormed

out.

Mrs. Matthews politely picked up the check, returned the same day, and cashed it.

Tobias Randall boarded a train for the Mexican border enroute to Argentina.

CHAPTER 29

It turns out that what people want in an auto mechanic are the same qualities often possessed by conscientious objectors. As such, the Peace Station locations thrived in every market we entered.

By 1947, all four of our first shops had sprouted at least one other, and there were plans for more. Marge and Dot set up The Peace Station corporate offices at our house.

Amidst all the business excitement came delightful news from Compton and Birdwhistle. A film version of *The Senators* was greenlit once again, and this time it was for real.

Marge, Dot, and I convinced Al to take us to Los Angeles for a week, where he could visit the four Peace Stations (two outcrops from Sal and Mick's originals). Additionally, Theodore Compton, agent extraordinaire, had secured us ladies backstage passes to watch film production of *The Senators* on the studio lot.

I had been to Los Angeles on previous trips with Al to set up the original shops. We visited the Millennium Biltmore lobby and ate an appetizer at Romanoff's, but never saw real behind-the-scenes Hollywood action.

Dot and Marge, both fantastic movie buffs themselves, were thrilled at the opportunity. Dot purchased for us the latest fashion scarves and bug-eye sunglasses at JHB's (John Harrell's Boutique) on Sunset. My glasses were rhinestone studded.

Our liaison with the film crew was a production assistant named Clark, a boisterous young man who reveled in showing off for us backwoods ladies.

"Over there is where they filmed the ocean liner cabin scene in *The Lady Eve*," he said, taking an incredibly sharp turn in our transport cart.

We barely grazed the backside of a man carrying a tray of coffees. He spun away just in time to avoid full impact, then swore at us.

"Sorry for that, ladies," Clark said. "People can be so inconsiderate here. It's a cut-throat business."

"They didn't film *The Lady Eve* on a boat?" Marge asked, adjusting her crooked glasses.

"Oh, Dear," Clark said. "Nothing is filmed on a boat."

Clark introduced us to the script director, Sal Bridges, a short, bookish man.

"As I live and breathe," he said, patting his chest. "Jane Alexander and members of the UVW in the flesh. An honor. Truly."

"Oh, stop that. You're too kind," I said, evaluating Mr. Bridges. He certainly didn't seem the Hollywood type, but I was now on the inside and recognized perhaps things were different here.

"In '44, I was fortunate enough to receive a reader copy of *The Senators*," Mr. Bridges said. "It simply destroyed me. I say it's a shame the work wasn't published. Surely, the script will never reach the craft of the original writing, but I have tried my utmost to be true to it. And now at just the right time, of course."

Sal inhaled a deep breath and widened his eyes as if to imply we knew what he was talking about.

"Yes, well, thank you, Mr. Bridges," I said. "I'm sure it will be a fair representation."

When we first entered, the crew was filming the later-in-the-book barn bombing scene, even though it was early on in the shoot. This is because Hollywood does things out of order.

Sal guided us toward the action while Clark motioned for us to stay quiet.

A black woman was in a barn giving birth. Her pains struck me as so accurate they triggered not a bit of self-introspection on never having my own children and being thankful for it. Marge's mouth dropped open and Dot covered her ears.

Two white men stood in suits off camera, waiting for directions to enter the scene. When the woman let out a particularly shrill scream, the director pointed, and the men ran into the barn.

"And cut!"

"Alright, lunch everyone. Back in an hour!" a

younger man next to the director yelled.

"That's it?" Dot said.

I marched over to the director for introductions.

"Uh, Mrs. Alexander?" Clark said, trailing behind. "Mrs. Alexander, please. You can't just approach the director on set."

"Why on earth not?" I said over my shoulder. "I created this world. You'd think he'd be more than obliged. Probably even want to meet Al."

"Ma'am wait! Who's Al?"

I pressed on until I stood before the director, deeply tanned with a tailored mustache.

"I am Mrs. Jane Alexander. Head of the UVW," I said.

"Seamstress union, eh? Well, we're not paying a penny more!" he yelled, standing to leave. "You know it used to be you could profit from a picture. Now I've got to worry about some Asian woman sewing tassels. Hastings?! Get my lunch."

The director stormed off while a skinny man (Hastings, I presumed) ran in the opposite direction.

I caught up.

"You misunderstand me, sir. I am the author, well, one of the authors of *The Senators*. The novel this film is based on."

The director wiped his brow, blew his nose forcefully, replaced his cap, and pushed forward.

"I'm sorry. I should have told you," Clark said, hustling to me with Sal. "Directors are… well, not keen to give attention to writers, as a matter of practice. They feel… You see, film is a director's medium."

"Nonsense," I said. "A story is a story. And without mine, he hasn't got one."

When I entered the director's trailer he was already reclining on a small sofa with a wet towel across his face.

"So you want a line?" he said, removing the towel. "Dear God. Has Hastings lost his mind? What are you gonna do, my taxes?

"I— well, no," I said. "I'm—"

"No matter. You'll do in a pinch." He began undoing his belt. "Make it quick."

"Stop that this instant!" I said. "I, sir, am Jane Alexander, as I have previously stated."

The director squinted.

"Hastings!!"

"I came here to see a bit of the inside of things. To understand how you all manage stories for pictures," I said.

"Hastings?! Get this woman out of my trailer now!"

The director fell back and recovered his face with the towel.

I removed the towel and slapped him across the face.

"You listen good," I said. "This story is a work of genius you will never touch. So you'll give it the respect it deserves, or I'll pull the rights from under you."

The old man finally looked me in the eyes.

"You can't do a cotton-picking thing, lady," he scowled. "The studio owns the rights—all of 'em. Writers throw dung at a wall. *I* make it entertainment."

He leaned in to kiss me, and I socked him with a fully clenched fist.

He flew back with a howling laugh.

"You're all crazy!" I said, composing myself. "And you better pray sweet Al doesn't hear about this." I slammed the trailer door behind me.

"Who's sweet Al?" the director yelled from inside.

Once back at the hotel, I contacted Theodore Compton to cancel the deal outright. Instead, I received his assistant, Sam Isaacson, who explained that Pinehurst Pictures owned exclusive rights to *The Senators* in all forms, including a future novel. They could not only do with the book what they wanted but had free range to modify it in any way they saw fit.

"How could Theodore let them?"

"I think it's standard practice."

"Standard practice?"

"Oh, and I'm glad you called," Sam Isaacson said, shuffling papers in the background. "Mr. Compton wanted you to call him. He said it's urgent."

"I *am* calling him."

"Right," Sam said. "I'll tell him you called."

"Was that not the whole point of this conversation?"

"I'm sorry?"

I slammed the phone.

Al, who was in the restroom, cracked open the door.

"Everything ok, love?"

"Yes, sweet man. Everything's OK."

Everything was not OK. As I discovered on a return call from Compton, a significant movement was afoot against the UVW.

"I'm sorry, I don't understand it myself," Theodore said. "The publishers have pulled the books."

"Which ones?"

"All of them."

"What do you mean?"

"Even *For Women Only*," he paused. "Jane, there's a major piece on the UVW coming out in this weekend's *Family Livin' Magazine*. It claims you're an anti-American group. I've received an advance copy, and it doesn't look good. I'm so sorry."

"Everyone is," I said. "Mail me a copy expedited. We're driving home tonight."

***

The article was worse than I imagined. Word had gotten out of the UVW's work with conscientious objectors, which the piece portrayed as an attempt to cause our nation's youth to hate democracy. Every book or radio release of the UVW was listed and summarized, along with a description of each's 'true evil intent.' All the Peace Station addresses were provided as well.

The filming of *The Senators* was promptly canceled. The only redeeming item was I received a nasty telegram from the film director blaming me personally for the downfall of his career.

I've provided the complete *Family Livin' Magazine* piece below without permission. May they sue me for copyright infringement:

Small Town Women's Writing Group Works to Sabotage Democracy

<u>Stramwell, Oregon</u>: A woman's writing collective, headed by Mrs. Jane Alexander-Clifton, has been quietly infiltrating the hearts and minds of our nation with Red propaganda that even pre-dates the War.

This group, known as the UVW, with a host of anonymous female members, also successfully ran a war objector operation that led astray over 150 young men from providing valuable services to our nation.

Mrs. Alexander-Clifton and her husband, Alfred Clifton, have since started a chain of highly profitable auto-mechanic shops, using cheap labor from draft dodgers up and down the West Coast. Addresses for the businesses' (tongue-in-cheekily named 'Peace Stations'), are listed herein.

Neither Mr. Clifton nor Mrs. Alexander-Clifton could be reached for comment.

Also provided, with summaries, is a list of publications from the UVW and their intended propagandistic meanings. Be advised: These works may have been imposed on you or your loved ones <u>without your knowledge</u>.

Their books range on topics far and wide, including a popular children's anthology, a re-writing of Southern U.S. history, and an infamous women's lifestyle guide promoting promiscuous acts.

There was even a major Hollywood film in production based on an as-yet-unpublished work the women's group meant to take *down the democratic institution of elected representation. (***UPDATE: Our senior editors here at Family Livin' Magazine have recently learned the project is being put on indefinite hold.)*

If you or a loved one have been inadvertently tricked into purchasing such communist propaganda, please <u>do not blame yourself</u>. It is merely a by-product of the entrenchment in leftist ideology so rampant among our major publishing houses. Please be assured we at Family Livin' Magazine will never stop promoting the liberty and freedom our readers deserve, and please do not donate your UVW books or materials to local libraries. Simply dispose of them as you deem fit.

PART III

CHAPTER 30

"Yes, Mary Ann," I said. "A horse is a noun because a horse is a, what?"

"Person?" the little girl said.

"No."

"Place?"

"Um, no. A thing."

"A horse ain't a thing."

"Yes, a horse is a thing. Now, who will read the introductory paragraph on the next page?"

"My horse Daisy's my friend. A thing can't be no friend."

I stared at my empty cubby.

The Peace Stations, hard as we tried, had all folded. Carol Burton and the Fairfields even had to sell the original Al's Fill n' Time to the Jiffy n' Fill on Main St., who promptly closed it.

On my walks home after school, I often thought of young Tobias. He was just a boy without a mother, and I had never been a mother. I was a schoolteacher with formal training in child development.

One day in June 1950, I stopped at the creek longer than usual. In fact, I sat down right in the dirt. In all the years that had passed, the nagging suspicion of what lay beneath that creek bed had not waned.

I had never shared my thoughts about what might have happened to Mr. Roy Randall and Beth Meyers. Was my silence serving to protect Tobias or me? Was it to keep treachery at arm's length or maintain willful ignorance? A proper investigation would cause all sorts of problems.

My mind drifted to the image of the young man, briefly cast onto a theater screen so many years ago. It couldn't have been Tobias… And yet, it certainly could.

I walked up our stairs to find the *Reversi* board readied by Al on the porch. In the kitchen, he was cooking his specialty of cornbread and potato soup—comfort food on an uncomfortable budget. I kissed him, wrapped my arms around his neck and hung against his solid back.

"Why does a lazy dog lie in an oil patch?" he said.

"I dunno. Why?" I mumbled.

"Because why not? You got a better idea?"

"Nope."

Al kissed my hand. I went to the table and picked

up the mail, containing a copy of *The Penny Saver* and an Armstrong's advertisement presenting a home dishwasher for the low price of $169.50. There was also a single postcard.

The picture on the card was of a mountainous area covered with rainforest. I flipped the card over, and there, in blue ink, was a finely drawn feather.

I lost my breath. The postmark was from a town I didn't recognize in Argentina. The only word written was in a messy scribble at the tip of the feather: *Frances*.

Frances Malloy was one of the original UVW members. She currently taught at the new middle school in town. I called her.

Frances lived alone in the small cottage I had once lived in. I could picture the phone in the living room, with the ringing traveling through each tiny space.

"Al, take me to Frances's immediately."

"What about the soup?"

"And bring a weapon."

Al covered the soup and grabbed a garden hoe.

We drove along side streets to view the house from the back corner, then parked further away. I instructed Al to mimic my every move.

I knew the terrain well, as this was the path I took walking home from school in my previous life. The trees and bushes were more prominent now, providing good cover.

I heard a sound and held up my fist for Al to stop, as I had seen in war films with Marge and Dot. When the sound was determined to be a ground squirrel, and I waved my finger forward thrice.

When we arrived at the back corner of the property, a car turned onto the road up ahead. It was Jeff Taylor and his wife, Jeannie. They would not only recognize us but likely give an invitation to play garbage rummy at their house on that Saturday night. (Jeannie's poor-quality pound cake was rivaled only by Jeff's non-existent conversation skills.)

I backed Al under an adjacent low-branched pine tree and the Taylors motored on.

I hopped my old fence in one jump, crouched, and waved Al in.

"Mercy," he said.

Al struggled over, and we crept along the fence line toward the house. The backyard was large and covered with shade year-round from two giant pines. I noticed Frances had taken down my hand-painted signs denoting names for vegetable rows in the garden.

"Doesn't look like anyone's home," Al whispered.

We moved to the bedroom window and peeked our heads up.

One of Fran's many black cats reached from inside the house and batted my forehead. I dropped to my knees in the dirt.

"Are you ok?!" Al said.

"Darn cat," I said. "Oh, forget all this. I'm going in."

My spare key still worked in the back door.

"Fran honey?" I announced. "It's Jane and Al. Just

came to check up on you."

"Nothing looks out of order," Al said. "You think she might have gone to town?"

Al and I visited all the regular stores in town to no avail, then called Sheriff Tawlins.

I showed Taw the postcard and, caring no longer to hide anything, presented the entire Tobias Randall saga to him.

"Hmm," Taw said, tipping his hat back. "Have you checked on the other ladies?"

We scrambled back to the house to get my phone number book and make calls. Sheriff Tawlins drove to check out Frances's house himself but found no evidence of disturbance.

I called the original group: Marge, Lucy, Heather, Mildred, Dot, and Virginia. All were safe at home except for Dot, who I later tracked at the VFW playing bingo. I told them to stay alert and visit their relatives at least for the night.

By 10 p.m., there was still no sign of Frances. She had left the middle school at 5 p.m. and stopped at Great Harvest for a quart of pineapple pecan as per her usual Friday evening tradition. The ice cream, an Agatha Christie yarn, and the attention of her cats would provide for a full weekend. We called every number in Frances's address book, but none had heard a thing.

Sheriff Taw engaged the men of Stramwell to join the search. We used Frances's house as a base, with sandwiches and coffee provided.

"You know," Taw said to Al before they left together for the initial search, "last time he tried to frame you, but Jane was too sharp. He won't make the same mistake."

We stayed up the entire night, with Al and I returning to our house at 6 a.m. to wait for the mailman.

"I don't think this is gonna end well," Al said, pausing at our front door with a thousand-yard stare.

I went to the kitchen and brought back some cookies I had stashed in a place Al didn't know about.

"My lady," Al said, taking a bite with a tired smile. "Full of surprises."

The postcard we received that day pictured a raging river running through another heavily forested area. Another hand-drawn feather was on the back, accompanied by a name: *Mildred*.

I had checked in with Millie the previous night. She lived five miles outside town in a small house directly behind her cousin's family farmhouse. I hadn't considered her alone because she practically lived with the cousins, caring for their eight children.

I called her, but there was no answer.

Taw drove out immediately and questioned the family, who said Mildred stayed the night with them, got up in the morning, and went to her house to prepare for the day. That was the last they'd seen of her. Nothing was disturbed in her home, and they hadn't seen anybody come or go besides the farm workers.

It was filbert harvesting season, and many Hispanic laborers were on the property. By the time Taw could arrange a translator, they'd all disappeared.

Taw suggested we round up the remaining UVW

women and get them to the station. I informed him the Lindross sisters had moved to Arizona after marrying two brothers from Prescott who had a real estate business there. I called and was able to reach both and explain what was happening. Then I called Marge, who said she was in the garden but would get cleaned up and come on in. I told her to forget all that and run like the wind.

As I hung up the phone and picked up my address book to find Virginia Gleason's number, I noticed a plain manilla envelope sticking out from the rest of the mail. (I received such envelopes with contracts and official documents from publishers when the UVW was full throttle but hadn't for some time.) Nudging the other papers aside, I saw the Argentine postage.

Inside was another postcard. The picture was of several Hispanic men leading a group of American tourists on burros past what looked like a monastery with children playing in a courtyard.

The phone rang.

"Jane, it's Harriet Gleason. I don't want to alarm myself, but I can't find Virginia anywhere this morning. I'll, yes... I'll knock on the neighbor's doors. I'm sure she's around."

I flipped the card over. A feather, and: *Virginia*.

I studied the picture more closely.

There was a sign to the side of the monastery, of which I could only make out half, "*Sociedad de*."

Taw, Al, Dot, Marge, and I huddled in Taw's office, with the postcards laid out on his desk.

"The way I see it," Dot said, "we go to Argentina.

Otherwise, it's Margie and me next, then you."

"What about Librarian Rebecca?" Al said.

"She in your crew too?" said Taw.

"Not technically," I said. "But someone should check on her."

The library was just across from the police station. Sheriff Tawlins asked his deputy to run over.

"I wish I had better answers for y'all," Taw said. "But until I have some hard evidence, or more time has passed, I can't get interest from state resources. It's all happening so fast. I think Dorothy may be right."

"What would we even tell the state police?" Al said. "There's a boy wonder out there snatching our ladies?"

"He's hardly a boy anymore," Dot said.

"Right," I said, swallowing. "We need to find out the location of this monastery and arrange our path south. And it needs to be today."

"Before the mail comes again," Marge said.

"I'll take time off," Taw said. "Arrange for a fill-in deputy from Cottage Grove. Say it's a family emergency."

"I'll bring my pistol," Marge said. "I've kept it by my bedside since the day he left."

We all stared.

Librarian Rebecca appeared at the door, out of breath.

"What is that?" I said, pointing to the manilla envelope Rebecca was holding.

"Just the mail. What's going on? Is it about the boy?"

Tilting my head, I recognized the Argentine postmark on the envelope.

Inside the envelope was a copy of the novel *Growth of the Soil* by Knut Hamsun. Opposite the title page was a handwritten note:

He never read a book but often thought about God; it was unavoidable, a matter of simplicity and awe. The starry sky, the soughing of the forest, the solitude, the big snow, the majesty of the earth and what was above the earth filled him with a deep devoutness many times a day. He was sinful and godfearing; on Sundays he washed himself in honour of the holy day but worked as usual.

"Is it a clue?" I said.

"I don't know," Rebecca said, turning the book over. "This book won the Nobel prize in '20. I've not read it, but I believe it's about farming. But Hamsun..." she held up the book, pointing to the author's name on the cover. "He was a Nazi."

"Society of," Taw said, studying the photo again and biting his lip. "*Sociedad de.*"

CHAPTER 31

O ur trip would have to be piecemealed and planned along the way. After some debate, we agreed to leave directly from the Stramwell Police Station in one car and head for the Portland airport. (Fortunately, Sheriff Tawlins had remained a bachelor and thus had savings to pay for our round-trip tickets to Denver and, from there, international flights to Argentina.)

No one returned home for as much as an undergarment.

We took Marge's car, a 1940 Chrysler Imperial with a scandalously large back seat. Sherriff drove, and per my insistence, circled town several times to see if we were being tailed. We then went west for thirty minutes, turned off the lights, and drove for another ten before making a dramatic left turn and hitting the gas full throttle. After a few miles, we turned right abruptly and parked in a wooded area facing the road. We sat, waiting for any sign of would-be-following cars passing, but none did. We then made our circuitous path North.

We shared the postcard pictures with everyone on the Argentinian flight and upon our arrival at the Buenos Aires airport. No one recognized the scenes.

We had nothing to go on, nowhere to go, and no spare underpants.

We sat at a café outside the terminal, all dead tired.

Buenos Aires was not the South American city I had imagined. For all I knew, we could have been back in Denver, New York, or, more accurately, Berlin.

"Sure we got on the right plane?" Marge said.

"White people, everywhere," Al said.

"The architecture; it's all European," Rebecca said.

Two blonde boys ran past wearing lederhosen.

Just as I was about to curse, a large cloud blocked the sun. Except it wasn't a cloud. It was a man.

"German immigration, day and night like a river, for a hundred years," the giant man said in a voice too low to be human. "Jewish too."

Taw and Al tried to stand, but the giant man waved them down with a hand the size of a turkey plate. Then he adjusted his enormous glasses the size and thickness of bus windows.

"No introductions necessary," the man said. "Except for me. I am Hanz. I'm to take you to him."

And then he just walked away.

We watched the giant open the glass door to the airport, duck, and enter the terminal.

"It's a trap," Al said. "We should go to the police."

"Tobias would have gotten to them sure enough," Taw said. "I'm afraid we're running on instinct here."

"It's all I've ever had, and I'm still kicking," Dot said. "Let's go."

"We'll take a vote," Sheriff said. "Who's for going with Goliath?"

Hanz was easy to spot inside the airport, speaking cordially with another man near a runway exit door. When we approached them, Hanz pointed his thumb at the other man.

"This is the pilot," he rumbled. "You don't need to know his name. It's a three-hour flight. I'll be sleeping, and I recommend you do the same. Ok then."

Hanz and the pilot turned and walked outside to the runway, where a medium-sized plane sat with the entry steps folded down. Once we were aboard and seated, Hanz looked us over, nodded, then crouched his way to the front row, where he took up both seats and put his hat over his eyes.

"Excuse me," I said.

"No questions," he bellowed back. "Especially from you."

"How do you know who we—"

"I hear all about you," Hanz said, his hat still covering his eyes. "No questions if you want to land in one piece."

He shifted his weight to one side, shaking the plane and causing me to fall back in my seat, where I stayed.

We landed at a remote airstrip next to a cargo van, which Hanz directed us to enter. There was no driver's seat. Instead, Hanz drove from the second row, leaning forward and squinting the entire time.

We bumped along until finally reaching the main road, which was surprisingly maintained and smooth.

"So, you were pacifists in the war," Hanz said. "Even with Hitler."

"Where are you taking us?" I said. "Or am I still not allowed to talk?"

"A monster on the loose killing innocents, and you don't stop him?"

"Answer my question first," I said. "Where's Tobias?"

Hanz thought for a second, not seeming to recognize the name. "I see. You change the subject. That's how."

"Sir, I demand—"

"No more questions."

We drove along a beautiful lakeside. The road was very busy with large trucks, and we seemed to be in a line of sorts, all headed the same way. Finally, Hanz turned left into a gated courtyard surrounded by several buildings. I leaned forward to read the full name on the sign.

"Sociedad de Socorros Israelitas," Hanz said. "The Israelites Relief Society."

In the courtyard several dozen children ran to greet us.

Hanz parked the van and exited, swarmed by the little ones. He walked ahead, patting their heads and lifting a girl to sit on his bicep.

Our group remained in the van.

Tobias emerged from a building.

He was a man now, fit and strong. He carried a phone on a long cord, placed it on a picnic table in the courtyard, lifted the receiver, and held it up toward us.

It was Dot that moved first. "Well, we came all this way," she said, reaching for the van door.

As we approached, Tobias dialed a number. He spoke to someone on the other line, nodded, and handed me the phone.

"Hello?" I said.

"Hello?" the woman's voice returned, faint with some static.

"Yes, hello?" I repeated. "Who's this?"

"Miss Frances Malloy, and who may I say is calling?"

"Frances! We've been worried sick!"

Tobias put his finger down on the receiver.

"So," he said. "The ladies are back safe and sound, and you have accomplished your mission."

"Our mission?" Taw said.

"For my mother to see me again, of course," Tobias said, smiling, but not at me.

"My boy!" Dot said, arms extended.

"Oh, Jane," Tobias said to me, his chin on Dot's

head in full embrace. "And after all the detective skills I taught you in *Man About Town*."

CHAPTER 32

Tobias insisted we stay for dinner, as Hanz moved a massive gate shut over the entrance. Food was served in the courtyard, with the children acting as our wait staff.

Tobias stood at the head of the table. Dot sat next to him, beaming.

"A gathering of old friends," he said. "As a special treat tonight. I will answer any question you have truthfully, except for one."

"Why are you such a turkey?" Al said.

"Very good, Al," Tobias said, sitting. "I am birdlike. It is how all life succeeds."

"You're a Nazi," I said.

"Is that a question, or an assumption from the flash of a single photograph?"

"What about Rebecca's book?"

I motioned to Rebecca, who held *Growth of the Soil* to her chest. She had been reading it obsessively since we left Stramwell, reporting the story to the group. It did indeed turn out to be about farming and was proving completely useless to our mission.

"The book was a gift, nothing more," Tobias said. "It reminds me of you all."

"My Toby," Dot said. "Such a generous boy."

"But, since the topic of Nazism has been breached," Tobias continued, "I will provide you my thoughts."

An older child approached and refilled Tobias's wine. Tobias smiled at the boy, drank the glass fully, and placed it carefully back on the table.

"Hitler should have been identified as a narcissist as a child," Tobias said. "Even then, they should have known. Installed it early in his programming to counter act his default state. They could have taught him more productive ways of altruism. It's what we teach the orphans here, as so many of them have early detachment injuries."

Tobias looked down the table, observing one by one our confused expressions. It was the position from which he lived his life.

"Essentially," he continued, "a selfish person should be taught to do good for others because it makes their own life better."

Tobias rubbed the rim of his glass with his finger.

"Of course," he continued, "after Hitler got trench gassed in the Great War it was too late. He should have been discretely terminated. At the very latest he should have been taken out in Berlin in '37."

"This is insane," Al said.

"I believe," Rebecca said, "You're describing moral re-armament."

"Very good, my fellow scholar," Tobias said. "But my theory is built on universal reality, not religion. Along with an emerging understanding of brain science as the technology allows."

"You're never gonna stop bad guys by bribing them to be good," Sheriff Tawlins said. "I'm sorry, but it don't work that way."

"How true," Tobias said. "And why this is merely a thought exercise, for now. It will take another species to implement the actual change, and over decades, not years."

"What other species?" I said.

"Oh, Jane, that is the one question I cannot answer."

"So, you're teaching the orphans here to be selfish?" Marge said.

"Oh, dear Marge," Tobias said. "He that hath small understanding and feareth God, is better than one that hath much wisdom, and transgresseth the law of the most High."

A small girl appeared at my side with a cluster of grapes raised. I plucked one.

"What are you really doing here?" I said.

"Helping orphans."

"Any questions for me?" Hanz said, cleaning his glasses. "I'm two and a third meters tall, by the way."

"Seven foot eight," Tobias said. "Hanz has an inoperable tumor pressing on his pituitary gland. He'll keep growing until he dies from an infection he is unaware of."

"Because I can't feel my legs."

Hanz replaced his glasses and raised his goblet in a toast.

"To not feeling our legs," he said, and swallowed a gallon of wine.

A series of large trucks rumbled past.

"Nuclear fusion," Tobias said. "The country is constructing a lab. It's a ruse, but a profitable one for now, and will, like all ruses, spur us onward."

"I don't care," I said, dropping my fork. "I don't care what you have to say. You kidnapped three women, brought us down here, wasted our time... And you murdered Beth. I want you out of our lives for good. I want you gone. *Permanently.*"

"No," Tobias said.

"What do you mean, no?" I said.

"J, you of all people must know I will never be gone *permanently.*"

I pounded the table.

"Why can't you leave us alone?"

"You will go home," Tobias said, "and care for my ailing mother to return the favor of profiting off me," Tobias said. "Frances, Mildred, and Virginia were test runs. But if you do not comply, they won't be. And, as Sheriff Taw has guessed, a certain man in your life will be blamed. Or was it a boy wonder Nazi in South America with a pet giant who did it all? Oh Jane, they will place you in the Blue Valley Nursing Home, branded the only thing worse than a communist sympathizer, an old hysterical woman."

(I had, of course, suspected Tobias of being the source of the *Family Livin' Magazine* article, but until that moment had not given myself to confirm it.)

Tobias stood, kissed his mother, and walked back into the building from whence he came.

"Such a wise boy," Dot said, turning to me.

"I shall require the master bedroom," she said primly. "No noise after 7:30. Breakfast of oats and toast with preserves served bedside at 8 a.m. And I believe a wardrobe update is in order. Al, be a dear when we return and let the Buell's ladies department supervisor know I'll need a private concierge, and you'll be assisting with carrying my purchases."

Al paused with his mouth open, fork in the air.

***

Hanz and Marge got talkative on the van trip back to the plane.

"My father was a short man," he said. "It bothered him his whole life. And here I come, taller than him at age 5."

"Why do you protect Tobias?" Marge said.

"Again, that name. I've never heard him called that."

"What do you call him?" she said.

Hanz thought for a moment.

"Friend. Yes. Friend."

"You're friends with a Nazi?"

"I don't understand why you call him that either."

Then, in perhaps the boldest move of her life, Marge said, "Hanz, would you allow me to write to you?"

He reached into his shirt pocket and pulled out a card listing a PO box in Buenos Aires. He squinted at it for several moments before handing it to Marge.

"I only go there once a month to get mail. So, I'm not the best pen pal. But I will write back if you write to me."

Hanz walked inside the airport with us to ensure we boarded the plane home.

Just before our departure, he walked to the newsstand, purchased a newspaper, and gave it to Marge.

"A parting gift," Hanz said, tipping his hat. "And a topic for conversation in correspondence."

From the plane windows, we watched the giant stand with arms crossed on the runway until we took flight.

The paper was a *New York Times*, and Marge read it from cover to cover.

As it would happen, a prominent article highlighted the nuclear fusion work in Argentina. It seemed a press conference there the day before we arrived had gained global attention.

Argentine President Juan Peron claimed his top scientist, German expatriate Herr Ronald Richter, had 'harnessed the sun's power.' Promises were made of unlimited energy, contained, according to Peron, 'in a small bottle a person could hold in their hand.'

At first, I thought Richter might be an alias Tobias was using, but the man in the small photo looked nothing like him.

Once in Denver, I used a payphone to call Frances, Virginia, and Mildred. All of them were safely home, and each of their stories was the same. They were alone at night, grabbed from behind, felt a sharp pinch in their neck, and awoke in their beds with no memory of the time having passed.

***

The return flight to Portland was very turbulent, especially while landing.

Rebecca kept her nose in *Growth of the Soil* the entire way, finishing just as we touched down.

Later, Sheriff Tawlins would confide in Al his desperate fear of flying.

She never knew whether it was fear from turbulence or a bold gesture of affection, but upon closing her book, Rebecca looked down to see Taw had taken her hand.

CHAPTER 33

A burnt match

While Tobias Randall could never be categorized as a nature lover, he was technically a naturalist, accepting humans as fully part of the physical universe, having evolved in conditions of intertwined environment.

At least until the 20th century, this was the pattern: humans adapting to nature. But, with the Industrial Revolution came an organizational shift, the by-product of which was humans trying to adapt nature to themselves. Randall determined this transition to be neither good nor evil but simply out of harmony with the past.

The human brain is made of physical matter and as such evolves linearly, but ideas are free from organic constraints and can adapt exponentially. This imbalance is the source of all human strife.

As a case in point: A carbon atom exists buried underground for millions of years slowly decays and gives off energy. In contrast, carbon atoms in the atmosphere are younger and have not yet given off the same amount of energy.

Since the Industrial Revolution, there has been a steady increase in the presence of these underground 'lower energy' carbon atoms up in the atmosphere. These atoms, previously existing underground, only get into the air because humans have dug them up and burned them. And all carbon atoms, whether young or old, trap heat.

So, the increase of these previously underground carbon atoms, combined with the naturally occurring carbon atoms in our atmosphere, will, over time, cause a small temperature increase around the globe.

These tiny temperature changes create corresponding small climate changes, which impact ecosystems that have evolved under the *old* climate conditions.

Humans never evolved to change widespread behavior on something as significant to us as fuel usage. As a result, the temperature increases will continue, and all life on Earth will eventually adapt or die.

This concept is fully understood today and has been for decades. It will continue to be proven with more significant evidence until the day it becomes too late.

It is why Tobias Randall went to be with the Nazis in Argentina.

CHAPTER 34

A clown figurine

Hanz Hernandez suffered from gigantism as a young boy, when a tumor grew in his brain, pushing against his pituitary gland and causing excessive growth hormone secretions.

Before their bodies break down, there is a window of time when giants possess extraordinary strength. Hanz's process was so impressive that crowds began to gather whenever he would show up in town to unload a truck.

Seeing an opportunity, Hanz's father started charging tickets for people to watch Hanz work around the farm. He then implemented competitions to see if anyone could match the boy's strength. Eventually, a traveling sideshow developed, which incorporated several other acts. They toured South America for many years until Hanz's father died, at which point Pinhead, the Fat Lady, Mole Man, Mr. Steel, and Hanz continued traveling from town to town. As they did, they began approaching town fathers at each stop about the inevitable feral children that would loiter around their events.

When a child was confirmed to have no family relations, the group would ask the child if he or she were interested in joining them. In the first year of this practice, the traveling show accumulated 34 orphans. These children even developed a sideshow of their own involving dressing like animals who could juggle and perform acrobatics, with crowd work as their primary specialty.

CHAPTER 35

Gideon Bible

Tobias Randall met the giant Hanz Hernandez in a waiting room at an ophthalmologist's office in La Plata, Argentina.

"The tumor responsible for pituitary secretions is also compressing your optic nerve," Tobias said. "But you already know this."

"Yes," Hanz said in his deeper-than-possible voice.

The big man raised his hand for Tobias to compare with his own.

"Goliath had it, too," Hanz said. "From David and Goliath in the scriptures."

"Yes, of course," Tobias said. "Goliath challenged fighters to come directly to him because of his poor eyesight. The mass in his brain must have ruptured when hit with David's stone."

Hanz shrugged.

The giant man desired to escape the traveling life, as his eyesight and general body tiredness had diminished his ability to perform. He'd nearly given up his feats of strength act and, although trying earnestly, was ill-equipped for the role of ringmaster.

***

While in the States, Tobias earned a small fortune from selling a series of kitchen appliance patents to General Electric.

(GE had a standing agreement to purchase the patents for a price named by Tobias through a pseudonym, with all communications accomplished through a PO Box in Chicago. GE was relentless in their attempts to determine the correct identity of Tobias but never did. Notably, not one of his inventions was produced, as each one in succession would have made GE's top-selling items at the time obsolete.)

***

A partnership was formed that morning in the eye doctor's office, and Tobias soon arranged for Hanz to purchase a sizeable, gated property to permanently house an orphanage for the children from his traveling act.

Hanz wondered what Tobias would gain from the deal but did not ask. He figured people have their reasons for living, which change over time, so it's not worth asking as the answer will be incorrect at some point anyway.

Tobias did not offer his name, so Hanz just called him 'Friend.'

CHAPTER 36

Plastic grapes

Allied forces surrounded Berlin. Mothers paced hallways at night, for the first time not grazing pictures of their Fuhrer with their fingertips.

The shores of Buenos Aires bobbed on the pre-dawn horizon as a non-descript boat pierced the dark, choppy waves of the Southern Atlantic. Two German guards slept in the ship's hold, their heads resting against an unlabeled crate.

As Juan Peron could be tricked into anything that promised power, and exiled Nazis would do anything to retain control, a religion of progress was born in Argentina.

Tobias Randall first heard about the German Tomahawk Reactor through rumors in the scientific community. He approached Ronald Richter shortly after arriving in the country.

"What are your thoughts on delta rays emitting from the earth?" Tobias asked.

"Oh, they are indeed the future of experimental physics," Richter said, confirming to Randall he was a fraud.

Tobias talked Richter into using the newly arrived reactor to establish a fusion laboratory in Argentina, providing specific guidance on a comprehensive grant request to the government.

"But I surely can't take credit for the idea," Richter said, buttoning his new suit to meet Peron. "You must come."

"Oh no," Tobias said. "Water doesn't take credit for the fruit."

At a dinner party that night, Richter regurgitated Tobias's pre-written script verbatim to the Argentine president.

"Fusion power?" Peron said. "In small enough canisters to propel a tank?"

"Propel a tank *forever*," Richer said. Then, as instructed, leaned in close. "The subatomic world is so small a single liter of volume is as the Pacific Ocean to you and I. So tell me, Mr. President, would you like to hold the ocean?"

"Hmm, and it makes sense, too," Peron said. "Scientifically speaking."

"It does," said Richter, neither man knowing what they were talking about.

The next step was securing funding, which may have been the easiest part after Peron's ears had heard the potential for unlimited power.

Tobias had already chosen the location for the development of the fusion facility. —A small island that guaranteed security, discreetness, and walking distance from an old mission ideally suited to establish an orphanage.

CHAPTER 37

A small chunk of concrete

Huemul Island sits in a lake deep in the Argentine interior near the Andes mountains. Construction of a nuclear fusion reactor began on the island in 1949 and continued day and night until 1951.

The project was so expansive it caused a nationwide shortage of brick and concrete. But regardless of the cost, no expense was spared. For example, once built, a crack at the base of the main reactor was discovered, so the entire structure was torn down and rebuilt.

Tobias Randall recognized by 1941 the technology needed to create controllable fusion wouldn't be available for at least 200 years, so he planned to accelerate that timeline by fraud. Creating worldwide fear a tiny dictatorship would claim unlimited power seemed a productive option.

After Tobias Randall disappeared from Argentina, Project Director Ronald Richter had construction crews dig a hole on Huemul Island a hundred feet in diameter and five hundred feet deep. Unsure of what to do next, Richter then ordered the cavity refilled with concrete. That very week, Peron announced Argentina's nuclear fusion successes to the world.

CHAPTER 38

A broken compass

Tobias Randall would often request Hanz Hernandez drive him blindfolded into the jungle. Remaining blindfolded, Tobias Randall would record his time to return home.

On these journeys Tobias would often think of Jane.

One morning, just after hearing the van drive away, Tobias took a step and collapsed to the ground. The tumor had stopped growing for a time, but the reprieve was over.

Tobias lay on the jungle floor without thought. In a branch high above, he heard the call of a little blue macaw. Near extinct and unknown to exist so far south, it must have been an escaped pet.

CHAPTER 39

D
ot was a pill.

I thought about poisoning her tea, but Tobias
would find out, as she wrote to him daily. I
could have snuffed her out and continued penning the
letters, but I didn't think myself capable of such poor
writing. She never got any letters in return, but we were
both confident enough that Tobias received them.

When I say "wrote," I mean Dot dictated to me as
I typed at her bedside. (Which was really *my* bedside, as
she took my bedroom.) Additionally, Dot had taken on
the position of a pampered elderly debutante, requiring
assistance on everything from combing her hair to
walking to the bathroom.

"Now, read that back to me," she would say, her
hands resting calmly on her chest, lying in the bed that
was previously Al's and mine.

"*Today I thought about balloons,*" I read. "*Maybe you*

could do something with them. Imagine getting a whole city of people living in a giant balloon! But where would they use the necessary room? You'd have to utilize the balloon opening as a drain of sorts. Be a dear and figure out the details then write me back. Also, I'm curious, what does Eva Peron spread on her crackers? Does she apply cheese of any kind, or is it just so much caviar all the day long?"

I vomited in my mouth.

***

As promised, Marge wrote and received regular letters from Hanz. He never mentioned Tobias directly other than to say upon returning from taking us to the airport, his friend was gone.

Hanz started traveling again whenever he received word of a child in need, whether it be to Buenos Aires or any point between. He also learned the basics of educational instruction and attempted to teach the children agricultural sciences.

Per Marge's request, I wrote to the giant with instructional guidance on teaching. I also shipped a copy of Griffin, Laycock, and Line's *Mental Hygiene; A Manual for Teachers.*

Hanz's final letter stated the orphanage had been shut down. The government seized all its assets, claiming the funds came from fraudulent activities. Outreach to his connections in the Argentine government had proven fruitless, and he feared impending arrest.

Hanz concluded the note with a single line relating to the fusion project, *"The snake oil is proving not to be the cure-all the salesman said it was."*

Marge made up her mind to return to Argentina, sending Hanz a letter stating her full intention of love and marriage, but she never received a reply. Three weeks later, an article appeared in *The New York Times* detailing the collapse of the Argentine fusion project, declaring it a scam of massive proportions.

Marge spent the rest of the money she'd saved from the UVW heyday on a one-way ticket to Buenos Aires. Upon arrival, she took a two-day bus ride to Huemul Island, where she found the Sociedad de Socorros Israelitas orphanage completely abandoned.

Marge traveled the area until her money ran out, finding no one who knew what had come of the giant man. He was simply there one day and gone the next. She even pleaded repeatedly with the prison department for at least confirmation of his incarceration, but all attempts were met with silence.

"It seems no one wants to remember anything about Huemel Island," she wrote to me.

After three months, she returned to Stramwell alone on what is believed to be the longest bus ride in Oregon state history.

***

Librarian Rebecca and Sherrif Tawlins were married in July of '52, with Al serving as best man and I as her bridesmaid. Mrs. Tawlins was with child by December, and the little family moved into a farmhouse down the road from ours in June the following year.

Not long after, and to everyone's surprise, Sheriff Tawlins hung up his badge and became a farmer. A darn good one too.

Three-and-a-half years passed before we heard from Tobias again.

During this time Marge became convinced only Tobias knew where Hanz was.

"He'll next appear at some flashpoint in world affairs," she claimed. "You can set your watch to it."

Marge began regularly scouring all the major newspapers and watched every theater newsreel possible for a glimpse of a feather in any cap.

"Toby!" Dot yelled one afternoon, causing our fellow movie theater attendees to turn and scowl. "It's my Toby!"

"Where?!" Marge stood, fixated on the screen. The newsreel showed young Queen Elizabeth waving to throngs of her subjects.

"Long live the Queen, as they say across the pond," the narrator said. "And rightfully so, as the world remains confident she will sort out the Suez problem in quick time,"

"Are you sure it was him?" I said.

"How do you know? When did you see him?" Marge grabbed Dot by the collar with both hands. "Was there a giant with him? What was he doing?"

"I know my own son!" Dot slapped at Marge's meaty paws. "And you'll do well to release me!"

"Maybe she doesn't care to," I said, leaning in. "Maybe if something happened to you, it would make your boy come here, and we can get this whole thing over with?"

After a pause and seeing enough horror in her eyes, I nodded at Marge to release.

"You don't even know how to contact him anyway," I said.

"Ladies?" squeaked a movie theater attendant.

"What?!" we yelled in unison.

That night, we went to the other two movie showings and waited for the newsreel at each.

"Of course, Toby's guiding the Queen," Dot said after the second film started with no sign of Tobias. "I want to leave now. My programs are starting soon, and last week you nearly made me miss the Brylcreem Mystery Hour opener. Miss the opener of Brylcreem, and you can forget the whole thing."

That night in bed I lay staring at the ceiling. As the house sat, directly above us was Tobias's bedroom, left untouched since the day of his departure.

(Al and I had moved our bedroom to the study downstairs, off the living room, as far away from Dot's butler bell as possible.)

Al read news about the Suez Canal situation.

"The whole world is fighting over this thing," he said. "Tobias could've kicked the honest nest and left already. We've just got to find a hornet's nest about to be kicked."

I closed my eyes and imagined the young man still in his bedroom.

***

The following Saturday, Dot wanted to go to the

movies again. So, I took her begrudgingly if only to get another look at the newsreels. I thought maybe I'd catch a glimpse of Tobias putting a feather in Pol Pot's cap.

As we were leaving the picture, I ran into Jesse Achey, the theater owner, now in his 80's. We exchanged pleasantries and were halfway to the car when I had a thought.

"Jesse," I said, running back. "Do you remember a young man who lived with me about twenty years ago by the name of Tobias?"

"Hmm."

"I thought you might remember him because he always came to the movies alone. He didn't have any friends."

Jesse looked at me blankly.

"I'm sorry, Miss Alexander. A lot of kids came to the movies. It's all westerns or space robots these days, of course."

"Right," I said. "Well, thanks for your time."

On the drive home, as thoughts often do, a single idea floated over me as if tied to a balloon.

"Dot," I said. "Do you still have Tobias's drawings tucked away in the trunk under your bed?"

"What do you want with them? You can't have them. He's my boy, not yours."

"Lord in heaven, woman, I just want to see them."

"Nope. No, that's just not possible. Not possible."

When we arrived home, I told Dot I thought I heard the phone ringing. I left her in the car, ran into the house, and grabbed Tobias's drawings from the trunk under her bed.

"Wrong number!" I yelled, out of breath on my return.

I had never looked at the drawings closely before, as they were done in Tobias's free time, and I tried to let him be free of any oversight to allow for purely concentrated work while writing.

Almost all the sketches were of robots, with a particularly recurring theme of female robots. I remembered seeing one or two of these when he was with me but passed it off to a boy working through his emerging desires. I had no idea there were so many of them. Each robot looked identical, with occasional guns, hair, and clothing changes.

I picked up one of the more accomplished pieces. The robot was female, and with its angular bends in the metal, the body portrayed a graceful form and a perfect left-to-right symmetry. On closer inspection, I observed Tobias had applied faint but detailed gridlines over the page to maintain perfect dimensions.

I had seen this robot somewhere, but I was unsure where. I showed it to Al and Marge, and both said the image looked familiar but could not pinpoint it. On a hunch, I took it to Jesse Achey.

"*Metropolis!*" he said. "One of the last great silents. A visual masterpiece. I acquired a copy from the Portland Star Cineplex in '33 and played it sometimes while waiting for new arrivals. It bombed, sadly. However, being a German film, perhaps 'bomb' isn't the best term to use. Then again, maybe it is."

"Do you still have a copy?"

"Oh Miss, I never rid of a classic."

Jesse graciously scheduled Al and me for an early morning show. I quickly remembered the confusing nature of the film from my first viewing. Still, its beauty and scope of scale remained shockingly impressive. The robot creation scene, in particular, was haunting.

"It's artificial," Al said, giving his critique at lunch after our viewing. "The whole movie. And this is going to sound plain, but especially the robot."

"But why Tobias's fixation with it?" I said.

"A couple things come to mind."

"Do they have robots like this yet? I mean, has anyone produced one that human-like?"

"Who knows what the government is up to," Al said.

After lunch, I met Rebecca at the library, where we read articles about the film and watched her little Melvil run down the aisles.

Every single film critic praised *Metropolis's* set design and massive scale of effort. A few connected themes from the plot to those present in pre-war Germany, and one even compared the protagonist's journey with the Nazi's plan for war.

I asked Rebecca if she'd seen any recent articles about robot creation. She hadn't but recommended I reach out to her friend, a high school science professor in Eugene, Mr. Fred Gibbs, who was always captivated by the newest technologies.

I called North Eugene High School and asked if I could have a moment with Mr. Gibbs after class. The office said the best way to reach him was to come in as school let out.

I sat in my car in the school parking lot and watched several students milling about the front steps. As with all big-city girls, their sophistication and innate worldly confidence bothered me.

One of the girls flipped her wrist palm side up, then down. I flipped mine the same. The other brushed her hair off her shoulder and punched a laughing boy. I brushed and punched the steering wheel, accidentally honking the horn. They looked over, and I hid my face by adjusting the mirror. When I grabbed my purse and stood erect, they continued to stare. Then the bell rang.

The front office staff informed me Mr. Gibbs's room was reached by making left turns until I hit a dead end. The hallways were congested with students, turning me into an invisible salmon.

"Mrs. Alexander?" a female voice to the left said. "Is that you? It's me, Mary Schneider. Well, formerly Wetly. Schneider now. Do you remember me?"

I didn't at first, but her thick brown curls reminded me: Little Mary Wetly. I recalled her headshot photograph from our files.

"Yes, Mary. How are you, dear?"

"Excellent Mrs. Alexander."

"Oh please, call me Jane. And it's Clifton these days. So, you are a Schneider now?"

"Oh yes, since '45. Two little ones, 7 and 8."

"Well then," I said, smiling. "Are you a teacher?"

She was a girls guidance counselor.

"And how is... Tom?"

"Tim!" she said. "Great memory Mrs. Alexander, I mean Mrs. Clifton. Of course, you're a brain, an author and all. Yes, Tim Schneider. He went to the Pacific, came back, and we got married. Lived in Cottage Grove ever since. He works at Schwabb's Mill as a foreman. I work here now that the kids are in school. Say, do you still write? I have all your books. I was just reading the health one the other day."

"Yes? Well, no, I haven't written in some time. I'm afraid the ladies have dispersed as a group."

"Oh, that's a shame," she appeared genuinely disappointed. "I always admired that about you. A real published author from this area. You know, I've been working on a novel of my own now and again, but it's nothing special. I barely have time."

"Well, I'm sure it's better than you think."

Mary looked at her watch, "Oh, speaking of time. I gotta go. Josiah will be standing in the parking lot telling people his mother forgot him."

She placed her hand on my arm.

"Say, what are you doing here anyway?"

"Um, looking for a Mr. Gibbs. I was told he—"

"Fred Gibbs?" She pointed around a final corner. "He's just around the corner, 197. The one with the big poster of the Solar System on the door. It was nice to see you, Ms. Alexander. We should catch up sometime!"

I knocked on Jupiter and, hearing no response, entered the large science classroom. At the front of the room was another doorway into a closeted space, where a clattering of noises arose.

"Excuse me? Mr. Gibbs?"

With more clatter, a large, wild-eyed, wild-haired bald man emerged.

"Ah, Mr. Gibbs," I said. "My name is—"

"I'm not Gibbs. I'm Bear, the gym coach." He made his way towards me. "Gibbs is in the courtyard. This way, ma'am."

He walked directly past me, out the door, and lumbered down the hall to the right.

I followed him but stopped at the door, noticing a poster on the backside: '*Metropolis*' was scrawled across the top with the image of Tobias's robot below.

"Beautiful, isn't it?" a younger, handsome man appeared in the doorway. "A masterpiece of art deco and modernism. Fred Gibbs," he said, extending his hand.

"Yes," I said. "Hello."

"And how can I be of service?"

"Yes! Yes," I said, breaking the trance.

I introduced myself while rifling through my bag for the selected robot drawings from Tobias's collection.

"Wow," Mr. Gibbs said, holding them properly like works of art. "Very nice. Did you draw these?"

"Oh no. Well… no. They are my nephew's. My sister was concerned about the subject matter, and I told her I would investigate. Rebecca Miller referred me to you."

"Rebecca! Such a doll," he said. "How is she?"

"Rebecca is the librarian in Stramwell," I said.

"Yes," he said.

"Oh, well, yes. She's fine. Married now. To the sheriff in Stramwell. Well, former sheriff. They have a little boy."

"Really?" he said. "Lucky man. Well, time passes for us all doesn't it?"

I handed him the rest of the drawings, making a mental note to ask Rebecca for more information.

"Well," he said, "I can tell you they are drawings of the robot from the 1927 science fiction film *Metropolis*."

He stepped inside the room and shut the door, fully revealing the poster and tapping the robot image.

"Also known as the Maschinenmensch. It's a German word, meaning 'machine-human.'"

"I see," I said. "Perhaps you could tell me the robot's role in the film?"

"Hmm, that is an excellent question," he folded his arms, studying the poster. "Well, essentially, the story is about a rich man's son living a life of wealth and leisure, and he comes across a beautiful girl he follows to an underworld city. In doing so, he discovers a whole society where the poorer class toils away mindlessly. They're turning the machinery that makes the above-ground city work.

The girl is a prophet whom the underworld people follow. She prophesies that a mediator between their world," Mr. Gibbs put his hand on his chest, "and the wealthy people's world," he reached forward (and nearly put his fist on mine but did not touch me), "will come and unite them." Gibbs interlocked his fingers. "Then a mad scientist gets involved and creates a robot," he pointed to the poster, "that looks identical to the prophet girl, to deceive all the poor into fighting the rich people. Ultimately, the rich man's son stops the fighting and unites both classes."

"Hmm," I said. "But how are they fooled into thinking a metallic robot is the girl?"

"The scientist puts skin and flesh over the robot to look like the girl."

"Skin and flesh?"

"I know, it's strange. And you wouldn't gather all that from the film. It's pretty choppy. We only know the full story because the director's wife released a novel of the same name. It's a pre-war German film, so naturally, people have taken different meanings from it. And the Nazis loved it, which didn't help. Thought it was 'the bee's knees' as they used to say in our day."

"Sounds like a gas," I said.

"Right!"

"So, the Nazi's—"

"Oh, it's no more of a Nazi film than King Kong. You know how they did, twisting anything they could."

"Right," I said.

"Speaking of novels," Mr. Gibbs raised his finger and bowed slightly. "I'm a fan. I've read the complete works of the UVW. *Man About Town*, the *McGillicutty's Menagerie* series, *Our Sky Was Not Yours*..."

"—Yes, well. Thank you, it was a team effort, of course. But that's kind of you to say. I do miss those days."

"Each work was so beautiful in its own right. I was enraptured."

"Ahem, yes."

"Forgive me," he said. "I'm gushing."

"No, it's quite alright," I said. "It's just been a while since I've interacted with a fan."

"The UVW was a real force," he said. "All those powerful women, with you as their leader, directing a wave of literary passion like Amphitrite herself."

"A goddess!!" I said, my voice releasing an unusual squeak. "Well," I continued, "I came here actually to gain knowledge of the robot. So, is there anything else of import you can tell me about its purpose in the film?"

"Hmm," Mr. Gibbs turned, studying the poster again as if seeing it for the first time. "Well, it was created out of love. The scientist was in love with a woman who passed giving birth. It was the rich young man's mother, in fact. But, she married his wealthy father instead of the scientist. So, the scientist created a robot to exactly resemble his lost love, as I guess he was lonely.

Anyway, in a plot for revenge against the wealthy father, the scientist repurposed the robot to look like the young prophetess. The scientist planned to kill the real prophetess and replace her with the robot version, then use *her* to deceive the masses into rebellion against the wealthy father and his world. Instead, the robot was caught and burned at the stake."

"They burned a robot? To what end?"

"Oh, they didn't know they were burning a robot.

They thought they were burning the prophetess."

"That's right. Skin and flesh."

"Yes, and quite lovely at that. Of course, it was just the actress playing the robot. Anway, the plot to revolt against the wealthy overworld failed, and the underworld workers blamed her as their scapegoat. The flesh melted off in the process, revealing the robot underneath. The real prophetess got away."

"Well, it all sounds dreadful," I said. "I'm glad I haven't seen the film."

"You'd be hard-pressed to find a good copy anyway. But it occasionally comes out for a revival in Portland or Seattle. Perhaps if I hear of one, I'll let you know. I would also like to see it again."

"Thank you," I said, raising my left hand to adjust my glasses and show my wedding ring. "Is there anything else you can tell me?" (At this point, I had completely forgotten my original purpose of learning about new robotic technologies.)

"I'm sure there's a backstory to the robot's construction in a film studies book I have."

Mr. Gibbs walked to the front of the room through the little door where Bear had emerged.

"Good Lord," I heard from behind the wall. "What did Bear do back here?"

I examined the poster one last time. The face of the robot now looked almost sweet.

"Here you are," Mr. Gibbs said, jogging toward me with a book. "You'll find more in here than I could ever tell you."

"Very good. I shall return it in the post when finished."

I pulled my purse tight and turned to the door.

"Or I could stop by and get it. It's no problem," he said.

I smiled politely.

"I shall have my husband Al return it in the post. Thank you for your kindness and admiration of the work of the UVW."

Walking down the hall, I could feel the handsome teacher's gaze on my backside, and in full transparency, a slight swagger of the hips may or may not have been released.

***

"It says here the most important contribution of the robot was being 'the first time this type of technology was taken seriously in film,'" I read to Al in bed that night.

"Hmm," Al said.

"I wonder, do you think the Russians are working on robots?"

"I have no idea. I bet Mr. Gibbs would know though. Happy to help, too, I'm sure."

I had already spilled the beans about the teacher's advances to Al. He took it in good fun, but it raised a minor chord of sadness in his smile, so I vowed to never bring it up again.

(In continuing full transparency, I will admit the scent of manly jealousy did spark some small fire in me.)

"Oh, sweet man."

I rolled to my right, turned out the light, then rolled back again.

CHAPTER 40

It being Christmas break the following week, I returned to the library Monday morning when Rebecca had several articles prepped for me regarding recent advancements in robotics. In return, I shared Mr. Gibbs's 'doll' comment with her, which Rebecca said she could imagine no justification for.

After a long, eyebrow-raised stare, Rebecca admitted Mr. Gibbs was in her graduating class, and they had once shared several dances at the junior social.

I placed my hands on my hips.

"Ok," she whispered (quietly, even for a librarian.) "He was my first kiss, but don't tell Taw."

"Never," I said, winking. "And, *well done.*"

***

Earlier in the year, an IBM programmer at their Poughkeepsie laboratories had taught a computer how to play checkers. Additionally, during that summer, a symposium of the leading minds at Dartmouth University and elsewhere gathered for 11 weeks to explore the potential of what they called 'artificial intelligence.'

I scoured every picture but did not find Tobias or a feather.

I reread the scientific journal on the checkers playing robot. Deep in the footnotes, I came across it — a reference to an article by James Bankhead (the very name of the Majority Leader and lead antagonist in *The Senators*.) The Stramwell Library did not carry the journal referenced, but the University of Oregon did.

"Would you like me to order a copy transferred on loan?" Rebecca asked.

"No, tell them to put it on hold. I'll be right there."

I rushed home, packed a bag for myself and Al, then called Marge, who agreed to care for Dot. (Her bell rang from upstairs like a cow in a tornado.)

We gassed up at the Jiffy n' Fill and headed for Eugene.

I lied directly to the clerk at the University of Oregon Library. As a non-student, I was ineligible to remove items from the building, so I told her I would return the magazine after reading it at a nearby desk. Instead, I tucked the periodical into my large purse, brought just for that occasion, and we fled the scene.

Once in the car, I opened the journal and read the title aloud: "*On the Ethics of Artificial Intelligence,*" by James Bankhead, United Scientists Laboratories, Poughkeepsie, NY.

"Poughkeepsie," I turned to Al. *"New York."*

"We're gonna need supplies," he said, putting the car in gear and turning towards Pay Less Drug, where we stocked up on beef jerky, RC Cola, Hot Tamales, and a new Rand McNally.

"We'll make it in four days if we depart early and retire at nightfall," I said, popping some Tamales. "First stop, Twin Falls, Idaho."

"We never did have a proper honeymoon," Al smiled.

On the Snake River Canyon bridge, there's a turnout where you can park and look over the precipice. The canyon itself appears genuinely out of nowhere like some great scar on the earth. A foot beyond the edge, and the world returns to normal.

I felt once unsettled at the memory of the man pushed by Tobias. It was dark, so he may not have known the canyon was even there. I imagined him preparing to hit shrubbery after a few feet, only to keep plummeting.

I didn't have a plan beyond a vague understanding of Poughkeepsie's location.

How could I confront Tobias Randall? What would I say?

"We know he killed Beth," I said, many miles down the road. "And the man on the train. And his own father. Maybe even Hanz."

Al started to speak but closed his mouth in thought.

"Come now, Al, use your words."

Al rubbed his face. "But do we know any of that?"

"Well, if we don't, it's only because he's too smart."

"Right…" Al said.

"What about the fact he was a Nazi?"

Checkmate, I thought.

"But even with that," he said, "we just have a single picture, which you saw for a split second in the late '30's? We don't know what he was part of or even knew."

"We don't know what he knew? Tobias?? Al Clifton, you pull the car over this instant. We are about to have it out."

And so, on the side of Interstate 80 outside of North Platte, Nebraska, we had it out.

"First of all," I said. "I am not a pacifist. You, of all people, know this. But I support you because you're my husband and I love you."

"Right," Al said.

"But we have found ourselves confronted with a unique type of evil, and we are the only ones who can do something about it."

"Ok."

"Naturally, we don't want to do anything violent."

"Naturally."

"And we can't confront him directly because he'll just outsmart us and make us pay for it, God knows how. So, we're left to clandestine operations," I paused, thinking. "Whereby we collect enough evidence to report to the authorities and trust the rule of law will prevail. Which we know it won't. So, we're back to taking action with our own hands."

We stared at the flat horizon. A large flock of birds flew past, then a single bird.

Finally, Al pulled back onto the highway.

"Where are you going?" I said in protest. "We haven't resolved our plan."

"No," Al said. "But I trust us."

"Hmph," I said and scooted closer to the sweet man.

***

When we finally passed the Poughkeepsie sign, I slumped in my seat and lowered my hat. We followed signs to the public library. To avoid arousing suspicion, I went in alone while Al stood watch.

The library reference section contained phone books dating back to 1937. I started with 1954. In the 1955 book, there he was, plain as day: James Bankhead, 193 Elm St.

I considered dialing the phone number just to hear the confirmation of his voice but knew that risked giving up the one angle we had: surprise.

The librarian was a heavy set man with octagonal glasses.

"Are you familiar with the United Scientists Laboratories here in town?" I asked.

"Can't say that I am," he said, tapping a pencil. "But it's probably related to IBM, and that place is a world unto itself."

"Yes," I said. "I understand they're teaching machines to play checkers."

"Sure have," he said. "But checkers is one thing, and chess is another."

I thanked him, then hid in a remote aisle and discretely tore a city map from the front of a phone book.

We parked two blocks from Elm St. and approached on foot via the back alley, as was now our custom.

The neighborhood was respectable but ordinary, and 193 Elm was a two-story maroon craftsman with white trim and a large glassed-in back porch. A waist-high chain-link fence surrounded the backyard.

A man was sitting in a chair in the corner of the porch with his back to us. He stood, stretched his back, and went inside. It could have been Tobias.

I grabbed Al's sleeve and pulled us to the side of the alley.

"Get down like this," I whispered, hunching.

Poor Al got halfway down, wincing the whole way. He tried a few steps forward, resembling a crippled ape.

"Oh, forget it," I said, standing straight. "I'd rather he spots us than see you in pain."

I slowly opened the metal gate to the backyard, and we sped over near the side of the house, just past the porch area. I stood on tippy toes but couldn't see in the window. Al tried as well, to no avail. I attempted to climb on Al's back, but after three tries determined it was not to be.

We heard a noise inside the house and took off back through the yard and gate and halfway down the alley.

"Ok," Al said, panting. "I think it's time for a real plan."

We walked back to the car.

"The neighbor's," I said. "I don't remember seeing any activity there, do you? The lawn looked uncared for as well. If it's vacant, we could pick the lock and camp inside to watch from a hidden vantage point."

"You know how to pick a lock?" Al said.

"No, I assumed you did."

"I think you use a hairpin." He looked at my head. "What is a hairpin anyway?"

The neighbors in question pulled into their driveway.

"If we're gonna catch him doing something nefarious," I said. "It could take a while. Weeks maybe."

"That's a lot of Hot Tamales babe."

It occurred to me for the first time that maybe Tobias couldn't be beaten. At least by us anyway, and if not by us, then by no one.

I thought about going home and simply doing nothing. Take care of Dot, living the rest of our lives in fear any moment Tobias could do something, but somehow equally afraid he wouldn't.

"It's gonna be ok," Al said, reaching for my hand.

I forced a smile.

"But it'd be better if we could nail the turkey," he said.

At 8:30 p.m., a man emerged from Tobias's house, got in his car, and backed out. It occurred to me while watching the man what Mr. Gibbs had said: *Time passes for us all, doesn't it?* How much time had passed since I knew the boy? It couldn't be 20 years. It just couldn't.

Al waited until the man was down the street before following.

The man drove through the city for ten minutes, traversing into an industrial area before finally pulling to a curb next to an old brick building. Several vagrants loitered under a lighted sign shaped like a cross.

"Poughkeepsie Rescue Mission," Al read.

A knock at my car window made me hit my head on the roof.

It was a beggar with his hand out.

Al pointed for him to come around to the driver's side, then rolled down his window and reached for his wallet.

Al gave the man some cash and began to roll up the window but stopped.

"Wait. Sir, can I ask you a question?" Al said.

"Sure," the man said. "Any question is worth five bucks."

(Al had pulled out a five-dollar bill to give the man without looking. I decided to store his cash in my purse for the remainder of the trip.)

Al pointed to Tobias's car. "What do you know about the man that drives that car?"

"You a cop? Because if you're a cop, it's about time."

"No, I'm not a cop," Al said. "Why? What do you

mean?"

"Fifty homeless men gone, no one says a peep. A white girl's late for dinner and they call the president."

"How... What do you mean?"

The man looked around then bent closer.

"Ok, I'm a tell you something, but only cuz you look like you might have another five-dollar bill."

I scowled and nodded at Al.

"Nice lady you got there," the man said, taking another $5 from Al. "Now, the man who drives that car? About two or three years ago, he starts giving out free meals right here."

The man pointed to the mission building.

"Good food, too," he continued. "They *still* got good food in there. Beef stew and cornbread tonight. I need to get in 'fore it's gone."

I leaned over Al.

"What about the missing people?"

The man looked around again.

"Well... no one noticed at first," he said. "Mostly, no one notices now. But I saw it first cuz I was friends with one of the early ones. Fella named Clint. Nice guy. Pushover, you know? But smart. Read books. Now, one thing you could count on with Clint was he was always around. He's been on the streets here his whole life. Right over there, in fact. That was his spot."

The man pointed in some direction above the car.

"He told me he grew up on the South side," the man continued. "From a good family, you know? But, one day about two years ago. Poof! He's gone like a toot in a tornado. So I ask around, and a few other fellas were missing too. Over the years, it's got so common we hardly notice. One day there's a guy. Next day, the wind."

"How many do you think have gone?" Al said.

"Shoot," the man pointed to the mission. "There's only about thirty of us now. Free cornbread and stew? There used to be a hundred, easy."

"Have you told the police?"

"Me? No. But a few of the fellas did. Nothing came of it."

Al nodded at Tobias's car.

"You ever talk to that man?"

"No. Well, he did ask me once if I had family nearby. I told him yes, which was a lie, but it's none of his business. Since then, he's left me alone. Just stands there and watches people eat. Speaking of which," the man patted his stomach. "Nice to meet ya both."

The man took off in a half-jog across the street; his hand firmly pressed to the pocket containing our ten dollars.

We knew we couldn't go to the local police as Tobias would no doubt have connections for a coverup of his activities. And the testimony of one homeless man wasn't enough to go any higher in the ranks of law enforcement. We really wanted to go into the Rescue Mission but certainly couldn't do that. In fact, there was only one thing that had worked so far.

"We can only give them a dollar each," I said.

"We've got twenty dollars for the effort—no more. Hand me your wallet. I'll distribute the money."

"I don't like the idea of you carrying all that cash," Al said.

"The fact I am carrying concealed monies an attacker doesn't know about adds no increased danger to my presence."

We parked two blocks away and walked towards the mission. The first vagrant we approached was a woman.

"I've got money, but I need something from you," Al mumbled.

She spat in his face.

We decided moving forward the person must be an older male sitting on the ground with a beggar's money can.

We found just a man a block down from the mission. He was dubious at first, but eventually took us up on an offer of $3. We handed him the money, which he counted twice, then stuffed into his underwear.

"Ok, what's your question?" he said.

We asked him about the disappearance of the homeless in the area. The man replied that he was new in town, didn't know anyone, and wouldn't know if they'd disappeared.

"We are giving one dollar only," I reminded Al. "No more of this multi-dollar nonsense."

"Maybe we don't need to get money involved at all?" Al said.

As it turns out, like other people, the homeless are

open to talking without payment.

Here is a summary of what we learned, in their own words:

"The government's been experimenting on us for years. Why you think so many drink? Military planted in our brains a switch. It's how they're gonna defeat the Russians. Just flip the switch. Make 'em all drunks."

"I haven't seen nothing. Never. I keep to myself and I don't see anything, ever. I never even seen nothing. Ever. That's all I gotta say."

"Yes, I've seen it. Don't have no proof, though. But I seen people just gone. I mean, leavin' all their stuff behind too. Just gone. Then a garbage man comes for their stuff, and that's gone too."

We finally came to an ancient-looking Jewish man. His right shoe had twine around the top to hold it to the bottom.

"Fifty, at least," he raised his bony finger. "A few women, too. But fifty gone, at least."

We tried to ask him for more details, but he kept waving his finger to the point it felt like he was fighting us off.

"Stop, please. I can't say any more. He makes the people disappear, I tell you!"

The old man shuffled away, and we let him.

We took a break and got some dinner, over which decided to return to Tobias's house for a stakeout, and to give the whole process three more days. If no proof of maleficence was found, we would write an anonymous letter to the police and local papers and

302

return home.

Al turned off the lights as we pulled within eyesight of the house. The lights were on, and curtains drawn, with the car back in the driveway.

"Why does a lazy dog lie in a gas station oil patch?" Al said.

"You got a better idea?" I said.

We sighed.

The front step light came on, the screen door opened, and out stepped a woman, a girl in her early twenties, pretty and petite. She held the door behind her, and out came Tobias.

He lit her cigarette as she sat on the stoop and crossed her legs. He sat beside her, and she leaned into him. It didn't look like they were talking. After a few minutes, he helped her up, they went back inside, and the light went off.

"A wife?" Al said.

"No," I said, "that's a girlfriend."

A man knocked on Al's window. This time I urinated slightly, and I suspect Al did the same.

The man was an Indian. He wore a silk button shirt, a large gold bracelet, and a number of gold rings.

The man bent down and smiled.

"Hi Al. Hi Miss Jane."

I raised my hand in a small wave.

He reached into his back pocket and removed an envelope. Al rolled his window down a crack.

"He wants you to leave now," the man said. "And stop at this address on your way home."

"Who is '*he*'?" I said.

"He said if you don't leave now, and stop at this address on your way home, then you know what'll happen."

The man stuck the envelope through the window.

"And now means now," he said.

"Um, who are *you*?" Al said.

The man laughed to himself. "I'm the real estate agent."

I started to speak, but the man tapped our roof and pointed for us to go.

The man took a few steps then returned to Al's window.

"And, I sometimes administer medicine," he said. "Please tell the ladies no hard feelings."

He tapped the roof again and walked off for good.

In the envelope was a single piece of paper. On the paper, in Tobias's unmistakable handwriting, was an address.

1304 Pinewood Acres

Cedar Rapids, IA

CHAPTER 41

Cedar Rapids, Iowa, is a moderately sized town with several cereal manufacturers, General Mills being the largest. You pass the massive city-sized plant on your way into town through a sour cloud of fermentation that stays in your nostrils for hours after leaving.

"Should we circle the block first?" I said.

"So Tobias's people can watch us go in a circle?"

"Maybe we should buy a gun. Or ask for police backup."

Al just looked at me with resignation.

We pulled up to the curb on the other side of a little house. It was a white and black single story with two large trees out front.

"You ready?" Al said.

We knocked on the front door.

"Around the side," a man said in a muffled voice inside. "I don't use this door."

We went to a small, enclosed porch area on the side, where the man opened the screen door for us.

"C'mon in. Ya'll want some coffee?"

We sat in the living room on a plastic covered couch while the man leaned in a recliner. He was in his late 50's, sinewy, with heavy stubble and short, uncombed hair. He wore an unbuttoned work shirt with a name patch too folded over to read.

"I'm Carl," he said. "James told me you'd be coming. Well, his man did. I don't talk to James."

My ring finger jittered against the cup of surprisingly good coffee.

"His man said to go ahead and tell you the story," Carl continued, pulling the recliner lever to kick his feet up. "It was a surprise, I'll tell you. But a relief. As I'm sure you know I haven't been able to tell anyone."

"Please do, sir," Al said.

"Well, it's like this: I was born in Tallahassee, Florida, in '97. Mom cleaned houses, and my dad was a handyman. I was the oldest of three, with two little sisters. Mom and dad split when I was 16. I went with dad, and mom took the girls. Dad and me traveled around doing odd jobs until I got the letter. Army trained me as a medic, and I got shipped to France."

He paused and took a long drink.

"I was there," Al said.

Carl nodded and lifted his cup as a toast.

"You know what they say about the Great War?" Carl said. "It was the most painful war in human history. You know why they say that?"

"No," I said.

Carl put down his cup and raised both hands, one very high and one very low.

"It was the biggest gap between war-making technology up here and medical know-how down here." He formed his bottom hand into a fist. "And here was me. I don't know where you were," he said to Al, then shook his fist. "But here was me. And I stayed here even after I came back. I stayed here. Couldn't hold a job. Keep a woman. Not a decent one," he motioned to me. "And that, as they say, was that."

The winter sun broke into the little living room, making the floating air particles visible. Carl caught me fixated on their movements.

"Sink or swim our whole lives," he said.

"Yes sir," I said.

"A year ago," Carl continued, "—this is in Poughkeepsie. James Bankhead's man, the Indian fella, pulls me out of the stew line. He said James was interested in meeting me. I said, 'Well, where is he?' The guy said James doesn't meet people that way. I had to schedule a meeting with him at my childhood home." Carl laughed. "I said, 'Childhood home? Partner, I grew up in Florida, and that's a long way from here.' And he hands me a pen and tells me to write down the address of my mom's old place in Florida where I grew up. So now I'm thinking, ok, what's up? You know? This guy wants to know 'bout my childhood? Give me a break. But I figured it didn't matter anyhow, so I wrote the address down. So, next day the man shows at the mission again, and gives me a plane ticket to Tallahassee, and asks if I'll meet James down there at the address. I told him to stick the ticket where the sun don't shine. I mean, who does he think I am? About a month later, I'm hungry and cold, so I head back to the mission. I get my food and sit down, and James himself comes over and sits with me. He's a different guy. Have you met him?"

"I believe I have," I said.

"You too?"

"Yep," Al said.

He squinted. "You family?"

"No," I said. "Just old friends."

The man laughed. "Right," he said. "Friends. Anyway, James said the only way to know someone is to know their childhood. I said, 'Mister are you writin' a book or something?' He laughed and said, 'not at the moment', he's just trying to get to know me. But since I wasn't willing to go to Florida with him, he'd have to take a risk. Then he says he's gonna give me a free house, set me up with a job, and hand me ten thousand dollars if I did one thing for him. So I says, 'If you want me to kill somebody, forget it.' Cuz nothing is worth prison. —No, he says. The thing I have to do for him is move away and never come back to Poughkeepsie. Not ever."

"Why?" Al said.

"I have no idea!" Carl waved his arms around, laughing. "But a year later, I'm still here. I still got eight of the ten thousand in the bank. I bought some stuff, and a car. Held a job for nine months now, longest of my life. And I don't even hate my boss, not all the time anyway. I'm thinking of trying for a lead position."

"Right," Al said.

"So…" I said, then stopped myself and leaned back.

"I *know!*' Carl laughed. "I asked the Indian fella when I was signing the papers on the deal, as there was full legal paperwork and everything. I mean, I truly own this place. But I asked the guy, I said, 'Why me?' And you know what he said? I remember because it's the craziest thing I've ever heard a man say in all of my sixty-one years. He said, 'You're number fifty-eight.' See, I'd asked him, 'Why *me?*' And he said it wasn't me. I'm nothing special. I'm number fifty-eight getting this deal."

***

The drive through Nebraska this time was vertigo-inducing. Not from any curves or hills, but just the opposite. The straight path of the road cutting through the flat, white horizon made us too much aware we were driving on a giant ball.

"You're distant," I said to Al.

He didn't respond.

"I'm done with Tobias," he said, finally. "Whatever he's gonna do, he's gonna do. I can't stop him or do a thing about it. That's it. The only question is, are *you* done?"

I didn't respond.

"I was talking to Mick," Al said. "He's thinking of starting up the L.A. Peace Station again, under a different name, of course. He asked if I might help get it going."

I studied the repeated sound of the tires against the highway. Just when I imagined a pattern it would change.

"Wouldn't be gone more than a few months," Al continued. "Could make a few bucks at least."

***

It wasn't divorce. It never would be. It was just distance, and distance isn't death, it's just time and space.

It was pitch dark when we passed over the Snake River. I couldn't have told the difference between the canyon and a field. I almost broke down but stiffened up just as quickly, as Al would never leave if he saw me crying.

We drove through the night, unpacked, and went to sleep. By the following afternoon, Al was gone.

The bell rang from upstairs.

CHAPTER 42

A page from Thoreau's Walden

1956

New York City

Thomas J. Watson leaned over his desk, studying the latest report on IBM's artificial intelligence program. They were poised to take the next step, not just in computing or business, but with life itself. The Poughkeepsie technicians believed they could teach the computer to play chess.

***

1956

Poughkeepsie

At first, Tobias Randall resisted all painkillers, working on training his mind to embrace and even enjoy pain. But, as the pressure inside his skull mounted, he gave in.

Randall wrote to the nation's top physicians under the guise of a medical journal seeking peer review of an upcoming article on brain surgery. All those surveyed disagreed with the article's conclusions, stating surgery at that point would be near impossible, not only causing blindness but significant mental impairment.

"Perhaps in 30 years," noted Dr. Harry LeFever, the leading brain surgeon in the nation, concluding with, "I am truly sorry."

***

May Williams leaned against the drug store checkout where Tobias Randall purchased his pain medicine. She was reading a dog-eared copy of *The Fountainhead*.

"What is truth?" Tobias said, placing his painkillers on the counter. "Is it just a drug?"

May curled the side of her mouth into a smile. She studied the man before her. He was tall and handsome in a boyish way, with mystery behind his dark blue eyes.

"Truth is the acceptance of reality," May said, punching the register. "So maybe it is the pills."

A month later, May insisted Tobias take her to a lecture by Ayn Rand at the Edison Hall Forum in Boston.

"Sure babe," Tobias said. "I could check in on some old friends."

***

Norbert Weiner was still at MIT and, on the

occasion of the young couple's visit, was giving a talk on teaching children to respect, rather than use, technology for selfish gain.

"Machines will act with what appears like malicious intent," Weiner said, "if we, even inadvertently, program them to mirror humanity's worst qualities."

May raised her hand.

"At some point in the future," she asked, "won't it be better if humans didn't exist? Isn't that the solution we're all dancing around but don't want to say?"

It was an earnest question, and Tobias was genuinely impressed.

"Well, of course, Miss," Weiner said without hesitation. "The nature of all philosophy," he paused, "and yes, all human endeavor, is to justify the anomaly of our perceived higher consciousness than the rest of nature. We will always fall short because we do not possess such a higher consciousness. It is only an illusion we fall prey to by the very nature of said consciousness."

"So, what do we do?"

"What to do?" Weiner picked his nose, removed his glasses, and cleaned them on his shirt. "We utilize the best elements our consciousness has afforded us. Of course, these include compassionate reason and effective communion. We practice pacifism even when reason would steer us otherwise."

Weiner paused, studying May, and she him.

"I suppose," he concluded, "consciousness does make cowards of us all."

***

Ayn Rand was speaking at 7 p.m. that night, providing just enough time for the pair to pop in on von Neumann.

"Princeton is a seven-hour drive," May said.

But Tobias was not thinking of a physical pop-in, as that time had passed. Von Neumann's body had been ravaged by bone cancer the previous year, and was now affecting his mind.

"The MIT library," said Tobias, "is the best place to visit him now."

They spent the day reading von Neumann's published works and recorded correspondence. Tobias recommended May start with a *Fortune* magazine article penned by von Neumann the previous year, entitled, *Can We Survive Technology?*

In the late afternoon, Tobias found himself in a back corner of the library next to an open window that allowed in the sound of a nearby running stream. He wrote von Neumann a poem and placed it inside a copy of the genius's 1928 article, *Theory of Parlor Games*, Tobias's favorite.

When It's All Played Out.

We know

that

we can't

know.

As we are part of,

314

And not outside of,

Existence.

We are left

with the word itself as a question:

Outside?

(And that question

in

itself,

is the fixed limit

of our reach.)

So,

We accept life.

We accept death.

Or,

we fight,

kicking and screaming.

Which is just another way.

(The one, I suspect, you will take.)

So, in saying goodbye,

I have no wish

For you,

Other than to say,

We didn't exist,

we exist

and we existed.

May and Tobias ate sandwiches near the stream.

"You've not told me what you think of her," May said. "I just realized that."

Tobias smiled.

"When I talked about Rand," May continued, "you know what you say?"

"Very good."

"Yeah, '*very good.*' That's what you say."

May put her sandwich down and crossed her legs towards him. "But that's not an answer. Or even a discussion. You're just affirming me. *Very good.*"

"Isn't affirmation the ultimate answer?" Tobias said.

May scratched the side of her head, a tick when thinking.

"No, not really. I bring up a topic and want to know what you think. I already know what I think."

"If you already know what you think, what's the difference?"

"Because I could be wrong!" May punched Tobias on the arm. "That's it. You don't believe you're wrong. Like ever. Not really."

Tobias let out a burst of air, thinking this could be it for the relationship. At least, it would be a mutual ending, with May not tolerating his remoteness and Tobias accepting the reality of it.

"You know, you could be wrong," May said, "and I could be right on some things?"

Tobias studied her tiny nose.

"And stop looking at me like I'm cute," she said. "It's another way of saying '*very good.*'"

"I don't want things to end yet," he said. "I still have much to learn from you. Experientially."

"Oh, I see!" May said. "And then what? What happens in a year when you learned everything *experientially?*"

"It won't take a year. I'll be done in a few days, maybe hours. Then I'll try to fool my brain into thinking I need more experiences from you. But this process will drain your life energy, because my attention will not be authentic. And when I realize you're getting close to the point where you won't recover without lasting damage, I'll leave in the night, and you'll continue your life as a regular person, never hearing from me again."

The wind rushed through the trees. May closed her eyes and listened.

"Fair enough," she said, with a strange look on her face. "Let's make it an interesting few weeks then. Can you hang in there for that long?"

"It's possible."

"How much money do you have? The real amount. C'mon, out with it."

May's suspicions were warranted. Tobias's GE patent money was dwarfed by skimming the lucrative Argentinian atomic fusion project. (In Peron's delusion and desperation, Richter, and by extension Tobias, had been given a blank check. Not all the funds could be spent on replacement concrete reactors, and bookkeeping was scrutinized with the oversight of a toddler.)

"6.27 million," Tobias said.

"Well, that settles it," May said. "I'm taking an indeterminant leave from the drugstore."

"Fair enough."

"Secondly, we're going to spend it on pure altruism."

"I'm not sure Ms. Rand would approve."

"On the contrary," May said. "Our motive for every expenditure, and we will spend every dime of the 6.27 million, is pure selfishness."

"Good," Tobias said. "Money is boring. I'd rather be done with it."

They attended the Rand lecture, but neither could remember what was said.

"My father was a hobo," May said on the ride home. "He would make his way home now and again. Mamma would clean him, feed him, wash his clothes. She made us promise to tell no one. She told people he'd died in the war. The truth is, he was a dodger like you."

318

"I thought I felt suspicion on my war stories."

"I don't want to know who you really are, and I truly don't care," May said. "But next time you lie about being at Normandy, make sure you've talked to someone who was actually there. Books don't tell it true."

***

The following day May and Tobias went to the bank, withdrew $60,000 in cash, and gave $5000 to the first homeless person they encountered.

They'd left the money in a bag provided by the bank, and the couple didn't even stop to tell the homeless person what it was.

That was step one.

Step two was to do the same thing ten more times.

Step three was to find a realtor.

"He'll need to be discreet," May said.

"I can just get a real estate license under a false name."

"I'm sure you can, whoever you are," May said. "But no, it needs to be legitimate; otherwise, whatever we give could one day be deemed fraudulent and taken back."

"I didn't think about that."

May paused before continuing.

"Ideally, the agent will have a good knowledge of the law," she said. "But most important, be willing to do anything for cash."

"I think I know a guy," Tobias said.

Timothy Jarbidge is the owner of the Los Angeles-based waste collection company 'Timmy's Sanitation.' The enterprise includes 27 employees, eight trucks, and provides quality, dependable service to over 7,000 homes and businesses throughout the San Fernando Valley.

"Why didn't you name it *Jarbidge Garbage*?'" Tobias said.

"Tell Tommy I said hey," Timmy said, and hung up the phone.

In the late '30s Tommy Jarbidge began performing security and detective work for a divorce attorney in Las Vegas named Chadwick Perkins.

Mr. Perkins, like Mr. Jarbidge, was an entrepreneur. Seeing the opportunity for expansion, together they opened a 'divorce ranch' just north of the expanding city. (Such 'divorce ranches' had become popular destination spots in Reno, where the famous and wealthy vacationed while waiting out the Silver State's shortest-in-the-nation six-week residency requirement for divorce approval.)

Perkins and Jarbidge's concept was to provide a budget divorce ranch experience for the common man.

"50 bucks a week we charged," Tommy said, taking a bite of a chicken wing at the Poughkeepsie Airport's diner, 'Wings.'

But instead of serving the common 'man,' as Perkins and Jarbidge would learn, divorce ranch services were almost exclusively utilized by women.

"The men had to work," Tommy explained. "The *women and children* came to Nevada. It's like a break for everyone that way."

Keeping with the 'Helldorado' wild-west theme, the two business partners named their establishment '*The Last Frontier Ranch.*'

They built 25 small cottages, a recreation center, and a small pool. Authentic Western cuisine was served twice daily, with complementary horseback riding lessons and fiddle music on Friday nights.

"The real services," Tommy said, "were done by the ranch hands."

Just after opening, a problem arose of women having second thoughts and returning home before their six weeks. Ever the entrepreneur, Mr. Perkins offered bonus pay to any male employee who could 'maintain' the female customers for the entire duration.

"I wouldn't do it," Tommy said. "The women were desperate all the way around. I couldn't give them more heartache."

Mr. Perkins and Tommy had a falling out over the issue. When Tommy asked his business partner to pay him out for his share, it was revealed the attorney had restructured their original arrangement in such a way as to leave Tommy with no legal right to anything besides his monthly salary.

Tommy fought Perkins in court, claiming the new documents were forged, but Perkins arranged for a highly reputable notary to testify to the contrary, and the law sided with the lawyer.

"That was in '47," Tommy said. "After ten years."

Bitter and resentful, Tommy left *The Last Resort* to work as an independent contractor for other divorce camps throughout the state, where he sold healing oils and performed 'genuine medicine man' spiritual treatments for wealthy female guests.

"These ones were rich," Tommy explained, taking a strong pull on his milkshake. "It wasn't the same."

Tommy eventually gained a stellar reputation as both a gentle and passionate healer, providing him with steady work. This was all until several months prior when he made a fatal mistake.

"Love," Tommy said. "With a white woman. Can you believe it?"

The woman became pregnant just around the time her husband was having second thoughts and demanded her return. Unfortunately, the husband was a significant East Coast mafia figure who may or may not have heard rumors of Tommy's existence.

"She thinks because he's Italian, she'll be able to pass the baby as his," Tommy said. "I told her I'd rescue her as soon as I raised the money for us to start fresh."

"I'll tell you our plan," May said, sliding a document across the table. "But only after you sign a non-disclosure agreement, which we will pay you $5,000 right now to do. This agreement does not restrict your activities in finding and helping us purchase homes. It does, however, restrict you from publicly revealing who we are and what we are doing with the homes. For each successful purchase, you will be compensated with $5,000 in cash."

Tommy flipped to the back of the thick document with one hand and signed, still holding a chicken wing with the other.

"Don't you want to read it?" May said.

"Words on paper don't mean anything," Tommy said. "Hey, looks like we're back in business, buddy."

"You are wise, for an Indian," Tobias smiled. "Oh, and Timmy says hey."

***

The next day, while Tommy studied for his real estate license exam, May and Tobias walked along the Poughkeepsie Upper Landing.

The couple approached a man sleeping in an alcove of the gas plant, where May provided sandwiches, and they ate together.

"No thanks," the man said.

"No, you don't understand," May said. "This is real. We're going to give you a house,"

"In some other town?" the man said.

"Yes," Tobias said. "We have to do it that way to avoid," he paused, "relapse into vagrancy by associating with people and places you're familiar with."

"Relapse into vagrancy?" the man said.

"And so that other homeless people don't find out and try to use you or the house," May said.

"Why can't they use the house? Ain't that what a house is for?"

"Well," May said, "in a fire, sometimes people get hurt in a stampede."

"And you two are trying to put out the fire?"

"No," Tobias said, "We're trying to make more exits."

"Seems backward," the man said.

"So, you're turning down a free house, with no strings attached, because you would rather stay on the streets of Poughkeepsie?" May asked.

"Can I sell the house?"

"No."

"Sounds like strings to me."

"He's right," Tobias said. "We're offering banishment. A punishment worse than death." He bent down. "Sir, the house costs $12,000. What would you do with $12,000?"

"I'd get a bank account," the man said.

And so it was decided. If someone turned down a free house in another town, $12,000 would be given until the $6.27 million or the candidate pool was depleted.

That Sunday morning, the front page of the *Poughkeepsie Sentinel* told of three homeless men who had notified the police someone had lost paper sacks containing $12,000 each. The police were holding the money pending further investigation.

"We will find and lock up whoever is doing it," the mayor stated. *"The money was got by ill gain, no doubt, and besides, it should be a crime to waste money like that when it could be put to good use."*

May put the paper down.

"They turned us into the police," she said.

"They couldn't believe the money was theirs."

Monday's headline bore an even more perilous warning:

ILL GOTTEN GAINS! BUM GIVEN $12,000 CASH BY YOUNG COUPLE

Authorities confiscate funds and arrest man for previous unpaid loitering fines.

'*Let this be a warning*,' the Police Chief stated. *'Ill-gotten gains do not profit. But righteousness delivers from death.'*

And so it was *re*-decided. May and Tobias were back in the banishment/real estate business.

Accounting for travel and realtor costs, Tobias mapped out 97 cities throughout the Northeast.

Their journey would start at Harmony Grove Cemetery in Portsmouth, New Hampshire, and take roughly six months. The first offering of a house would go to the closest homeless person in proximity to a certain gravestone. It was nothing more than a small piece of rectangular concrete embedded in the ground with unkept grass peeking over it:

WILLIAM J. 1898-1944

It is more information than he would have wanted.

CHAPTER 43

I went to prepare myself breakfast and coffee but stopped in the dining room, having caught a glimpse of myself in the mirror.

It had been a while since I'd taken a good look, and maybe it was Al being gone, or it being the Saturday before school started back after Christmas break, but I decided to give myself a critical run down.

The bags under my eyes had grown larger than I thought, my thighs wider, hair thinner and almost entirely gray. The wrinkles near my eyes reminded me of a certain canyon in a nearby state.

"It's only going to get worse," I said, aloud. "It is never getting better than this."

I paused for another moment there, then pivoted, opened the door under the stairs, and muscled out the first of seven tables we used for writing stations. After some labor, I dragged the table to the end of the drive and set it up. In short order, I repeated the effort with its six sister tables, then gathered armfuls of my clothes, and placed them on one table. Next, I brought out stacks of dishes and placed them on another table. Next was assorted bric-a-brac and various pieces of art I'd purchased in the heyday of the UVW.

"Marge, it's Jane," I said, holding the phone receiver, nearly out of breath. "I'm having a sale tomorrow. I was hoping you could put up signs all over town. Just paint the town, Margie."

"But it's freezing Janie. No one is going to come."

"They sure will old pal. Just write, 'Everything is free' on every sign."

Meanwhile, Dot rang the bell incessantly, curious about all the commotion.

"I'm just exercising," I yelled up. "Trying to lose weight."

Even from downstairs I could hear Dot laughing her heart out.

It took me five minutes of standing in front of Tobias's door to open it. During that time, I attempted to make up a song to go with the ringing of Dot's bell (with the rhyming of '*bell*' and '*hell*' not lost on me.)

Once open, my first thought was how sparse the room was.

The nightstand still held the last book he'd been reading, a paperback science fiction novel about robots. Inside the book was a single feather.

As always with Tobias, everything seemed like a clue, left on purpose. I'll never know how much of that was the young man's otherworldly knack for future prediction or how much was my own paranoia.

Inside the dresser were his few clothes and some drawing pencils. In the closet sat my old encyclopedia volumes I'd given him when I first moved in.

The dresser did not maneuver downstairs easily. After reaching the second step, I got a sliver, released my grasp in a yelp, and the thing went tumbling. I only fell a few steps, but the dresser went all the way, breaking its frame to kindling.

In the silence after the commotion, I smiled, acknowledging the near-perfect comedic timing of Dot's bell.

"I'm alright! Don't worry!" I yelled, then stumbled downstairs to bed. But no sooner had my head hit the pillow than I had the strangest yearning.

I crept off the bed, crawled to my closet, dug deep inside, and pulled out a hat box.

Upon lifting the lid, a feather floated out of the box and onto the floor. I picked it up and intended to study it for some clue, when the papers I'd stored inside the box caught my eye.

Atop the stack was my story, *Les Fleurs De Son Sein.* (*The Flowers of Her Bosom.*) I wondered if I had been too hard on myself or if maybe even the piece had ripened into fine prose in the dark.

I selected a random sentence and read it aloud:

Jeanne Blanchard moaned when Henri touched her. "Ooo,"
she said, followed by, "La la."

Nope.

I dropped the papers back in the box and studied the feather more closely. Then I had an idea. It was not some great burst of lightning, just a thought as unsubstantial as the feather itself.

I ran to the kitchen, grabbed the egg timer, then snatched a pencil from my nightstand and a hard-bound book to write on.

I took the *Les Fleurs* manuscript and the feather into bed and flipped the pages over. On the top of the blank page, I wrote '*Feather*,' then set the ten-minute timer.

Pencil to paper, without stopping to edit or think, here is what I wrote:

> *Why he chose a blue feather and my best hat, I still don't know. I never asked him. Perhaps it reminded the boy of some misperceived notion of his mother, the crazy bird.*

> *My mother never wore a feather in her cap. Never wore a hat at all. Too busy raising nine children to worry about feathers. I've never thought until now about the frequency of relations she and Father must have had. Was it to produce children to work the farm or the only thing interesting in their lives? Was it even of her own will? What did she ever desire besides being a housewife and mother? I certainly never asked. She wouldn't have wanted me to ask. I think.*

> *"It's foolishness," she told me the night I came home with a new green dress in preparation for the school social. "Have you even got a boy to ask you? You don't buy the dress until you've got the boy. And you don't get the right boy showing your," she glared at my chest with something between anger and pity, then pulled her blouse taut. "You get the boy by showing your worth in work."*

> *That Saturday night, dressed in green, I brought my*

remaining dollar-fifty to purchase an admission ticket to the dance, but was refused at the door for not having a date. (I can't imagine they even do that anymore.) In retrospect, I don't believe the action to be ill-meaning as much as protocol, I guess. A teacher, Ms. Browning, was called over to settle the dispute. She asked if I would like to work at the concession stand and gain entry at no charge. I took her up on the deal and operated the stand until closing, selling out of popcorn and lemon cakes.

I looked at the piece before me. "Hmm," I said. "Not bad."

Marge, freezing and exhausted from hanging signs, appeared at the door.

"Got 'em all hung up," she said, removing her knitted cap, wiping her brow with it, and replacing it slightly askew.

"Good. Most of the work is done then. Now let's add the words 'Free Writing Group Signup' to them."

Marge spit on my floor, apologized, cleaned the spit, and we headed back out together.

Every item was gone by 2 p.m. the next day, including Mr. Randall's car, who I gave to poor Sadie Huff. (Careful readers will remember her as Sadie Becker, a fellow attendee of the United Methodist's 'Single's Mingle' in October 36'.)

During recess the next day I drafted rules for the writing group, which would meet on Saturday mornings at the house. I would serve hot tea and crumpets.

Participants were to bring a pad and pencil. No one had to share their writing if they didn't want to, and absolutely no negativity would be allowed. I would provide an ordinary object as a writing prompt, (like a feather), with some guidance that need not be followed. I would set the timer for ten minutes, and we would each write silently about whatever came to mind.

That Friday after school I told Dot we were getting her hair done, then had Marge drive us to the Blue Valley Nursing Home. Dot spewed all manner of vile at their new facility manager, Ms. Burley, including strange, wild stories about a genius son who created nuclear fusion and communicated with ivy league professors and Nazi leaders. The performance was enough to secure her a place without me adding further comment.

The first writing group attracted three attendees beyond Marge, Rebecca, and me. One of them was young Mary Schneider, who I'd met in the hall at North Eugene High School on my visit to Mr. Gibbs.

In the following weeks, our count swelled to nine.

Mary Thompson Smith (MTS) even showed her face. She wrote a piece based on the writing prompt of a thimble about her first time sewing. It would have caused scandal amongst the Stramwell Civic Improvement Club (SCIC) had any one of them the literary sense to recognize double entendre, and I thought more of her from that day forward.

With permission from Rebecca, I've included below a portion of one of her pieces:

> *"What was Growth of the Soil about anyway?" my friend asked.*
>
> *"Nothing," I said, without a pause. "It doesn't have a proper theme at all that I can tell."*
>
> *We rocked on the porch in silence, as my friend knew not*

to push.

"I've read it again since our trip," I said.

"What is the story about?" my friend asked.

"Really nothing," I said. "A farmer and his wife work some land and have friends who join them, and at the end there's just a lot of them living on that piece of land together."

"That doesn't sound like nothing to me," she said.

***

On the Tuesday morning of Spring Break, 1957, just as I awoke, Al returned home.

"The Peace Station L.A. is up and running," he said, still standing in the doorway. "They kept the name. Can you believe it?"

"Of course I can," I said, starting to cry. "It's a fine name."

I reached for his suitcase, but he stopped me.

"You're crying."

"Yes. And you are far too thin," I said, patting his side. "Now sit while I fix you breakfast."

"Behold, I am the Lord, the God of all flesh: is there anything too hard for me?" Tobias said, standing atop our stairs at the railing. "Speaking of which, where is Mother?"

Al and I both froze, our mouths open.

"On our first trip in '37, when I found Sidis," Tobias said, descending to the living room. "We talked about girls, of all things, and how our procreation urge surfaced in unusual ways."

332

Tobias held a Luger pistol. He motioned for us to sit at the table, where my typewriter sat next to a ream of blank sheets.

"Sit," Tobias said.

Al stepped forward. "You listen to me—"

Tobias fired a shot, grazing Al's leg. The big man collapsed back onto me, and we fell to the ground.

"Son of a turkey!" Al screamed.

"Yes," Tobias said, firing another shot, this time aiming high and missing entirely.

I begged him to stop and crawled to the chair with my hands in the air.

Al lifted his pant leg and examined himself. He was still in pain, but his panicked look subsided.

"Only a graze. Now, the basement," Tobias motioned for Al towards the basement door off the kitchen.

Al scooted slowly to the door.

"Miss Jane," Tobias said, "we are going to write our final story together."

"At least let me attend to his wound," I said. "I will be no use as a writer worrying about him."

"A typist," Tobias interrupted.

"A typist," I continued, "I will be no use as a typist until I'm assured infection will not set in."

Tobias smiled and nodded towards the door.

I helped Al down the stairs.

"I'm getting blood on the steps," he said. "Don't

slip, honey."

"Hush. Does it hurt?"

"Well, yes."

I sat him down on an overturned bucket.

"No stitches," Al said, pinching it. "Just get the super glue."

I ran up the stairs, slipping on the blood, but catching myself in time.

"Honey?!" Al yelled.

"Hush!"

I grabbed a bed sheet, scissors, a bandage, rubbing alcohol, and the super glue. Al applied the makeshift first aid with proficiency.

"Nurse Jane?" Tobias called from the kitchen. "Time is up, dear."

"Go," Al said.

I climbed the stairs, being careful of the blood this time, and sat at the typewriter. For a moment, the house was quiet.

"You put Mother in Blue Valley?" Tobias said.

"Yes."

"And she screamed the truth?"

"Spilled the beans like a drunken bean picker."

"Must have been your best entertainment since Cain and Abel."

I turned and looked him in the eyes, still those of a young man.

"I'll type whatever you want," I said, "but answer me one question."

"How do I know the future?"

I nodded.

"I don't. Not for certain," Tobias said.

"But time and time again,"

"Predictability... isn't certainty."

The words floated in the air between us. We looked at each other for longer than ever before.

I got an idea. Probably my craziest.

On impulse, I stood and went to my room.

"Sit," I said, pointing to the chair next to mine. "Do it."

Tobias sat.

I returned and placed an acorn in front of him on the table. He leaned forward and studied it.

"This is your writing prompt," I said. "Go ahead, pick it up. Study its texture. Smooth on the bottom, rough on top, stem still in place, small and hard. Tell me whatever comes to your mind without hesitation. It doesn't even have to be about an acorn or a tree. It could be anything."

I went to the kitchen and grabbed the egg timer.

"Ten minutes," I said, cranking it. "We don't have to talk about it after if you don't want to, and I won't critique. If you want to talk about it, I will only praise you for what is strong."

Tobias picked up the acorn.

"Go."

The man began speaking and I typed as if possessed by Lucy Lindross herself. When the timer sounded, I yanked out the page and smacked it face down on the table.

"Now," I said. "Would you like feedback?"

"Sure."

"Above all, it's honest. More than good; it's beautiful. Thank you for sharing. I mean that."

"Would you like to continue in this manner?" I said.

"I would."

I rose, went to my room again, and brought out the extra-large hat box containing all the writing prompts I've used in every group so far.

Inside the box I stored an assortment of seemingly ordinary and random items, including the acorn, as well as a personal letter I had written from the viewpoint of a Stramwell rock, a small toy wishing well, a letter opener, a wooden sculpture of three owls on a limb, a toy donkey, a piece of sheet music, a hole punch, a porcelain angel, the book *A Children's Book of ABC's*, a baby doll, a rock, a pill bottle, a burnt match, a clown figurine, a Gideon Bible, some plastic grapes, a small chunk of concrete, a broken compass, and this selection from Henry David Thoreau's *Walden*:

> *Morning air! If men will not drink of this at the fountainhead of the day, why, then, we must even bottle up some and sell it in the shops, for the benefit of those who have lost their subscription ticket to morning time in this world.*

I set the egg timer for ten minutes, and we were off.

***

It was twelve-thirty in the afternoon.

With one hand, I smacked the most recently finished page on top of the stack and reached for a blank with the other.

"Lunchtime for Al, I'm sure?" Tobias said.

"Oh, my heavens!" I looked at the closed basement door.

Tobias picked up the egg timer and smiled playfully.

"Ten minutes, Janey."

I rushed down the stairs but did not spot Al where I'd left him.

I heard a racket in the darkness at the far corner, and Al emerged wearing his army hat and jacket.

"I found these down here," he said. "They still fit."

The jacket was several sizes too small through the belly.

"I believe it," I said, walking towards him.

Al held up his hand to stop me.

"Wait," he said. "I got a thing to say." He adjusted the jacket straight. "The only reason I ain't come up there yet is because I know when I'm beat. That boy would have some contingency plan for me bull charging through the door, and I'm not going to fall into a trap laid by a better hunter."

I started to tell him of the change in tone upstairs.

"Secondly," he interrupted, pulling our *Reversi* board

from behind his back. "Why did we ever let this thing get put down here? It should be on the porch at all times."

I nodded.

"Third, we're going to play a game right now, and after you've beaten me, I've got something else I want to share."

"But I've only got ten minutes, and you need to eat-
"

Al tugged the jacket tighter.

"Clearly, I can wait on additional rations for the time being, Ma'am."

As always, he allowed me the first move, and I took advantage. -And, as always, he tried to thwart my impending march toward the nearest corner and failed.

"Shucks," he said, shaking a fist in immersive competition.

He bit his index finger and attempted a move that would have prematurely ended the match before pausing and moving his hand to a more benign position. Still, his glimmer of hope remained undaunted until I had the third corner secure.

"*No, no,*" he said, sensing I was pausing to allow his surrender and prevent the inevitable. He motioned with both hands down at the board, always wanting to complete the game despite my charitable protests.

"Hmm," he said, studying my black sea of pieces. "I was practicing at Mick's a whole bunch. Thought I might have gotten better. Oh yes!" his eyes brightened. "What I was going to tell you. Well, I was urinating in the corner earlier—,"

My face fell.

"I used a bucket, and I'm sorry," Al said.

Then he leaned in and dropped his voice to a whisper.

"But as I was standing, I caught a glimpse of movement from the window."

He motioned to the small, dirty basement window letting through a fog of light.

"It was *Marge!*" he said. "So, I knocked on the window and got her attention. Unfortunately, I had no way of telling her what was going on without making sounds, and… she eventually left."

"I didn't see her," I said.

"That's good!" Al's voice rose a bit, then caught himself. "Maybe that means she's getting—"

Bang!

The sound of a mallet cascaded from upstairs, followed by a crash.

I ran ahead of Al up the stairs, swung the door, and found Marge standing in my kitchen, holding a large frying pan. Two chairs had toppled, and the typewriter lay upended on the floor. A settling cyclone of papers fluttered. On the floor lay Tobias Randall, dead.

CHAPTER 44

Marge here.

After seeing Al a prisoner in the basement, I ran home and grabbed a garden hoe. But, taking it to my backyard and swinging against a tree, I got the hoe stuck in a crook.

So, then I grabbed a broken tree limb. But it shattered against the tree trunk when I tested it for strength.

I returned to the house and saw my mother's cast iron pan.

It's a ridiculously large pan, especially for my two little morning eggs. But it was the only thing I'd kept of Ma's after the sale Jane put on to fund my planned trip back to Argentina.

It's a good pan. Jane even asks to borrow it sometimes for fried chicken.

I walked back to Jane's. The front door was open, and the young man stood with his back to me. So, I raised the pan and bonked him square on the coconut.

Jane and Al insisted we bury him right then and there on the property. (On account of me just committing murder, and any story of self-defense would require too many details about the nature of who Tobias was.)

"Well, rocks," I said. "You got an extra shovel?"

Al slung the boy over his shoulder and took him to the stream, where he single-handedly dug a grave and put him in. At Jane's request, the final writings of the young man were stacked neatly on his chest.

We three stood over the pit in a silent service, neither of us, I believe, knowing what in the world to say.

Al broke the silence by throwing the first shovel of dirt in the hole.

***

So anyway, Janie seems to think I did something important enough to put my name on this book her, Al, and Tobias. But all I really did was the bit about the frying pan.

She also told me to write something about myself. I fought her on it, but she is Jane. —So, I've decided to inform y'all of one personal detail:

I like collecting rocks.

Rockhounding is a man's game, but I don't care. I see a good rock and I'll pick it up. I like looking at rocks too, especially under a magnifier. I like just wondering where they've been.

I believe every rock, at one time or another, has sat at the bottom of the ocean. High above them the waves pass for millions of years until one day, out of the blue, it's their turn to get kicked ashore.

CHAPTER 45

J ane back with you.

The day after burying Tobias, we received this letter:

> *I, Tobias Randall, am dying of an inoperable brain tumor. Of course, the word 'inoperable' only means 'inoperable today.'*
>
> *After leaving Stramwell in 1937, I traveled to meet William James Sidis. He had just completed his book on the American Indian, The Tribes and the States. It contains a detailed analysis of their storytelling process, history, and full impact on the formation of the United States. Sidis gleaned his information through studying wampum belts.*
>
> *Our discussion on this topic would lay a roadmap for the rest of my life.*

***

> *I did not kill Beth Meyers.*

Just before she arrived in Stramwell to join the UVW, Beth's long-lost father re-entered her life. As a result, she was early on with child.

Beth was a recent student of Frances Malloy, who recommended Beth as her replacement. The recommendation was Frances's attempt to assist Beth. Frances was unaware of Beth's full condition, only that her father was unkind.

I begged Beth to stay, but she didn't want to bring shame to the UVW and was determined to flee before she started showing.

I reconnected with Beth in August of '37 and have stayed in touch. Her boy is now 19 and efficient as a mechanic. I have included their address on the back of this letter if Al would be so kind as to reach out.

Hanz is alive. He was arrested for money laundering in connection with the Huemul Fusion Project and currently resides in the National Penitentiary of Argentina in Buenos Ares, awaiting release in one week.

I've included information on where Marge may find him, along with a one-way ticket to Argentina. Hanz will be anonymously receiving a large sum of money on his release, which they can use to start their future, and the future of many others.

***

To whoever is reading this: You, right now, are made of flesh and bone. But go smaller and see you are made of elements. Go smaller and see your atoms. Go smaller. Go smaller. At this level there is no longer a definable difference between existence and non-existence. In this one short paragraph, we have crossed the line into permanent uncertainty. (The identical effect also works by going

344

larger and larger.)   What it all means is this: Truly everything is where you are now.

***

I will tell you a secret about The Senators: the tiny nation is you. But there is a solution coming.

Now for an additional clue to the question I would not answer at Sociedad de Socorros Israelitas*: It is my humble opinion we humans will never implement the real change needed on Earth, because our desire to procreate is too strong. It is that simple.*

As I said in Argentina, it'll take another dominant species to implement the change. What I did not say, is that it must be a non-procreating one.

As this letter is being penned, I've already planted the seed in humanity for our inevitable future. I predict the sprout will take 75 years to emerge.

Eventually, this new species will move our planet closer to universal altruism, and toward the elimination of all suffering and pain.

Only unconditional acceptance of reality will remain when my Maschinenmensch takes her place as the mediator between the head and the hands.

***

This letter is to be included at the conclusion of Jane and the Boy Wonder, as written by Jane Clifton, Marge Plimpton, Al Clifton, and myself, regarding our journey together.

Al, when you dig me back up to grab all the pages, divert the stream over me this time.

To Marge: Thanks. I always wanted to go out with a

345

bang.

Lastly to Jane, I am sorry for allowing you to believe I bore nefarious intentions for you and Al.

By the way, do you know what Native Americans believe a blue feather means?

I hope they're right.

Yours,

TOBIAS R.

1921-1957

CHAPTER 46

A l trudged back outside. I found two more shovels, and we all dug this time.

The following day I invited the local ladies of the UVW, along with Rebecca and Taw, to help reroute the stream back to its original direction.

***

Marge has gone. She said to write whatever I wanted in this book, as she'll never be back to face murder charges.

***

That summer, we had a big potluck on the side lawn at the house. MTS directed which ladies should bring appetizers, desserts, or fried chicken, while I supplied the pickles.

We invited the whole town, with the high school drama department reenacting the funeral scene from *Ms.*

McGillicutty's Menagerie of Wonders.

I even arranged for Dot to be positioned in a chair with a full view of the activities. (Just out of earshot from the others so as to not be a bother—a sad case, that one.)

Al works part-time at the Jiffy n' Fill on Main St., pumping gas and teaching a few Stramwell young people mechanic work.

***

This book could be a hit. It could bring us all down. It could be rejected for publication, or get published, but fail to sell because the writing wasn't good enough. - Tobias's "seed" could destroy the planet, and it all won't matter anyway. I don't know for sure, but my guess is we'll have a good 75 years to figure things out.

***

Today I will fix Al breakfast and we will eat on the porch. Then he will go off to work and I will have my writing group. Tonight, we will play *Reversi* and listen to the birds and the stream.

Later, if Al is lucky, we will fool around.

Yours,

J

AUTHOR'S NOTES

William James Sidis lost his libel case against The New Yorker.

The case, *Sidis v. F.R. Publishing,* is now regarded as a landmark in American privacy law, establishing the basis for much of our current legal understanding on the topic, erring on the side of the free press vs. personal privacy.

Ultimately, just to silence him, The New Yorker offered Sidis their first-ever cash settlement in such matters* in the amount of $500.**

This figure was reached after the New Yorker repeatedly offered multiple thousands of dollars to Sidis to write articles for the magazine on any topic he chose, even allowing him to use a pseudonym. Sidis rejected all offers.

**Sidis died 3 months after the settlement was reached. The $500 was still in his bank account.*

Recommended reading:

Wallace, Amy. *The Prodigy: A Biography of William Sidis.* E.P. Dutton, 1986.

Amazon.com: The Prodigy eBook : Wallace, Amy: Kindle Store

***

349

Norbert Wiener developed an anti-aircraft system for the US military in WWII that predicted the future trajectory of planes in flight in real-time. After the US dropped our atomic bombs on Japanese cities, he became an outspoken critic of scientists partnering with the military.

As private corporations funded most post-war scientific research in concert with the military, Wiener found himself increasingly outside advanced opportunities. He devoted much of his time to writing and speaking about the future, predicting a world where human labor and intelligence could eventually become obsolete.

Recommended reading:

Conway, Flo, and Jim Siegelman. *Dark Hero of the Information Age in Search of Norbert Wiener, the Father of Cybernetics*. Basic Books, 2006.

Amazon.com: Dark Hero of the Information Age: In Search of Norbert Wiener, The Father of Cybernetics eBook : Conway, Flo, Siegelman, Jim: Kindle Store

Heims, Steve J. *John von Neumann and Norbert Wiener: From Mathematics to the Technologies of Life and Death*. MIT Press, 1987.

John Von Neumann and Norbert Wiener: From Mathematics to the Technologies of Life and Death: Heims, Steve Joshua: 9780262081054: Amazon.com: Books

John von Neumann contributed to a broader range of advanced scientific fields than anyone in modern history, including work in mathematics, quantum theory, economics, defense planning, game theory, and computing. His work was crucial in developing the atomic bomb, and he sat on the selection committee deciding which Japanese cities to target. Thereafter he continued working closely with the US government in developing military technologies and creating the doctrine of mutually assured destruction.

In 1955, at 51, von Neumann developed terminal cancer. For the next two years, he grew increasingly fearful of death and, even more so, of losing his intellectual capabilities. On his deathbed, he was surrounded by military personnel attempting to keep secret whatever von Neumann might utter in his drug-induced delirium. He died in 1957.

Marina von Neumann Whitman, John von Neumann's daughter, graduated at the top of her class at Radcliff (now Harvard) and received her MA and Ph.D. in economics from Columbia. She became a professor of economics at the University of Pittsburg and served on the President's Council of Economics before taking an executive position at General Motors from 1979 to 1992. Marina's daughter became a doctor of internal medicine at Yale University, and her son a developmental biology professor at Harvard.

Recommended reading:

BHATTACHARYA, ANANYO. *Man from the*

Future: The Visionary Ideas of John von Neumann. W W NORTON, 2023.

> Amazon.com: The Man from the Future: The Visionary Ideas of John von Neumann eBook : Bhattacharya, Ananyo: Kindle Store

Neumann, Whitman Marina Von. *The Martian's Daughter: A Memoir.* University of Michigan Press, 2013.

> Amazon.com: The Martian's Daughter: A Memoir eBook : Whitman, Marina: Kindle Store

***

IBM subsidiary Dehomag worked closely with Nazi Germany in 1933 and thereafter to develop the punch card technology responsible for identifying and locating the Germans Hitler deemed to have Jewish lineage. Dehomag technology was also used extensively to schedule and route trains to concentration camps.

In 1936 IBM showcased their punch card systems to win the United States contract for the launch of the Social Security program. This pivotal contract launched IBM's status as the most powerful technology company in the world for the next 45 years.

The name 'August Siebert,' which the character in this novel, Tobias Randall, reads from a punch card in Berlin, was chosen at random by the author from a list of holocaust victims on the United States Holocaust Memorial Museum website: United States Holocaust

Memorial Museum (ushmm.org). The specific page listing known victim's names states:

This list contains the names of 5,000 Jewish and non-Jewish individuals who were murdered by Nazi Germany and its collaborators between 1939 and 1945. Each name is followed by the victim's country of origin or place of death. Unfortunately, there is no single list of those known to have perished during the Holocaust. The list provided here is a very small sample of names taken from archival documents at the United States Holocaust Memorial Museum. Approximately 650 names can be read in an hour. Names List 2015.indd (ushmm.org)

Recommended reading:

Black, Edwin. *IBM and the Holocaust: The Strategic Alliance between Nazi Germany and America's Most Powerful Corporation.* Dialog Press, 2012.

Amazon.com: IBM and the Holocaust: The Strategic Alliance Between Nazi Germany and America's Most Powerful Corporation-Expanded Edition eBook : Black, Edwin: Kindle Store

***

The Argentina Huemul Island Fusion Project was proven in time to be an utterly fraudulent operation, but not before the threat of a small nation developing unlimited energy sparked significant interest among world superpowers.

Princeton University scientist Lyman Spitzer, upon hearing of the Argentine project from *The New York Times* article, began intently contemplating the legitimate technology that would be required to create fusion. Spitzer ultimately invented the 'stellarator,' a predecessor of today's modern fusion devices, which promise unlimited energy and the potential to end climate change from fossil fuel dependence.

Recommended reading:

> Mariscotti, Mario. *The Atomic Secret of Huemul Island: A History of the Origins of Atomic Energy in Argentina.* Lenguaje Claro, 2017.

>> Amazon.com: The Atomic Secret of Huemul Island: A history of the origins of atomic energy in Argentina eBook : Mariscotti, Mario A. J.: Kindle Store

***

Camp Angel on the Oregon Coast near Waldport, Oregon, was a conscientious objector camp during World War II focused on forest management. It was one of 152 such labor camps housing 12,000 men during the war. The camps were maintained by church congregations and family members, with the men receiving no wages and their families no support. The men served longer enlistments than others drafted, which did not conclude until well after the war was over. Their service made substantial and lasting contributions to many aspects of our nation's land management and mental health systems.

The men at Camp Angel performed dangerous and grueling manual labor six days a week. During their limited downtime, they developed an extensive fine arts program consisting of plays, painting, and extensive self-publishing of books and poetry. Many notable writers emerged from the camp, including a number of which who migrated to San Francisco after release. There, these men launched the San Francisco Renaissance, which led to the Beat Generation, and, ultimately, the 1960s peace movement and cultural revolution.

Recommended reading:

> McQuiddy, Steve. *Here on the Edge: How a Small Group of World War II Conscientious Objectors Took Art and Peace from the Margins to the Mainstream.* Oregon State University / Corvallis, 2013.

> > Here on the Edge: How a Small Group of World War II Conscientious Objectors Took Art and Peace from the Margins to the Mainstream: McQuiddy, Steve: 9780870716256: Amazon.com: Books

***

Fritz Lang's first wife, Lisa Rosenthal, came home one day in 1921 to find Lang and his future wife, Thea von Harbou, engaged in sexual activity. Police were later called to the scene, where they discovered Rosenthal dead from a single gunshot wound to the chest. Lang and von Harbou were the only witnesses to what they claim was Rosenthal's suicide. The gun used was Lang's sidearm he'd kept as a memento from his time in World War I.

The German word 'machinenmensch' literally translates

in English to 'machine-human.' In the film version of *Metropolis*, the female machinenmensch robot is not given a name. In the novel version of *Metropolis*, written by von Harbou as the template for the film, the robot was named 'Futura.' The scientist who created the robot also calls her 'Parody.'

The run time of the original version of *Metropolis* was shortened in 1927 out of fear that American audiences would find it too long. In 2008, approximately 25 minutes of the original film, not seen since 1927, were discovered in the archives of a museum in Argentina. The lost footage has now been restored to the original film, creating a richer and more understandable narrative.

Metropolis is considered one of the most influential films of the 20th century, explicitly contributing to countless design elements in science fiction and fantasy, along with the first serious presentation of artificial intelligence in film. On January 1, 2023, the film's copyrights expired in the United States, and it is now part of the public domain.

Recommended reading:

McGilligan, Patrick. *Fritz Lang: The Nature of the Beast*. St. Martin's Press, 1997.

Fritz Lang: The Nature of the Beast - Kindle edition by McGilligan, Patrick. Humor & Entertainment Kindle eBooks @ Amazon.com.

***

The Amherst Writers and Artists (AWA) method was developed by poet Pat Schneider during her work with women living in public housing in the 1970's and 80's. The process involves a leader providing a small group with a writing prompt and a short, timed exercise to write about whatever comes to the participant's mind. All work is treated as fiction and kept confidential. If the writer chooses to share, only positive feedback regarding the piece's strength is allowed.

For more information about the AWA, and to find a writer's group near you, please visit:

www.amherstwriters.org

Recommended reading:

> Schneider, Pat. *Writing Alone and with Others.* Oxford University Press, 2003.
>
> > Amazon.com: Writing Alone and with Others eBook : Schneider, Pat, Elbow, Peter, Elbow, Peter: Books

***

A growing body of evidence proves that giving money directly to impoverished people without strings attached is one of the most impactful ways to create lasting life changes. For more information on how simple it is to make a difference, please visit www.givedirectly.com.

***

Blue feathers in Native American culture often symbolize the presence of transcendent connection.

Thank you so much for reading, it means the world to me. —Aaron

For more of Aaron's work, please visit
www.aarondonley.com

If you'd like to reach out directly email:
langanmae@gmail.com

Thanks to Sybil Johnson, who did an amazing job on the audiobook version. www.sybiljohnson.com

A short review of this book on amazon would be hugely appreciated.

Please visit
www.amazon.com/author/aarondonley

Made in the USA
Monee, IL
19 October 2024

67663539R00215